TARGETED VALIDATION

Ron Vergona

Published by:

Coeur d'Alene, Idaho

To my wife Addie, and children Jessica and Michael, for their love and support.

PROLOGUE

San Francisco Bay Area

The Kessler Foundation

BEFORE HEADING HOME, SHE HELD a final breath and remembered that first day.

The tears had stopped flowing, but distinct etches marred once delicate facial features. How long had she lived in this filthy hovel? Going from one fix to the next; not caring whether the next hit could kill her. Maybe that's what she prayed for.

The stranger, a nurse, had walked into the room. Mesmerized by the visitor's stark, white uniform, she'd answered every question.

Did it matter if she once lived in her family's rusty trailer on the reservation? She'd gone from one wretched pit to another. She barely recalled her own name and had long since abandoned any hopes of crawling back home.

Home? Yeah, whatever that meant.

The nurse had smiled and stroked her arm. She would be saved. Of all the decrepit souls, she had been chosen. She had no real family. No one cared if she existed. The nurse promised to take her to a place where all her medical problems could be addressed by a new government program. The nurse had called it ConnorCare.

She had started that day like all the rest.

Not knowing if it would be her last.

She remembered the stained, putrid mattress. Her bed. The stench of urine and other bodily fluids clung to the atmosphere like a ghostly apparition. Screams, moans, and bitter spurts of laughter echoed about the squalid chambers. The paper bag holding her worldly possessions lay crumpled and torn. Last night someone had rifled through it again. What did she have to lose?

Of course, she agreed to go to the clinic.

For a while, she felt almost human again. The withdrawals had been tough, but the medical staff didn't tolerate failure. This new facility became a salvation, like a fantasy, banishing her past life. They tended to her every need. She allowed herself to dream of a future.

And then things changed.

Her health problems worsened. But not to worry, she was in one of the world's finest clinics. The doctors knew exactly what to do, and she believed every word.

Ignoring the astringent odors and the bleeping hospital monitors, she had imagined herself in a luxurious resort. The food was first class. At least to someone who had spent most of her life fighting for scraps in rat-infested dumpsters. And they treated her like a princess. But despite the lavish care, her health continued to spiral downward.

Yesterday, she had stolen a brief look in the mirror hidden beneath the tissue box on the bedside table. She screamed at the vision of a once pretty face. She'd been aware of the blotches spreading on her arms and chest, but when she saw the changes to her olive complexion, accentuating sunken cheeks and reddened, swollen eyes, it froze her in fear.

And now, she released the long-held breath and stared at the ceiling, once again feeling frightened and alone. Just like back in that hovel—before the nurse had stepped into her life.

A sudden coughing fit subsided, but a wheezing breath tickled and clawed her burning throat. She blinked away the fuzziness and tried to twist her neck, but her upper body felt restricted. Through a wave of returning tears, she saw a heavy strap stretched across her chest. When she tried to move her arms, she realized they too were restrained.

This was something new.

Long strands and matted clumps of hair lay scattered about the sweat-soaked pillow. Again, she struggled to move. Another bout of heaving coughs wracked her body. She pictured armies of insects chomping at every organ. She agonized with the need to rip away the scaling skin trapping them inside. The pesky creatures needed to go. Why didn't these people do something to stop it?

Through a waxing, waning consciousness, she sensed nurses and doctors hovering nearby. They raised and spread her legs. Cold hands and even colder metal instruments prodded. She begged them to stop. She got a few brief smiles; firm pats on her arm. An occasional damp washcloth eased the incessant suffering.

They administered even more drugs. Claiming it was necessary. All expenses covered by this new healthcare law.

The side rails clicked into place and, for the moment, they left the room. She heard voices mumbling in the hall, right outside the door.

The young woman never quite grasped what was happening. From the beginning, they insisted these tests were all routine. Part of a special program aimed at improving tribal medicine and assuring proper healthcare for the more unfortunate members still living on the reservation.

All sense of time and reason vanished.

This new sensation confused her. She tried moving her legs. Something warm and sticky blossomed. Metallic, yeasty odors floated through the chambers in her deadened nasal cavities. In a desperate effort, she twisted her head enough to see. Spreading red stains between her legs contrasted with the crisp white sheets. A scream stuck in her throat. If not already flat on her back, she would've collapsed in terror.

A nurse's hand tapped the side of a slackened cheek. She couldn't make out the words spoken. A cold rush of liquid moved up her arm, fighting the mass of insects swimming through her veins.

What was that smell? The accompanying taste seemed familiar but not pleasant.

She could not comprehend that unlike the perceived insects assaulting her body, a tangible alien substance now tumbled through her bloodstream. A portion of the tiny, injected molecules collided with and attached to sensitive nerve receptors, stimulating olfactory and gustatory centers. Only a part of their intended mission.

All fluid motion stopped as icy fingers caressed a weary heart. A few useless beats lingered, and then the muscle no longer compressed. The tingling and itching ceased. The insects had escaped.

She released one more breath and fled her ravaged body.

At long last, she'd be going home.

* * * * * *

The silver BMW stopped in front of the clinic's emergency room entrance. No screeching brakes or crying tires. A security guard ambled forward and stood by the vehicle as the driver opened his door. In no particular hurry, Dr. Kessler stepped out and looked at his watch. He shook his head. Almost two A.M. He threw the key fob to the guard and walked inside. The nurse met him, and they headed down the hall.

"Let me see the charts, Doreen."

"Yes, Dr. Kessler." She handed him the clipboard as they crossed the threshold of the patient's room. After a brief glance at the lifeless woman, he concentrated on the information in the charts.

"Same as the others?" he asked, but already knew the answer.

Doreen nodded. "The incidence of these side effects is holding steady. Statistically, it all matches our estimations. High enough to be certain of the correlation, but not so high as to jeopardize the clinical study." She took a deep breath and stood straighter. "We've got things under control, Dr. Kessler. There's no way to link these specific events to Uteroprost. Separate databases; different subjects."

Dr. Kessler glanced at the bloody sheets. "You get the last biopsy sample?"

Doreen gave a quick nod. "Yes, Dr. Kessler. We've already labeled the vials and sent them to the lab. I've logged it into the Uteroprost trial system. The patient's ConnorCare codes have been changed. Like the others."

Dr. Kessler handed the charts back. She took them with a grim smile. "These will be taken care of."

There was a knock on the door. Doreen walked over and ushered in two security guards. They nodded at Dr. Kessler and got to work. They'd done this before and understood what to do. No questions asked, no instructions needed.

CHAPTER 1

THE LENGTHY SHADOWS HAD RETREATED, softening the contrasts but not easing the tension. The clock chimed closer to noon than the early dawn hour that started the president's day.

Granted precious time with the leader of the free world, the woman had practiced her speech during the long flight from the West Coast. In a strong, clear voice, she delivered her opening lines.

The president asked only one question before walking to the windows behind his desk in the Oval Office. For the longest time he stared at the South Lawn. He watched the first lady and his youngest son playing with the family's new puppy. The Irish Wolfhound, still gangly and small, in several months would rival the president's physical stature but would never match his tenacity. The president longed for the family photo op scheduled for later in the day. A rare opportunity to spend time with them.

Facing the fireplace, the woman appeared lost in the regal atmosphere of the White House. But her words had forced the president to take a step back and fight the sensation of being boxed into his oval sanctuary.

The president saw the tossed ball disappear over the low hedge into the Rose Garden. He shook his head as two secret service agents scrambled to grab it before the puppy dug up the closest flower bed. One of them ran up to the president's son, knelt down smiling, and handed him the ball. At least, the president mused, the agent hadn't tussled the boy's hair. Lately, those guys spent more time with his family than he did. This made him pine for his secluded retreat in the western foothills of the Garden State.

He mumbled to himself, "That's not why I'm here." A little louder, but still looking out the window, he said, "Your ten minutes are up, Edie."

But instead of ushering her out, the president turned and picked up the phone to cancel his meeting with the house majority leader.

Edie Pauling's amber eyes remained fixed on the portrait of George Washington. President Tyler Griffin sensed the apprehension radiating from her normally confident demeanor. He'd lost count of all the people parading through this office with personal quests and absurd ideas. But Edie Pauling wasn't one of them. She was anchored in reality.

He took a deep breath and stepped toward her, knowing her former words had been only a brief prologue to a more frightening story. The stiffness of her posture made his own head spin and his stomach churn from the potential consequences of her visit.

"Now take as long as you need."

Edie Pauling jumped as President Griffin stepped closer, his booming voice catching her by surprise. The president motioned for her to take a seat across from him near the marble fireplace.

"You do know that was just a figure of speech?" he added, a grim expression set in place.

Edie brushed back strands of straight black hair, picked up her notebook, and recited the entire proposal to the president.

The president prided himself on reading behind the words, picking up the smallest nuances of body language tells, or even the most subtle changes in facial expressions. He needed to listen to this whole story without any distractions.

Her eyes stayed riveted to the pages in her notebook, avoiding Tyler Griffin's penetrating stare—known to slice his adversaries to pieces. She was far from being the enemy, but the story she brought today promised to be more controversial than the upcoming senate vote to repeal ConnorCare. It would definitely provide additional fuel for the growing backroom talk of impeachment as Griffin fought a bitter battle to strip away the divisive healthcare law.

She completed her speech with no interruptions. When she finally looked up at the president, Edie Pauling sighed and gave him a slight shrug. "Details still need to be worked out, but this is the deal—what they're prepared to do."

The president looked from Edie to the portrait of George Washington. He strained to listen to the playful shouts of his son and the escalating barks of his new puppy. The office closed in around him. The flames in the fireplace begged to be stoked, making him think of the splitting maul sitting in the metal shed at his retreat in Stillwater. He shrugged it off.

"I'm guessing they'll probably be dead before this ends," the president murmured. "But they already know that."

It was all he could say.

In response, Edie Pauling nodded.

It was all she could do.

* * * * * *

Edie hadn't planned on it, but she accepted the martini from the flight attendant and settled back in her seat. Not an unusual reaction for someone who'd just spent the last hour with the president of the United States. But Edie's apprehension didn't stem from intimidation; she only called him Mr. President in public. They'd been on a first name basis for a while. Edie worried about the impact her visit would have on President Tyler Griffin's legacy, but even more critical was how the nation would respond to the chain reaction of events certain to explode.

"Can I offer you another drink, Ms. Pauling?"

The flight attendant must've watched her suck down the first martini. Not the public image Edie welcomed. That snapped her back to reality. She took a deep breath and smiled at the waiting young man. His eyes fixed on the empty glass.

"Thanks, but no. Perhaps one of those bottled waters? Guess I'm thirstier than I realized."

"I just love watching the news segments when you battle it out with those know-it-all politicians. And…you're way… *way*… more gorgeous in person." He said this as he plunked several ice cubes into a glass, twisted off the bottle cap, and set the items on her tray table. The drained martini glass already whisked away.

Edie attempted to flash her ring finger, when the flight attendant continued.

"Love your hair. My significant other is a hairdresser. I can't wait to tell Eduardo that… Edie Pauling… our favorite political journalist… was on my flight." This time the word 'love' stretched into two long syllables, sporting a catchy tune.

She grinned and thanked him. As he moved the cart down the aisle, Edie relaxed and started feeling her old self again. She shook her head, considering how unforgiving any social media coverage would've been if she accepted a second martini. Luckily, nobody had any smartphones aimed in her direction.

And she found herself a little bit disappointed. Not from the guy not trying to hit on her, but from missing the chance to show off her rings. He probably would've appreciated the delicate design and styling. More so than Steve. Steve never even noticed the tooth marks on the tiny black box when he'd pulled out the engagement ring and proposed. That made her smile again.

Edie watched the Washington Monument shrink and fade below as the airliner banked gracefully around and climbed to its cruising altitude for the cross-country flight back to San Francisco. The receding landscape housed a unique blend of the American saga: history, power, patriotism, corruption; mixed into a vast urban scene of riches and poverty.

Just before she had left the Oval Office, the president threw out a proposal of his own.

Was it time for Edie to replace her favorite New York harbor icon? Unlike the Statue of Liberty, this new one didn't even have an expression on it.

If things worked out, she could ask Steve to rappel down the side of the Washington Monument and scribble on a happy face or two. Although he probably wouldn't be smiling at the prospect of trading one East Coast town for another one a little farther south.

President Tyler Griffin's new offer might just complicate an already adventurous relationship. Edie understood this, but remained oblivious to the circumstances that would soon unfold—and once again threaten her life and those she loved.

Chapter 2

At the end of his shift, Steve Casella, first-alert hazmat coordinator for the Dogpatch fire station in the Potrero Hill section in San Francisco, knocked on the open door to his captain's office. Leaning back, hands grasping his thinned and graying hair, Capt. Jordan looked up from the cluttered mess on his desk.

"Good work last night, Casella. Things could've gotten ugly if you guys hadn't secured those flammables right off."

"Would've been less of an issue if the owner had come clean from the start. But you know how it goes." Steve nodded at the pile of papers on Jordan's desk and dropped the latest incident report smack in the middle.

Jordan sighed. "Thank God it wasn't a wannabe terrorist like the call from the panicked neighbor hinted."

That's why he'd ordered Steve's team to respond to the scene in the first place. Steve was in charge of a specialized hazmat crew trained to deal with the growing risk of potential terrorist activities in the San Francisco Bay Area. They assisted local and federal law enforcement agencies in identifying risks and coordinating manpower. As first responders to many dicey situations, it made sense to have these guys trained to assess the threat potential from any given incident and be prepared to take action before the situation got out of control.

"You've probably got it all spelled out in painstaking detail," Jordan said, glancing down at Steve's report. "You sure you're not getting editorial help from Edie?"

"You know I hate writing these reports almost as much as you hate reading them," Steve said. "The facts just get in the way of a good story. Always left the investigative reporting to Edie."

"Nobody does it better than she does. Oops—I forgot. Should've used the past tense. Looks like her journalistic talents have been displaced. How the hell did that happen?" Jordan pushed his bulldog frame back in the chair, stretching his bulky arms. "An advisor to the goddamn president himself. So, she's found a way to avoid all the middlemen and preach directly to the choir."

Steve pressed his lips together. "The way things have been going in D.C., there's no time for any middlemen. And if anybody can make a difference…." Steve shrugged as his words trailed off.

Jordan filled in. "You got that right. But I can appreciate your approach too. Never imagined you'd find any use for that underused muscle between your shoulders. You heading home to work on your next novel? We're all waiting to see what that damn dog and her dimwitted handler are up to next."

Steve smiled. "Yeah, I was surprised to learn you could actually read. Always figured you were faking it with my reports. I'll try to remember to use simple words; maybe add a few pictures."

Before Jordan put together his response, Steve's phone chimed. His olive-toned Sicilian complexion turned two shades lighter as he read the text. Pushing back his scattered brown hair, he headed for the door.

Over his shoulder, Steve mumbled a shrilly sounding, "It's showtime."

CHAPTER 3

EDIE PAULING VAGUELY REGISTERED THE sounds of the screeching tires, the pounding footsteps, and the front door to their cozy one-bedroom cabin slamming open. In seconds, she recognized Steve's gasping breath as he stood staring down on the scene.

She watched his typical calm demeanor in dealing with a potentially dangerous situation evaporate faster than the fading twilight behind the western mountains bordering the Sonoma Valley.

How much longer can this go on?

"She look okay to you?" Steve blurted out for at least the fifth time in the last two minutes. "I still think we should've taken her to the clinic." It appeared to Edie that second-guessing himself had been honed into a new art form.

"I told you I've done this before. This is all very common on the reservation." Catori Torrence smiled and patted his arm. "Besides, I remember you telling me about assisting the paramedics on more than a few occasions yourself. Isn't that right, Edie?"

Catori's voice cut into Edie Pauling's distress, but all Edie could do was nod. On the verge of passing out, she blinked in time to her bobbing head while her black hair lay matted against cheeks, sheened in sweat. Rivulets of dampness trickled between her breasts. This was a new and terrifying experience. Maybe Steve was right. It wasn't supposed to happen like this. On a worn and battered bed.

What the hell were we thinking?

All of a sudden, she wished her Nana was here.

Edie cried out with a gasp. "Oh God—here comes another one."

Catori got into position, easing Steve to the side.

Several moments later Catori smiled and said, "I think that about does it. Let me make her a little more comfortable. Here you go, Steve. You got him? Careful now."

Steve's finger pointed down the line, lips counting in silence. "Huh. I guess they were right." He eased the last one onto the make-shift bed, nudging the blanket on top.

"I was beginning to think we'd get all black ones, but this last one's white. Just like they said." Steve coaxed out a weak grin. A bit of his Sicilian coloring returned.

Wiping the sweat from her face, Edie kneeled down and kissed her husband's cheek. "Steve? I hope you're not expecting me to deliver this kind of assortment if I'm ever pregnant. For now, I'll even ignore your racially insensitive comments."

"Hey. I'm just working out all these genetic details. That's all. We got Amber, a white female German Shepherd. We got one black male German Shepherd. Now we got six black puppies, and only one white puppy. Makes the Casella family genetics seem elementary."

Catori picked up the last clean towel and dried her hands. "Several of those black ones will probably turn lighter as they grow up."

With a guarded expression, Steve looked at the two young ladies. He ignored Catori's last comment. "So, Amber's doing okay?"

Chapter 4

THE SUN ROSE ABOVE THE redwoods on the ridge behind the training facility. Inside the steel building, Steve glanced at Amber's yelping twelve-week-old puppies in the exercise pen one more time before turning his attention to the students lined up against the rear wall.

He studied the paperwork and called out the names, "Harley, Misty, Ruby, Max, Ziva," and then checked off the appropriate boxes on his worksheet.

Although he'd been instructing these early morning canine training sessions on a regular basis for the last six months, he never understood why it seemed easier to remember the names of the dogs, while it got more difficult to keep the handlers' names straight.

About to start teaching today's class, Steve reacted to a tap on the shoulder. The person plunged into an animated dialogue. He coughed and looked at his watch, interrupting the woman in mid-sentence.

"You've got a great idea, ah…." Steve struggled to put it together. *Border Collie? Named Misty.* "Ah, Carol—"

The young lady in her late twenties and dressed as if she should be out on the town, barhopping, instead of taking a dog training class, tried not to look disappointed. "It's Nancy. Carol is the *older* woman who has the Springer Spaniel."

"Of course, Nancy," Steve said, trying to glide over his mistake, thinking those damn dogs looked alike. Hopping all over the place like jumping jacks. "I know we have the space to set up an agility training course, but that's not the purpose of these classes."

Nancy moved in a little closer, as did her dog. Steve expected the dog to lick his hand and sniff his crotch, but he sensed Nancy was about to perform a similar stunt. She bent over in front of him and grabbed hold of her dog, at the same time presenting him with an eyeful of her ample cleavage.

"I could give you a few key pointers on the sport." She droned on about bringing in her own agility training equipment and working with him in private.

Steve envisioned her putting new meaning to agility exercises. He tried blocking images of tight tunnels and swinging teeter boards. Visions of weave poles made his head spin.

Edie had talked him into building this new canine training center on the relatively flat piece of land across the dirt road from their house. She had witnessed firsthand how he worked with Amber, changing her from a wild, unmanageable, potentially dangerous animal by channeling her instincts and making her one of the best trained canines in the fire service. As a team, Steve and Amber rivaled the best police K9 squads in the country.

Several years ago, Steve spearheaded an innovative program in his department aimed at increasing the utilization and cross-training of canines in a number of service areas, including an assimilation of how firefighters interact with law enforcement agencies for handling terrorist threats.

At first, Steve had balked at the idea of firefighters carrying firearms on duty, but with Edie's perseverance, his thinking gradually adapted to the needs of what his special squad required to perform its new duties. An even steeper learning curve had been required before department officials came around to the same mentality.

These new first-alert hazmat teams were becoming a critical part of the arsenal in the war on terror. In dangerous situations, they were more often than not, first on scene. Having the ability to defend oneself, plus the added value of working with trained and motivated canines could often make the difference in a deteriorating situation.

Most dog training facilities in the surrounding North Bay area concentrated on teaching basic obedience techniques and classes enabling dogs to compete at American Kennel Club, or AKC, sanctioned obedience trials. Steve did not try to compete with those instructors. His mission was to establish classes geared to personal protection training for civilians.

Before his untimely death, Steve's uncle, a retired San Francisco police department K9 trainer, had given him great insight into the canine world, as well as the confidence needed to handle his first problem child, a white German Shepherd named Amber. Until his uncle stepped in, Steve had been ready to give up on dealing with the troublesome dog he had rescued from a house fire which took the life of Amber's owner.

Today's class was for puppies. Even though the end game was to have a well-trained protection dog, Steve's philosophy was that first and foremost, these were also family pets and needed the appropriate socialization skills and bonding with their handlers. This approach was not universally accepted. Many trainers believed a protection dog should be treated as a weapon, and any socialization or casual contact with other people should be vigorously avoided.

By the end of today's class, Steve had remembered most of the handlers' names; except they weren't always linked to the correct team. He wouldn't be forgetting Nancy's name anytime soon—but he wasn't associating it with the breed of dog she owned.

His assistant, Catori Torrence, was much more proficient at getting those details correct. She always had the paperwork in order and up to date for Steve when he entered the facility.

Steve taught today's class by himself. Earlier, he had seen Catori's car pull up in front of the training facility, but she'd dashed across the narrow country road and disappeared inside his A-frame cabin that overlooked the Sonoma Valley. When Steve peeked inside the door to see what was up, Edie shooed him away and walked Catori into the kitchen.

After class, Steve climbed up the steps to the wraparound deck and stepped through the front door of the home he shared with Edie. Amber, padding along at his side, picked up the pace and charged ahead into the kitchen. He scooted the puppies through the patio door and onto the fenced-in rear portion of the deck.

Edie and Catori sat at the table, sipping out of large mugs. From the aroma hitting Steve in the face, the mugs didn't appear to be filled with coffee.

"Care for any herbal tea?" Edie asked Steve. "Catori's brought over a special blend." She bit her lower lip after a furtive glance at Catori.

Steve and Edie met Catori Torrence at the same time Steve's uncle stumbled onto some terrorist activities up in the Idaho panhandle. His uncle had paid for the confrontation with his life. While investigating the suspicious death of his uncle, Catori, a young Native

American girl, had helped Steve and Edie uncover and eradicate the deadly terrorist plot.

From birth, Catori's life had been woven between the mysterious ancestral teachings of her prophetic grandmother and the trappings of the modern world. Recently turning eighteen, she had become a stunning beauty. Her olive-toned face, high cheek bones, and dark brown almond-shaped and distinctively slanted eyes had gradually matured. And she had lost none of the mysterious abilities that beguiled and astonished anyone who crossed her path.

Steve froze in place, sizing up the situation. Like on duty with his hazmat team, he took in the scene, trying to pick up signs of any immediate danger. Edie turned back to Catori, who had been petting Amber. Amber's head rested in Catori's lap. The dog shifted her eyes toward Steve.

"Thanks, but I think I'll put on a fresh pot of coffee," Steve said, deciding on his next move as he got to work measuring out the scoops.

He didn't know where the next words came from. "Anything wrong?"

Edie and Catori looked at each other; a silent signal passing between them. Catori nodded and turned toward Steve. Edie did the same and leaned back, arms folded.

Steve noticed that the coloring on Catori's face looked a little off; not an easy deduction with her dark complexion. He wondered if the 'special tea' had anything to do with the change and rendered a quick glance at Edie. No help there. The African American features of her face rarely gave any clues.

After a slight hesitation, followed by another quick glance at Edie, a familiar Cheshire smile emerged on Catori's face. "Steve, I'm sorry about missing class today."

"Blame me, Steve," Edie said, jumping in. "I wouldn't let her go."

Edie then held her hands out and apologized for the interruption. She lowered her head and bit her lip again.

Catori resumed, eyes taking on a hooded appearance. "I've been getting these awful headaches and cramps. About once a month?"

She placed her hands low on her abdomen; right above where Amber's head had just rested.

"And then the menstrual bleeding—along with the extremely bad headaches—did I mention the cramps?"

"Oh. And what about your breasts?" Edie helped out.

Catori nodded and cupped both hands under her breasts. "Yeah. See how swollen and…."

Steve turned away from the now evident rising flush on Catori's face and focused on the coffee pot, waiting for the chance to get the hell out of his own house.

Over his shoulder, he mumbled, "Ah, no problem, Catori. Next time, just call. I understand what you're going through. I mean, it's fine… really. I understand."

"Can I stop now, Edie?" Catori playfully pleaded and fanned her face with an outstretched hand.

Edie smiled. "I guess. By the way, Steve. Did you say you understood the symptoms? Huh. Must mean you think I can be a little bitchy at certain times of the month?"

Taking a breath, he stood his ground. "Nah. I'd say you got that covered pretty much twenty-four-seven."

Steve still looked for an out. He eyed the distance to the French doors leading to the deck, wanting to join the puppies and forget about the coffee.

Then it hit him.

No come-back from Edie. She'd never let him get away with that response.

Resigned, he walked over and sat down at the far end of the table and waited. He noticed the reddish hue on Catori's face had gone into full blossom.

All games over, Edie got down to business. "Catori needs a ride to the women's health clinic in Napa Valley tomorrow morning. The Kessler Foundation? She'll be checking in for a series of tests."

Glancing apologetically at Catori, she said, "I'm sorry I can't take you, Catori. But the president insists I'm standing in the Oval Office before his speech is scheduled to start in the morning."

With a concerned look, Steve leaned toward Catori. "No problem, Catori. What's going on?"

The color of Catori's face started returning to normal, but she still wore an awkward expression.

"Those things I just kidded about? They're kinda true. And it's been getting worse over the last few months." Catori held up her empty mug and managed a weak smile. "These ancient tribal remedies don't cut it anymore."

"So this is serious enough for you to go to a hospital?" Steve asked.

Catori placed her mug on the table and shrugged. "Several weeks ago, I went to the campus healthcare facility. I had a long talk with one of the visiting nurses. She asked me a ton of questions. A lot about my family background and even more about my tribal ancestry."

Pausing, Catori glanced at Edie. "As I just told you, Edie, she gave me a bottle of pills—said they were just the usual over-the-counter stuff—and told me to come back a week later. The pills didn't help much. If anything, things got even worse. When I went back, she sent me in to see a different doctor. From the clinic; the Kessler Foundation."

Confused, Steve said, "This doctor works at Sonoma State University, too?"

"No. Not directly. I got the impression the nurse called him in to help. He was very thorough and asked a lot of the same questions the nurse did. Told me because of ConnorCare, clinics specializing in female healthcare are now more accessible." Catori looked at Edie and raised her eyebrows.

Edie stood up and poured Steve a cup of coffee from the fresh brewed pot he'd all but abandoned. After placing the mug in front of him, she leaned back against the counter by the sink. "Before I began working for the government like you, Steve, and became part of the problem, one of the last stories I researched, centered on how ConnorCare could erode away the fundamentals of our healthcare system. I focused on female healthcare, since the new law, when it took over—imposing the single payer system at the federal level—appeared to have its most significant impact in that area. It represented the epitome of what an overreaching government could do."

Almost burning his tongue from the hot coffee, Steve said, "Yeah, I remember you did several interviews with that activist—the feminist. What was her name?" The name *Nancy* popped into his head. "The one with the humongous—"

"Earrings?" Edie interrupted.

Steve almost disagreed, but instead said, "Right, she wore those big earrings. They bounced whenever she talked."

After a slight pause, Edie replied, "That would be Tiffany Liebermann. And by the way, she'll be at the Kessler Foundation tomorrow."

CHAPTER 5

BENT OVER, HANDS RESTING ON his knees, Dr.
Dequain Johnson inhaled the cool, dry, early morning air.
After growing up across the Mississippi from the
sweltering humidity of New Orleans, the Napa Valley's
Mediterranean climate proved addictive. Although born
on the island of Jamaica, Dequain Johnson relied on his
family's recollections of its warm tropical climate since he
was only seven when the family of eight siblings moved
to America.

Dequain retained enough of his Jamaican lilt to garner
attention from strangers. He sometimes dialed it up when
the appropriate situation arose. As he did two months ago
when he'd gone through the BioCoGen's orientation
program organized by the company's public relations
director, Clarissa Mendelschein. He had gotten only a few
brief moments to speak with her during the tour of the
Kessler Foundation; the clinic affiliated with his new
employer, BioCoGen, and responsible for the Uteroprost
clinical drug trials.

In the rare moments when he allowed his mind to
free itself from mulling over problems connected to his
research projects, he considered every lame excuse for
giving her a call, but never did. And then he read the
email last night from Clarissa Mendelschein requesting a
late morning breakfast meeting.

Cooling down from his two-mile jog along the
meandering sloughs of the Napa River, he pulled in one
final lung-filling quaff, catching a briny taste and hint of
decay. He arched his back, and with a spring to his step,
walked up the path to his rented townhouse.

The one-bedroom unit stood two blocks up from the river, but faced the noisy highway, not the landscaped courtyards overlooking the private docks and river. That didn't matter because Dequain's busy work schedule never allowed him to take full advantage of the local amenities anyway. These morning workouts represented the only personal concessions he stole from the all-consuming research efforts at his new job. He had the habit of working well past the usual dinner hour.

A Harvard graduate with a PhD in molecular genetics, Dr. Dequain Johnson secured one of the four post-doctoral appointments at BioCoGen. BioCoGen was a well-established boutique pharmaceutical company, one of many in the San Francisco Bay Area. It had been singled out to participate in one of the new federal government pilot programs aimed at streamlining the clinical development of noteworthy new therapies.

These post-doctoral research positions were funded by the federal government through the new controversial healthcare law, ConnorCare, which slipped through congress during the final months of President John Connor's administration. This occurred right before the president and other key personnel in the White House had been forced out of office.

A poorly understood part of this law, of which there were many, was the establishment of a new regulatory agency, the Public Welfare Agency, or PWA. It possessed broad powers over all aspects of the administration of ConnorCare, including oversight of the FDA and all primary phases of both preclinical and clinical research. Under this law, government funding directed specific areas of research and co-opted private institutions to fast-track new therapeutic approaches through streamlined approval processes. The PWA currently directed enormous amounts of funds to promote research into female healthcare, and private companies had been chafing at the bit for a piece of the pie. It was the new venture capital system in play, with endless reserves of cash on tap.

BioCoGen, on the verge of capitalizing on the bottomless market of fertility control, pushed a revolutionary treatment modality. If the regulatory agencies approved the preliminary results with Uteroprost, the founders of BioCoGen stood to make billions from the acquisition of the patents by a competing stampede of any one of the major pharmaceutical companies.

Dr. Dequain Johnson was excited to have landed this post-doctoral position. It would give him an opportunity to resume his research on the investigation of key modulatory mechanisms of the ubiquitous prostaglandin system. This important biological pathway had paved the groundwork for BioCoGen's Uteroprost program. Dr. Johnson's area of expertise was not in reproductive biology but complemented the company's interest in prostaglandin research. That was why he'd been selected for this particular position.

Dequain smiled as he entered his condo, recalling his most recent attempt last evening to explain to his mother exactly what his research efforts entailed.

In her usual fashion, his mother had said, "Dequain, your father and I are so proud of the work you are doing. I have described to our friends that your work will do much to save the American Indians from the unpleasant suffering due to their dry and itchy skin."

"Yes, Mother. I cannot thank you and Father enough for your support to provide the opportunity for me to go to the finest schools and pursue this line of work."

If they didn't understand his field of expertise by this point, he decided that his mother's misguided version was close enough for them all.

CHAPTER 6

THE COFFEE HAD TURNED TEPID as Steve Casella's large, rugged hands swirled the mug on the kitchen table. He smiled at Catori and then looked back at Edie.

"Tiffany Liebermann? What the hell is *she* doing at this clinic?" Steve asked.

Edie focused her eyes on Steve. She told him about Tiffany Liebermann's scheduled appearance for a publicity event at the Kessler Foundation tomorrow morning.

"If you promise to behave, I'll give you my ticket, since regrettably, I can't attend."

Edie walked over to the trash container next to the refrigerator and grabbed the crumpled envelope, handing it to Steve.

Steve pulled out the invitation and started reading.

Edie shrugged and said, "Since Catori's going to be treated at the clinic, it can't hurt to find out a little more about it. If I were driving Catori there tomorrow, I certainly would want to listen to what Ms. Liebermann had to say at the rally. She's been traveling the country, giving speeches at all the clinics involved with ConnorCare's efforts to expedite the clinical development of innovative female healthcare therapies."

Steve made a point of flattening out the paper as he nodded. At least the coffee stains splattered over it had dried. "And with my renowned expertise in all female matters—what exactly might I be looking for?" A note of challenge crept into his voice; backed up by a slightly raised brow on an otherwise poker face.

Edie ignored Steve's comment. "I've still got my notes around here somewhere if you'd like, but one of the things that concerned me about ConnorCare involved the new federal agency named in the law. The PWA. And its role in driving private-sector research activities. They've already started partnering with drug companies and pushing new therapies through. Right now, fertility control is a hot venue being pumped up and pushed by the government."

"What does that have to do with this clinic?" Catori asked.

"Well," Edie said, "the Kessler Foundation was one of the first to receive a huge funding grant. But before I start, Catori—that's a whole different matter. You shouldn't be concerned about any of this. The clinic itself happens to be one of the best facilities in the world."

Edie smiled supportively and resumed. "This government program is why their new fertility control program, Uteroprost, has progressed so rapidly. They've entered into a special agreement with the federal regulatory agencies. This expedited program jumpstarts the clinical development plan to move potential drugs from the lab to the market in record time."

Knowing he'd hear more than he bargained for from Edie's response, Steve asked, "And you're against this? Why? Instead of weakening our healthcare system, doesn't this give more people and, in this case, I mean women, better access to medical care?"

"That's what you'd think, right? The government stepping in and providing on-the-spot oversight— pouring in millions of dollars—deciding what therapies are important. Specifying which strategies to follow. Did I mention on-the-spot oversight?" She leaned back and folded her arms. "What could possibly go wrong with that?"

"What time do you need to be at the clinic, Cat?" Steve ventured, ignoring Edie's challenge. His mind erased visions of the desperate attempt to find Edie, through miles of mining tunnels in the Idaho panhandle: safe and secure under the watchful eye of the Environmental Protection Agency. Another one of Edie's favorite government agencies.

CHAPTER 7

Syria

Twenty-five miles south of the Turkish border

(six months ago)

THE LIGHTS SNAPPED BACK ON, but for Farid the darkness remained. His consciousness blinked as a cold hand slapped across his face. Thick, dried blood stuck to his eyes, blocking out the harsh glare from the overhead fixtures. The stench of human waste filled his nostrils. The screaming had stopped. But the silence he understood to be more threatening.

Then he remembered—the blood was not his.

"You are back with us just in time." A familiar voice spoke to him in English, not his native Farsi.

The man's next words were spoken in Farsi, but not aimed at Farid. "Do not cut the girl down. First, you must lower Farid. We would not want him to miss this."

With a sudden rush of air, the unseen blade sliced at the rope stretching Farid's bloodied arms above him. Knowing what would come next did little to quench his fear. His mind retreated, attempting to mute the sudden sting of the putrid slime as his naked, bruised body plunged into the squalid pit.

His submersion lasted only seconds but seemed more like an eternity. Farid's arms were once again wrenched, his body dragged from the depths of the cesspool over the muddy and reeking surface. A chilling rush of icy water cleansed the filth, clearing away most of the crusted blood. He held his eyes shut to ward off what he feared the light would reveal. The smell of death still clung to the heavy air blanketing his sanity. Something slapped onto his prostrate body with a sickening thud. He knew what that was as well.

They expected him to open his eyes. So, he obliged. The cooling, disemboweled body of the young girl rested against his torso. They had been at this monstrous game for hours. In a savage motion, they slid the girl's body away toward the pit, smearing a path of blood and bodily fluids across his chest.

Farid's outward expression remained blank, hiding the fear and distaste. The brutal killing of the young girl did not disgust him. Death meant nothing to him. The death of another female warranted no reaction. But the defilement of his own body with that of the bleeding female corpse almost caused him to beg for it all to stop. Instead, Farid kept his silence and bit his tongue hard, his own blood mixing with the coagulating fluids of the dead female.

He forced himself to concentrate on the one thing that drove him. The hatred. The revenge he sought. This temporary distress represented a necessary path to his life's mission. His own personal jihad. All this, he convinced himself, was trivial.

Before the girl's body reached the pit, the words Farid expected echoed in his ears. He propped himself up to a sitting position and watched one of the men hacking the girl's breast. He stared at the man who had spoken to him in English.

"Do it," the man hissed.

Without blinking, Farid pushed himself off the floor. He took the offered knife from one of the men and, in a practiced motion, severed the dead girl's head. The knife cut through the soft tissue, cold metal striking bone. The lack of spurting blood made the job less fulfilling. He completed the task of kicking her remains into the slimy pit. Next, Farid jammed the head onto a rusted steel spike near the wall, in line with the others. There was no need to keep count. This would not be the last.

"Remember, Farid. Here in Syria, you are among friends. If you are caught in America, this will all seem insignificant. Our enemies are capable of much more defiling acts. They tell the world they would not stoop to our proven methods. But I know better than to accept their lies. Do you think you are ready to face the Great Satan?"

Farid nodded, but questioned the infidels resolve in dealing with the brave jihadists. He doubted they had the stomach for the real fight. Especially when the holy warriors showed up on the shores of the Great Satan. He knew this day drew near. And the numbers would be staggering. Of one thing he was certain. When the final confrontation commenced, he would be rejoicing the moment from a coveted place in Paradise. At the side of his father and the countless other jihadists that had come before.

* * * * * *

Halfway around the world, the psychologist listened to the man seated across from her. She jotted down a few notes and nodded. When she looked back up, her eyes blinked once.

"And how did this make you feel?" Dr. Saperstein asked.

"Are you fucking serious?"

Dr. Saperstein's expression remained neutral, her emotions veiled as she wrote on her notepad. "So, you are bothered by what you are doing?"

In an exaggerated motion, the CIA agent's hands lowered from his weathered face, and he stared at the doctor. His lower lip quivered. He took in a deep breath, but no words formed on his lips. From his shadowy countenance, the doctor knew he struggled with a desire to rip the notebook out of her hands. Or worse. In a reflex action, she tightened her grip and glanced down at whitened knuckles.

"Look, Doc," he said, bouncing out of the chair and searching for a window he couldn't find. He looked trapped, pissed-off, and helpless. He turned back to the doctor, his eyes dark and hooded.

Dr. Saperstein remained patient. Brutally so. She pretended to browse through the thick folder on her lap and chewed on the pencil between deliberate twirls of the instrument. The folder contained a lot of information, but none of it new to her. She had been following the details of the man's actions since this latest assignment had gotten under way. Her face reflected none of the concerns she fostered. This was her job. Trivial, compared to what they asked this man to do.

Her office sat in a non-descript building in the middle of the isolated complex. It did have a window, but it was hidden behind an interior oak panel. At this juncture, any glimpse at the tranquil setting in this remote mountainous retreat in the backwoods of Maine might've been the last step to catapult the man over the edge.

This military base housed the Navy's training site for the SERE program. That stood for survival, evasion, resistance, and escape. Dr. Saperstein's patient was a CIA agent and instructor in the level C component, or resistance phase, of this grueling training regimen sometimes referred to as the Big Boy program. It was aimed at providing military personnel with an unwanted degree of exposure to what would happen if they found themselves in the hands of the enemy. And unlike past conflicts, the nature of the current enemy presented a far more horrifying image of savagery. They followed no rules, and the game they played had roots planted by their prophet, Mohammed, in the seventh century after the death of Christ.

Another role for the CIA agent included his involvement in the use of enhanced interrogation techniques previously carried out at the U.S. military facility in Guantanamo Bay, Cuba. Dr. Saperstein remained one of the few individuals who could answer the question of whether or not these techniques were still sanctioned on the Ronald Reagan; the aircraft carrier whose classified location now housed the latest crop of detainees.

The doctor ratcheted things up. First, she pointed to the chair, and the man sat back down. "Do you think what you did," she paused after the deliberate use of the past tense, "saved lives?"

His eyes narrowed in confusion, and then he shook his head. "What the hell are you talking about? We both know damn well that's not the issue on the table."

"Go on," she prodded, her face still blank.

"We're not talking about using uncomfortable interrogation methods to extract information from fanatical savages. These are our own people; not some— and what I'm doing goes way beyond a little discomfort. This here is real fucking torture. Forget all the politically correct propaganda babbling from the media. This is what they'll face when those fucking barbarians grab hold of them. Not to mention the obvious."

He got no response to the bait and pounded a fist on the table between them. The doctor held her ground but couldn't stop her eyes from blinking shut. She recovered and allowed them to widen, still not moving her body.

He rubbed his hands and grasped the back of his head. "You know exactly what I'm talking about." His eyes narrowed. "And what in the hell is wrong with the Defense Department? Not only allowing women to participate in special ops—Navy SEALs, in particular—but signing off on this operation. The men will be facing the cruelest form of torture you can imagine. But a woman? Those fucking savages don't even consider females to be human. And if she ever makes it back alive, which I seriously doubt, she won't be anything even close to human again."

Dr. Saperstein did something she rarely did. She leaned forward—as close to a challenge as she'd ever gotten. "And how did this female respond to your techniques?" She knew the woman's name was Angela, but refused to use it in her question.

She got the reaction she expected.

He stood, returning the challenge, a tight smile on his face. "She asked for more."

The doctor nodded as he walked toward the door. Placing his hand on the knob, he turned and said, "What the hell drives someone to volunteer for what's clearly a suicide mission?"

He didn't wait for her response. The door slammed shut. As Dr. Saperstein listened to his footsteps fading away, the expression on her face no longer hid her emotions. She didn't make any more entries in her notebook. She looked down at the pen held in her hand, surprised to see her fingers steady, no visible tremors.

* * * * * *

In a rusted metal building at the north end of the military base, the room remained dark. By her rough calculations, this was longer than any of the other times. She knew no other way to do this. Whatever they did, she would endure. Almost welcome, because it would bring her that much closer to her goal. She'd survive this, and what was to come—the real evil.

Her intense training as a Navy SEAL would only get her so far. She'd then retreat to somewhere deep within herself. She'd tune everything out, except the memory of her father, and will her body to separate from her mind.

The footsteps sounded in the distance. Hesitant at first. But as they got closer, she sensed a building resolve in the pattern. Possibly, he'd survive this too. No one had ever discussed who he worked for. She presumed CIA— but just left it at that.

In her darkest moments, she allowed herself to think what it would be like when it was over, and to return and shake his hand. Deep down, Angela knew it would never happen.

CHAPTER 8

SHUTTING HER EYES, BUT NOT expecting to sleep, Edie listened to the embodying engine sounds and the increased vibrations as the jumbo jet started its takeoff run on her late-night flight from San Francisco to Washington, D.C. She whispered a brief prayer for her friend, Catori, knowing she was in good hands with Steve. Her mind then refocused on what would unfold after the president's address to the nation.

Since first presenting this idea to the president, an overwhelming weight of responsibility pressed on Edie's shoulders for its potential consequences, coupled with the ungodly sacrifices being made by the two men and one woman who had first come to her over a year ago with this insane plan.

She barely fathomed the pain and suffering that would be unleashed on the two men. As for the woman, she was without reference as to the degree of defilement she'd be forced to endure. Edie didn't think any female who confronted this madness could remain even remotely sane. No matter how many times Angela had spoken to Edie about her motives, the reality could not be grasped.

Against all odds, Angela had fought her way through the stringent training program to become a Navy SEAL. She was one of the first females to qualify in the special operations forces after the Department of Defense lifted the gender restrictions.

No one in the ranks considered it a good idea to allow women in these positions, and many had remained vocal in their objections through the entire process. Angela shrugged it all off. She figured if she couldn't take this kind of heat—they were right—she didn't belong.

Only the president and a select few individuals knew the plan's true nature. Steve Casella happened to be one of those people. Edie had made it clear to the president, that whatever she knew, her husband needed full clearance as well. Based on past interactions, President Griffin had no problems with that arrangement.

The bizarre path leading to the White House for Tyler Griffin had been filled with a dangerous series of conspiracies and partisan politics instigated by a few corrupt political leaders and labor union bosses. At the top of the original list of enemies was President John Connor, only the third president ever to be impeached, and the only one to be removed from office. The former president now served time in a federal prison for his crimes.

Connor had tried to destroy Tyler Griffin, the then senator from New Jersey, as part of a plot to discredit a new grassroots movement called the Restraint in Government Alliance, or RGA. The goal of this fringe coalition focused on reducing the size and the power of the federal government. And Tyler Griffin had become their leading advocate.

While Connor's initial plot had wounded the RGA, Griffin came out unscathed, and perhaps stronger from the ordeal. Both parties were terrified of what Griffin could do to the political status quo in Washington. The labor unions, in particular, had plotted against him. A failed assassination attempt headed by two corrupt union leaders, and potentially backed by an unknown, but deadly consortium, actually helped spearhead Griffin's rise to the White House. The discovery and unraveling of those events, in large part, resulted from the efforts of Steve Casella and Edie Pauling.

* * * * * *

President Griffin delivered a forceful speech. He outlined the behind-the-scenes negotiations that had led to the return of three Navy SEALs captured by an offshoot of Al Qaeda two months ago in Afghanistan. This particular terrorist organization had strong ties to the Muslim Brotherhood. Jihadist groups were on the rise and were becoming the more virulent terrorist threat. There was growing concern that similar groups with more subtle ties to the Muslim Brotherhood had already spread their tentacles into the United States. Homegrown Islamic terrorists might be hiding out and training within our borders; in plain sight and protected by our constitution.

According to the president's words, in exchange for the safe return of the captured SEALs, he had released four top Al Qaeda leaders. The jihadists had been detained by the United States military for the last two years and held on the Ronald Reagan Nimitz-class super carrier, the current administration's answer to the forced closure of the facilities at Guantanamo Bay.

While the United States had a longstanding policy of never leaving a soldier behind, the president's negotiations with a terrorist organization were viewed by many, including members of his own party, as an open invitation to the world that Americans were valuable kidnapping targets.

Tyler Griffin's campaign rhetoric on promising a tough foreign policy agenda had been one of the reasons for him beating out his opponent in a fierce and close presidential race. While the nation was weary of the endless wars and conflicts, and watching our brave soldiers being killed or disfigured, they knew that a weakened, tentative approach by America would only lead to further escalation of Islamic terrorism throughout the world.

One could not ignore a threat of this proportion. Griffin had vowed to oppose the Islamic jihadists from a position of strength, not weakness. The greatest risk of precipitating an aggressive action by your enemies, he had touted, was an indecisive and appeasing leader, coupled to a weak and retreating military.

And now, as the nation listened to President Griffin announce he had secretly negotiated with the enemy, many feared we were caving to terrorist threats. Another example of the continuing decline of our role as the leader of the free world. To make matters worse, the fact that one of the SEALs was a female, reopened old wounds and a national debate about the consequences of sending females into the heat of battle.

President Griffin's immediate predecessor, Alice Andersen, had her hands tied in fighting the war on terror after the Senate Intelligence Committee released a report detailing how American intelligence services used enhanced interrogation techniques, described by the media as torture, in their quest to obtain vital information from post 9/11 detainees.

The consequences of publicizing these activities did widespread damage to the credibility of the United States in the world community, but in Tyler Griffin's mind, it also gave our enemy an added incentive to carry on their jihad. Not in the sense they were appalled by what they heard, but by the fact they no longer feared being captured.

Not all Islamic jihadist leaders trusted us to be so ignorant as to give up any viable means of combating their efforts. They continued to warn their troops about the dangers of being captured. Better to die in the effort and take as many infidels as possible.

Exactly what activities took place on the Ronald Reagan remained a mystery. The administration hand-fed periodic briefings to the congressional intelligence committees and only allowed them infrequent visits to the detainee cells on the carrier. The current location of the Ronald Reagan remained classified, and Tyler Griffin was doing everything in his power to make sure it stayed that way. They couldn't let political expediency win the battle to subrogate the war on terror.

The president's announcement this morning came as a complete surprise to both sides of the aisle. Both his supporters and the opposition failed to understand his end game. On the surface it appeared Griffin's efforts in negotiating with a terrorist organization were at complete odds with everything he had done thus far.

Everyone smelled blood in the water, and the sharks circled eagerly around President Griffin. To long-time insiders in D.C., to accomplish this prisoner exchange with no one outside the inner circle of the White House included in the discussions did not seem possible. Cries of executive overreach and abuse of power echoed throughout the political heart of the nation. It appeared that the strife between the executive branch and congress was about to get a lot worse.

In the shadows of the Oval Office, while the president delivered his speech announcing this unprecedented and dangerous action of negotiating with terrorists, Edie hunched forward on the sofa, covering her face with both hands. Eyes squeezed shut, she summoned up the image of her own father, the last time she saw him, the last words he spoke to her. Whether or not he recognized the danger he was heading into, Edie knew it wouldn't have mattered. He would've still walked through that door. The love of his country and the responsibility he lived every day was all he considered.

Edie saw that same strength and resolve in the three Navy SEAL prisoners the president talked about today. Angela was the daughter of one of the best friends Edie's father had ever known. Like Edie's father, he too had died saving others in the name of the United States of America, the country he loved. Angela was prepared to do the same. Not for glory. Not for fame. But because she was taught to do the right thing.

The events that would be made public over the next several days would challenge not only the president but would target the loyalty and integrity of these three Navy SEALs. The scathing accusations would be too much for any ordinary person to bear. But not to the three Navy SEALs at the heart of this issue. They understood what they had done. That was all that mattered.

Edie knew that the president's speech, while not exactly a lie, was by far nowhere near the whole story. The next part of this saga would hit hard, as a series of carefully planned leaks found their mark.

CHAPTER 9

CLARISSA MENDELSCHEIN TOYED WITH HER cup, listening to the melodic lilt of Dr. Dequain Johnson's Jamaican cadence. Sitting in a corner booth of the BioCoGen cafeteria, they presented a shockingly contrasting image. Dequain Johnson stood just shy of six feet. With his shaved head, pencil-thin frame, and black skin, one imagined a cue stick poking at the eight ball.

Across the narrow table sat Clarissa, not considered short, except in comparison to Dequain. Her finely honed body, accentuated by her outfit, still maintained a professional appearance. Clarissa possessed a pale radiance with natural blond hair that had been notched down about four shades lighter. This framework transformed her nominally thick, black-rimmed glasses into a magnet that kept Dequain's attention on her blue eyes. A light jasmine-scented aura surrounded her.

"So, Dr. Johnson, are you finding everything to your satisfaction at BioCoGen?" Clarissa interjected, regretting the need to interrupt the musical intonations of his speech.

A broad smile transformed Dequain's face. "Please, Clarissa, you must call me Dequain."

She blushed, the reddish wave disappearing beneath her white blouse. The name, Dequain, sounded like a song. She sensed an underlying shyness in him, as well, and nodded in response.

"Everyone has been most helpful. The equipment in the lab has been set up and I have started doing pilot studies." His engaging smile faded. "There may be, however, certain things that are not going as planned. I've encountered a few minor issues, but once I can determine the problem, I'm sure the experiments will start to move in the right direction. I'm positive these new studies will help to better understand the concepts behind the Uteroprost treatment protocols."

Clarissa observed that as he spoke about his work, his voice turned less lyrical, even as his speech became more animated. To keep him talking, she asked, "If I remember correctly, your research involves the investigation of genetic profiling in certain populations, and their susceptibility to scleroderma. How does this work fit in with what we do here at BioCoGen?"

She had spent considerable time last night reading Dequain's Curriculum Vitae, so she had some idea of the work he had done for his PhD thesis. Although the part about not understanding how it fit into her company's research interests was true.

Dequain looked again into Clarissa's eyes. "I know you are familiar with the biological molecules in the prostaglandin pathways. Your presentation during the orientation made that clear."

"Of course. Prostaglandins are the basis of Uteroprost. By modulating how they interact with the female reproductive system we can control fertility, as well as correct deficiencies or problems with any part of a woman's cycle." She wondered if any of those damn prostaglandins had instigated these sudden tingling sensations. She sensed her face getting hotter and squeezed her legs tighter together. Thank God the gasp she heard was only in her head.

Dequain gave her a strange look and said, "You are right. And your scientists have developed agents to modulate a key factor—"

"Transuteroglobin," she blurted out the word, trying to rein in her own hormones. Since when did prostaglandins turn her on? "Prostaglandins are powerful hormones, right?" Clarissa had just about lost her ability to think; she needed to put back on her company hat and stop acting like a schoolgirl.

Dequain's jaw slackened. "Well, yes. You're correct about the importance of transuteroglobin being the key. But one point of clarification, Clarissa. Prostaglandins are not hormones in the general sense. They work locally in the tissues where they're produced. They don't travel through the bloodstream to exert their effects. So, they're not considered to be hormones in the true meaning of the term."

"Oh." The single word tumbled out. She liked being corrected by Dequain, finding it difficult to concentrate on his words as a droplet of sweat trickled a path between her breasts. She picked up what he had been saying in mid-sentence.

"—responsible for regulating which prostaglandins are activated and in what sequence. But prostaglandins are important in regulating a host of other biological functions. They work locally in almost every tissue of the body. My research is involved with studying the role of transuteroglobin in predisposing certain ethnic groups to scleroderma. There is a specific genetic alteration in some Native American tribes that may be responsible for the high incidence of this disease."

Right now, Clarissa didn't care about Native American gene pools. She wanted to find out more about Dequain. At the same time, Dequain, apparently forgetting about prostaglandins, turned the conversation to Clarissa's personal life. She toned down that aspect by discussing her responsibilities at BioCoGen. This gave those damn prostaglandins a chance to sneak back to the local tissues where they belonged.

The main part of her job description included the coordination of the public relations aspects of disseminating company propaganda to the general public. While her science background was limited, she was phenomenally gifted in making technical and scientific jargon understandable to the lay person. She was at home dealing with physicians, research scientists, accountants and business managers, the media, and the general public.

Because of her ubiquitous activities, she was a visible fixture in many of the inner circles of the company. Her accessibility to most aspects of the business gave her considerable powers that neither management nor Clarissa herself had ever considered.

Today, sitting in this booth, legs still held tightly together, she was having trouble remembering her own name, but she was glad she'd initiated this first move. And from the expression on his face, so was Dr. Dequain Johnson.

CHAPTER 10

TWO HOURS BEFORE THE PRESIDENT'S scheduled speech, Steve and Catori began the early morning drive to the Kessler Foundation. He guided the light green Tahoe through the remaining primal redwood groves that did their best to shutter out the dawning skies—in juxtaposition to the scattered vineyards awaiting the sun's radiant heat to lick away the evening's dew and sweeten the upcoming vintage.

The Tahoe crested the ridge dividing the Sonoma and Napa wine producing regions, and the expansive Napa Valley stretched below them, ablaze in the morning sun. After the winding descent onto the valley floor, Steve crossed the flat terrain and linked up with the Silverado Trail about two miles north of Yountville. A bronze sign posted on a triangular granite slab on the right side of the road indicated the entrance to the Kessler Foundation.

A stern, but polite security guard at the gatehouse confirmed Catori's admission code and check-in time. Steve needed to present two forms of identification, including a photo ID, and fill out a two-page questionnaire before being provided a guest pass. He thought that flashing the ticket Edie gave him to attend the rally would speed up the process, but it wound up delaying the guard from allowing him access, as it necessitated an additional phone call to have the appropriate substitution made on the rally's invited guest list.

As the gate cranked open and Steve edged the Tahoe forward, Catori smiled and said, "How'd you think that would've gone if Edie was here to critique their techniques?"

"Careful what you say, they've probably got listening devices attached to my pass," Steve joked, but his hand unconsciously rubbed the visitor pass clipped to his shirt pocket. He had an unwelcome flashback about a supposed militia compound in the Idaho panhandle that turned out to be a front for an even more frightening operation. The guards at the Kessler Foundation didn't look anything like Muslim terrorists, but then, neither did the group in Idaho. They were disguised as a red-necked right-wing organization. Steve shook his head. Not this time. Not in California. He chanced a cautious glance in his rearview mirror.

The paved drive climbed to the edge of a broad knoll where a complex of interconnected buildings formed an intricate maize overlooking Lake Hennessey, the reservoir for the city of Napa's municipal water supply. Even at this early hour, the parking lot looked full. Steve assumed it was because of the women's rights rally due to start in about two hours.

After finding a spot for the Tahoe, he grabbed Catori's bags from the back seat and gave her a slight hug with his free arm. "You okay, Cat?"

"Without going into the gory details, I'm fine. Thanks for doing this. You're a sweetheart," Catori said, managing a weak smile.

"Now you got me worried. I'm not used to any of my girls being so deferential. Yesterday's attitude was much more like it."

Catori raised her head and glanced around. "A little advice, Steve? You might wanna lose the 'my girls' line. May not go over so good at a female healthcare rally. Especially if you're trying to impress Ms. Liebermann with your progressive modern male attitude."

Steve smiled. "Oh, I intend to keep a low profile at this rally. I'll just sit in the back of the room and take notes. Not planning on getting anywhere near the goddess of fertility."

"I'm thinking you got that backwards, but aren't you going to ask Ms. Liebermann any pertinent questions from your enlightened sexist point of view?"

Shaking his head, Steve said, "I doubt there's anything Ms. Liebermann can reveal that I haven't seen before."

"My senses tell me you should be careful today," Catori said with a slight smile and fluttering eyes.

"Yeah?" he countered. "And my senses think Edie told you to keep an eye on me."

She shrugged. "Love to, but I have to check in to the clinic before the rally starts. So, you'll be on your own."

The admissions process proceeded on schedule. The staff had most of the forms completed, requiring only several signatures from Catori. Steve thought he detected an abrupt change in attitude when he asked for copies of the documents to take home with him. The moment passed quickly after Catori approved his request, but a sense of uneasiness haunted him as they escorted Catori down a long corridor, and she disappeared behind a large steel door.

At the last moment, she turned and gave Steve a brief smile and a wave.

The clanking of the door swinging shut still echoed in his head as he sat in the clinic's cafeteria and sipped his coffee, waiting for the rally to start. Steve shuddered at this last sight of Catori—now replaced by a past image of her running through a web of abandoned mine tunnels and recalling how confident she had been in leading him on a dangerous path buried far beneath the earth.

Although certified to work confined space rescues, he'd never be as comfortable as Catori in navigating an underground environment. Catori's father had taught her everything she knew about the mining networks in the heart of the Silver Valley, deep in the Idaho panhandle. But ultimately, those same mines took her father's life.

Working in the Bay Area, Steve had only rare opportunities to test his underground stamina again. And that was a good thing. He'd never been at ease riding BART, the Bay Area's rapid transit subway system. He couldn't remember the last time he'd even been on a BART train and had no intentions of doing so in the near future.

* * * * * *

Alone in the small room, stripped down to a hospital gown, Catori Torrence became more nervous than she would've guessed. After all, she was just here to undergo several minor tests to get a better handle on her symptoms and the best approach for managing them. She never considered her medical problems to be anything serious.

Then the nurse in the Sonoma State clinic had begun lecturing her on a host of potential complications. After listening to all the doom and gloom, her symptoms magically intensified. Of course, all that might be in her head.

When she came back for the follow-up visit, the nurse whisked her in to see this new doctor. She hadn't paid any attention to the doctor's name until today. Dr. Kessler. Dr. Kessler—the head of the Kessler Foundation. The head of one of the most prestigious clinics in the country, if not the world. For some reason, he found it necessary to respond to a school nurse's inquiries about her health.

"Oh God! What the hell could be wrong with me?"

Catori leaned back on the pillow and started taking long, deep breaths, eyes closed, hands on her cheeks. She panicked, with a sudden need to gulp for more air. The blanket felt like a dead weight on her chest, and she yanked it down, pushing the half-eaten tray of food aside. At first, she had been hungry, but the lingering smell of the mystery breakfast meat and rubbery eggs coagulating on the plate turned her stomach.

Probably didn't agree with the regimen of pills the nurse's aide forced her to swallow right after being deposited into this room and stripped of her street clothes. Several sour burps floated up. Trying to shove them back down with a dry swallow, a coughing fit took over, making her eyes sting, but no tears came.

"This is just great," she murmured, "I've been here less than an hour, and I'm becoming a hypochondriac. Jeeze, get a grip on yourself."

With a few cleansing breaths, she relaxed and turned her mind to images of the past. The stirring visions whirling about her head had the paradoxical effect of anchoring her body, while releasing her mind to soar and meld with her ancestral family. As of late, dark, unbidden images penetrated her visions, assaulting the pleasant memories.

Before accepting the scholarship at Sonoma State University, Catori Torrence had been spending more and more time with Bobby Smithfield, a young man on the reservation. He shared her dreams of embracing their cultural heritage in a way that would help merge them into a modern world and surmount the stereotypical boxes stifling those on the reservation.

They had also shared more intimate physical manifestations of their attraction to each other. At first, with a blundering inexperience and innocence; but without any embarrassment, a whole new world of exploration emerged, and they eagerly embraced their emotions.

Catori never told Bobby about her going to this clinic. Right now, Catori felt empty without him here, but selfish for this weakness. She was having trouble opening her eyes and remembered it was probably the medications. They had told her to relax. The doctor would be in to see her later today to explain what they were going to do. The testing was scheduled to start first thing in the morning. She longed to return to the traditional herbal remedies of her ancestors and unchain herself from this so-called modern medical facility.

She picked up the small mirror on the bedside table and lightly ran the brush through her hair. That always helped relax her.

"What the hell?" She gazed at several clumps of hair clinging to the stiff bristles on the brush. She tossed the mirror and brush into the table's drawer, slamming it shut.

"It's a good thing Bobby's not here to see me in this condition."

But she really needed to be held right now. She believed her entire body was falling apart.

CHAPTER 11

BEFORE EDIE PAULING REALIZED IT, the cameras were gone and the bright lights were off. The Oval Office emptied. The drapes behind the president's desk slid open and the outside world intruded. Edie sat still as the president took several deep breaths and turned from the natural sunlight that briefly provided the man a rare moment of peace.

As he headed toward Edie, Tyler Griffin snatched the handset from the phone cradle and brusquely issued a few short commands. His final halting steps before sinking into the sofa across from Edie displayed how heavy all this weighed on the man.

To the uninitiated, his next words bordered on an attack on the young woman he faced, but Edie knew better and took no offense, only compassion for what he needed to do. She let him spill it all out. She understood what would happen next, once they carried out his orders.

Leaning forward, the president looked at his hands, alternately making fists and rubbing them harshly in his lap.

"You know Angela… don't you, Edie?" The words hit her harder than his previous rant.

Saying nothing, she stared back into his eyes.

"I've thought about those three SEALs every day; from the moment the terrorists captured them to the day we got them home." He shook his head. "Yeah, that was a big help. I visited them when they first got back. I know you did too. I also remembered shaking their hands before sending them into Hell. Don't think they'll ever be the same."

"Tyler," Edie started, "I—"

"Let's just get the rest of this done," he interrupted.

Edie glanced aside as the president wiped away the gathering moisture from his eyes.

"Things are going to heat up now. Think we can count on our friends on the hill for squeezing this for all it's worth?" The president paused to let out a gruff laugh. "This may be our only chance to observe congress acting as the singular body they're supposed to be. Too bad it will probably just lead to a quicker road to impeachment."

Following President Connor's disgraceful departure from office, the vice president, Alice Andersen, took over the top spot in the White House. In a surprising move, she appointed Tyler Griffin, the republican senator from New Jersey and unofficial leader of the Restraint in Government Alliance, as her new vice president.

Alice Andersen, like her prior boss, John Connor, was a democrat. It was a bold move aimed at restoring the citizens' faith in their federal government to work together and begin the healing process after seeing their top leaders indicted for murder and a series of high crimes and misdemeanors. Unforeseen health problems with Andersen paved the way for the election of Tyler Griffin.

This process had done little to steer the nation back on track. Griffin narrowly squeaked through the primaries, upsetting the traditional republican candidates. And then in the general election, the heated campaign resulted in an even narrower margin of victory for Griffin. In the end, the man now seated in the White House faced a fierce battle against both parties in congress.

To make matters worse, the attorney general, now an elected official, appeared hell-bent on weakening the president at every step. From Griffin's perspective, his presidency represented the final attempt to restore the nation to its original values.

The president's goal to rein in the vast powers of the federal government appeared distant and unsurmountable. ConnorCare was the first critical wound that needed to be fixed. But right now the blood was spilling hard and fast from the revelation that he'd negotiated with a terrorist organization over the release of several high-profile detainees.

CHAPTER 12

Somewhere in Mexico

(one month ago)

THE ENDLESS HOURS OF SUFFOCATING heat could not be fathomed. The stench of human waste hung like a second skin and stuck to the lungs with every breath. Underlying traces of decomposing flesh darted about like bony fingers pointing at death. The darkness did nothing to hide the suffering, just as it failed to mask the fear of the wretched riders. The truck bounced and shook those inside into varying states of paralysis, the only hint of relief for the living dead.

Farid drunk it in like a tonic, strengthening his resolve. He'd endured far worse to arrive at this point. Every fetid breath took him one step closer to his destination and the culmination of his personal jihad. If it pleased Allah, it would be a one-way journey to complete a task that had driven him from the moment his uncle brought his family the dreaded news.

He had listened to every gruesome detail regarding the death of a father he had hardly known. He had identified with his father as a brave jihadist driven by faith and a consuming hatred of the vile infidels. The young Farid did not weep at the news of his father's demise. Instead, a fiery rage built within him. It was surely the soul of his father igniting in him the need to pick up the sword and honor the prophet.

Endlessly, the American government argued the case to secure the borders and to reform immigration policies. At the same time, officials chose to remain ignorant regarding the extent and efficiency of a dangerous network of complicated routes organized by an enemy that had vowed to bring the fight to America's backyard.

As a result, Farid now hid among this pack of desperate, but hopeful creatures from countries such as Nicaragua, Belize, Guatemala, and other third-world points of origin. This represented the final trek of his long journey. Even if he had been on his own, once reaching the southern border of America, his options would be plentiful and far less dangerous. Due to his grasp of the English language and inherent light complexion, with proper clothing and grooming he would easily blend in with the infidels. But his leaders left nothing to chance, and the next phase of Farid's mission had been carefully orchestrated.

Farid knew he embodied the spearhead of the coming wave of Islamic jihadists to America. At long last they would take the fight to the homeland of the Great Satan. A critical mass would soon be reached, and the ultimate jihad would be launched. His task was to stoke the embers of fear until the day of reckoning arrived. Farid did not care if he lived to see that day, he would rejoice with the other jihadists in Paradise.

Farid had one other goal that superseded all else. This all-consuming quest challenged his allegiance to the greater jihad of Allah. Either way, he stood willing to pay the consequences for his actions. He knew when the time came, Allah would guide him down the correct path.

Chapter 13

Dr. Dequain Johnson stared at the stack of laboratory notebooks on his desk. Clarissa Mendelschein had come through as promised. At the time of their breakfast meeting, sitting across from her in BioCoGen's cafeteria, he thought he'd overdone it a bit. He always got carried away whenever the topic focused on his research. And he usually found the exact path to end up there.

That same day, Dequain had talked to Clarissa about one of the professors at Harvard University who he had worked with on a major portion of his research. Always a character, Dr. McBride liked mixing things up in the lab and pulling pranks on the newcomers. He had a favorite trick of sneaking up behind new students while they toured through the large-animal research facility. This was where they housed the dogs, sheep, and primates, either in cages or pens, in climate-controlled rooms. While the new students listened to the facility manager's speech, from behind, Dr. McBride would grasp someone's calf, and utter a shrieking, snarling sound. This was especially fun when the new student was a young female.

Dequain always wondered how Dr. McBride had gotten away with those antics. Anyone else would have been dragged into the dean's office and fired. Dequain credited this as a strong testament to the integrity and the stature of Dr. McBride. No one ever questioned his motives, and respected the work he did at the university.

Another tidbit of wisdom about Dr. McBride he chose to pass on to Clarissa was an important lesson he learned about analyzing the data from experimental results. Dr. McBride told him the only way to gain a real feel for any scientific study was not to look at the reports, but to grab the raw data and feel it in your hands. He said you needed to smell the numbers to understand what conclusions could be drawn from the data.

When Dequain finished telling Clarissa that last story, she had remained silent, staring at him for quite some time before she responded.

"Dequain, did you know that when you talk about your work, you no longer have any accent? Isn't that strange?" Then she whispered, "This is something that definitely needs more research."

As she got up to leave the booth, Clarissa had turned back to Dequain and said, "I have access to all research files in the company. If you'd like, I can obtain the preclinical Uteroprost data from the archives and send them to your office."

Coming back to the reality of the moment, Dequain was now troubled by what he'd been looking at since the notebooks had been delivered to his office. He read every research report and then compared the executive summaries to the raw data files. On the surface, everything appeared to be in order; but then he started to smell the data.

He reached for the phone and called Clarissa.

CHAPTER 14

STEVE HAD TIME TO KILL before the women's rally started, so he wandered about the non-restricted areas at the Kessler Foundation. The queasy sensations in his gut got stronger. Probably that second donut he forced down. No. Something just seemed off about this place. Of course, he'd never spent a whole lot of time at a women's health clinic before. Hospital emergency rooms—that was something he unfortunately had way too much experience with.

According to Edie's notes, this place was a world-renowned private clinic. And it did look expensive. The buildings, grounds, and interiors were all extravagant and well-appointed. The atmosphere—not all that friendly, but everyone was at least polite and professional. The security—that had gotten him nervous from the start. It was conceivable the high level of security was necessary because of the government oversight and partnership since ConnorCare became the law of the land.

This was one of the first clinical trials performed under the expedited guidelines using the new regulatory criteria set forth by ConnorCare. Edie had highlighted that information in bright yellow in her notes. Evidently, a lot rode on the success of this particular therapeutic approach to fertility control. And that's what Tiffany Liebermann's rally was all about.

Walking back into the main lobby, Steve was pulling out his ticket to check on the location for the rally when—

She smacked into him from the left as she literally flew out of the restroom.

If he'd been paying attention, he might've caught her before she fell, but it was doubtful he could've avoided the collision altogether.

He stood by with a dumb expression, gazing at Tiffany Liebermann's large, bright red leather shoulder bag and watching the contents spill over her cream-colored knee-length tent skirt, which at the moment flapped about her waist. At least her navy-blue sleeveless blouse remained tucked in place.

Steve didn't get much opportunity to evaluate this transitory image. A fraction before the barrage of obscenities aimed at him exploded, two thoughts buzzed through his head. One was that Ms. Liebermann did not have on her earrings. And the other was that while he honestly tried to look away from the unfolding drama below him, he noted the absence of a particular article of clothing.

Tiffany Liebermann came up swinging, at least figuratively, and Steve tried to minimize the damage. He reached out his hand, and she rewarded him with an additional array of unkind suggestions. The contents of the red bag tumbled down her legs as she peeled herself off the floor. In a clumsy attempt to help gather up the spilled articles, he tried not to look at what had been in her bag. Steve really didn't want to know what she carried around. He wisely backed away as she finished the job and marched away.

Watching her storm down the hall, Steve noticed several squares of white perforated tissue paper hanging out the back of her skirt, her blouse still half-heartedly tucked. Steve considered his options, gave a sheepish grin to the small, but attentive group of onlookers, and elected to remain silent.

He counted to ten and then marched after Ms. Liebermann, finding it no longer necessary to check his ticket to determine the location of the rally.

Steve handed his ticket to a mean-faced woman at the door to the auditorium. He put on his most gracious smile as she stared him down and checked that the change in his ticket had been approved by security. He didn't feel entirely welcome at this event.

Forgetting his promise to Catori, he smiled and said, "I've no need for birth control pills, but my union's health insurance policy does cover those medications."

That comment didn't help his situation, but as the line backed up behind him, the woman relinquished her stance and allowed him to enter. By the look on her face as she thrust his ticket into the container, he imagined he was damn close to being shepherded out the door by security. Probably what he'd been aiming for with his last remark.

Just inside the door, he caught a glimpse of Ms. Liebermann's backside. A man's hand was retrieving the pieces of tissue paper from the waistband of her skirt. The hand showed a good familiarity with her anatomy. It appeared to linger longer than necessary, and Steve spotted the fingers subtly massaging the area a little lower than her waist. He recalled the lightweight skirt provided little interference.

The man's head turned in Steve's direction.

"Holy shit," Steve said loud enough for the lady in front of him to swing around with an annoyed expression. He offered a brief apology and lowered his head.

Right after Steve's dad had died, or more correctly, been murdered by rogue federal agents, Steve had gotten involved in politics. In an effort to distance himself from what he considered his dad's misguided political association with a growing right-wing movement, the RGA, Steve had jumped in and campaigned for the opposition. He had spent many hours working in the race for the Twelfth Congressional District in California. That's where he met this man in his San Francisco election headquarters and helped out with his campaign.

And now it looked as if Congressman Derrick Pranchard was showing Tiffany Liebermann a lot more appreciation than any of his ardent campaign supporters ever got. Or at least the male campaign workers.

Steve's attention, along with the other attendees, was drawn to the sound of a sharp tap on the microphone centered on the podium in front of the room. An attractive young lady introduced herself as Clarissa Mendelschein, the head of BioCoGen's public relations department. She went on to give a long, glowing introduction to today's keynote speaker, Tiffany Liebermann, and then took a seat in the front row.

Finding a seat in the last row, Steve tried to disappear into the huge crowd. He attempted to look away whenever Ms. Liebermann's eyes riveted in his direction. That got old pretty quick, so he returned the favor and sat there stoically with a small but noticeable smile. Apparently, it would take a lot more than that to force a blush on Ms. Liebermann's face.

Congressman Derrick Pranchard never gave Steve a passing glance.

The rally itself turned out to be a poor sequel to his previous encounter with Ms. Liebermann. The theme of the speakers carried a unifying cry for more government funding of research into improving the options for fertility control, giving women the maximum number of options to exercise the right to choose. Living with Edie had chipped away at his perception of the role of government in healthcare, and he was beginning to wonder what the tipping point would be, or if it had already been reached.

After the rally ended, Steve tried to take advantage of the turmoil and confusion from the presence of the large crowd and attempted to gain access to other areas of the clinic. But security remained tight, and he got the picture of an efficient and well-organized security department.

Walking down a quiet hallway, Steve stopped at the sounds coming from a small conference room. He didn't like to snoop, but the door was open about an inch, and he did promise Edie he'd take a close look into all activities at the clinic.

As he peered through the narrow opening, the frenzied voices escalated. Derrick Pranchard's hands grasped Tiffany Liebermann's butt, which was bare and scrunched on top of a conference table, her legs in a vice grip around the backside of the congressman's boxer shorts.

Steve had learned enough about undergarment preferences for one day and walked away thinking at least Tiffany practiced what she preached. And Congressman Pranchard apparently took government oversight quite seriously.

Steve finished up his undocumented tour with a walk around the exterior. Feigning interest in the scenery and views of Lake Hennessey from the back of the clinic complex, he grew aware of close scrutiny by several security guards. He observed that the site was guarded by a sophisticated network of cameras and sensors, supplemented by well-armed and serious looking security guards.

On the upper right arms of several of the guards who were wearing short-sleeved shirts, Steve thought he noticed similar looking tattoos. While, for the most part, the symbols remained hidden, what he saw had a disturbing familiarity to it. But he couldn't place the meaning or where he'd seen that particular tattoo before.

All-in-all, while he was surprised by the clinic's tight security, he had nothing concrete to report to Edie. He doubted she would be interested in Ms. Liebermann's wardrobe choices, but that at least might provide him with some interesting pillow talk. He wondered if Edie was interested in the fact Congressman Pranchard was a boxer man.

Before getting back into the Tahoe, Steve glanced around one more time, trying to shake his underlying uneasiness. He returned his focus on how Catori's tests would go tomorrow.

CHAPTER 15

Northern California
Mendocino County
(one month ago)

THE LAST LEG OF FARID'S long journey starkly contrasted from the earlier hardships he had endured. Still, he chose to make the trip in silence, ignoring even the minimal hospitality of the man who had met him in the desert near the southern border of the United States. Farid accepted the water and rations with a silent nod and got into the back of the Jeep.

During the trip, he had occasionally gazed outside the window at the passing scenery, but the beauty of the mountains and the rocky coastline with the pounding Pacific surf below the narrow winding road held little interest. For the last thirty minutes of the journey, they appeared to be swallowed up in a maze of giant redwoods; the road had withered into a damp, needle-covered path broadcasting a mossy aroma. Staring up at the monstrous trees towering above, his only consideration was to learn the final details of his mission and fulfill his destiny. He did know that this camp specialized in training attacks led by single jihadists.

When he was finally alone at the camp, Farid allowed himself a grim smile. "They call this a lone wolf attack." The smile turned into a sneer. "I do this alone. The wolf kills for sport. But this is no game. I kill for revenge."

He leaned back on his cot and waited impatiently to learn the location and timing of his strike. Of more importance was to acquire the information he needed to carry out his personal jihad. They would keep this from him until the last possible minute. Perhaps they were smart enough to sense his true commitment.

They had given him maps and brochures of the San Francisco Bay Area. They circled a location where he would eventually stay and prepare to execute the plan. He was told to study the pages and become familiar with the area's roads and other items in the documents.

In the coming weeks, his instructors would demonstrate the techniques and proper use of the specialized equipment needed to carry out their mission. He would examine the diagrams and practice the assembly procedures, making sure his enthusiasm and skills convinced his leaders he was capable of handling this important jihad.

He had gotten one step closer, and this stoked his rage.

* * * * * *

There has been much speculation regarding the number of Islamic terrorist training camps located within the borders of the United States. Most people fear they are on the increase, and this has been supported by leaked reports from the government. In the past, these camps were not the starting point for the breeding of homegrown terrorists, but rather one of the final steps. For many years, state and federal prisons represented the initial path on the road to jihadism.

The structural organization of radical Islamic gangs within the California state prison system rivals the vast network of U.S. military recruiting centers. While prison officials gripe about insufficient funds to staff these same prisons and house the growing inmate population, ample monies exist for converting and radicalizing the best and most talented among the eager and susceptible souls within these government run facilities.

Once the strongest, most highly skilled, and fanatical personalities have been selected by the Muslim gang leaders, the rest go to the competition; the Aryan Brotherhood and the Mexican Mafia, to name a few.

Prison officials inadvertently facilitate the indoctrination programs by their preferential approach to house and feed the new Muslim converts in a separate cell block, importing and distributing collections of jihadist training manuals under the guise of Arabic language religious materials. Prayer rugs are the least deadly items on the list.

This system is nothing new. One needs only to look to the nineteen sixties and seventies to view the consequences of the Black Panther Party or the Symbionese Liberation Army.

Although Islam is steeped in historical doctrine and beliefs, when it comes to the art of persuasion, they are well adept at using modern social media and hip-hop music in addition to the traditional sacred materials provided by the prison officials. Once the conversion and radicalization process of the inmates is complete, graduation into the real world involves the infiltration of certain mosques and Islamic communities, and of course the hidden network of training camps within our borders.

At one time, when the final training was completed, the majority of jihadists disseminated around the world to wreak havoc on the non-believers or other Muslims less committed to the holy war. Lately, these home-grown terrorists have stayed, amassing one of the largest terrorist networks in the world.

The American prison system no longer needs to be the primary route to radicalization. Recruiting jihadists who have no criminal record afford the terrorists an even better means of blending into the American culture. Based on constitutional rights, there are no valid reasons to monitor the activities of innocent American citizens.

A gradual, yet insipient process has largely gone unnoticed in this country. Violent radical extremism in the name of Islam is not the only means to wage war on the infidels. Since its inception in the late 1920s, the Muslim Brotherhood has become a formidable and deadly political power. Not only providing the framework for state-sponsored terrorism in the far corners of the world but serving as the basis to infiltrate all nations designated as enemies of Islam. To this end, they rely on seemingly peaceful organizations whose sole purported purpose is to expound the virtues of Islam and assure that Muslim citizens are treated fairly and not subject to undue religious bias and hateful rhetoric.

The number of these Islamic organizations within the United States is on the rise. Some have the legitimate aim of helping the Muslim population blend into the community; others do not and have complicated ties to terrorist groups. Many leaders of these Islamic community-based organizations have worked their way into all aspects of our government, including political advisors, as well as elected officials.

Several have been named as unindicted co-conspirators in legal actions where convictions have been handed down for the funding of named terrorist groups. With the current climate of political correctness, authorities sometime neglect due diligence and refuse to question any potential ties of a particular group to the doctrines of the Muslim Brotherhood and their support of terrorist activities around the globe.

In the absence of any violent terrorist attacks, it is easy to ignore the power of politics and dogma to coerce the population. In the greater scheme, it is far easier to build a bomb; it takes a village to create the radical ideology of a jihadist.

During the last days of the presidential campaign, candidate Tyler Griffin made one of his most powerful speeches regarding foreign policy and the ongoing war on terror. He concluded his remarks by saying, "The threat of radical Islam is the ultimate weapon of mass destruction."

Those words resonated with a frightened constituency, and political pundits argued it might have catapulted him into the White House.

CHAPTER 16

OUTSIDE THE HOTEL SUITE, THE morning sun rose high enough to ratchet up the temperature, complementing the unbearable humidity that lifted the discomfort level of the tourists walking along the crowded National Mall in Washington, D.C.

"Even he can't be that stupid," Senator Henry Whitcome scoffed. He was older and cruder than the two other men in the sitting room of one of the Willard Intercontinental Hotel's residence suites. He continued to pace, holding a gin and tonic in one hand, while spearing shrimp from the buffet cart and stealing envious glances out the window at the White House. His squeaky, grating voice, a constant source of annoyance to both younger men in the room, was only one of several key flaws in his character that would preclude him from achieving his presidential aspirations.

More to the old senator's companion, Arthur Constantine said, "This comes from one of the best sources we have. It appears the imbeciles redacted this part in the initial reports."

The senator interrupted again. His conduct was trying Constantine's patience. "Nothing like this crossed my committee's desk. As chairman of the Senate Intelligence Committee, the administration is required to provide me with this information."

He ignored Constantine and looked to the other man in the room. "I know you're just a junior member, but did anyone inform your committee about these negotiations?"

Congressmen Derrick Pranchard, newly appointed to the House Permanent Select Committee on Intelligence, shrugged and shook his head.

The senator turned back to Constantine. "I hope this source of yours has a better track record than those stupid clowns you had working for you in New Jersey." He shook his head in disgust. "Those fucking idiots almost got us thrown in jail. We should've ended this whole fucking nightmare before it started."

"For chrissakes, you and everybody else were well shielded from that mess. I should know—I had to come in and tie up all those loose ends." Constantine neglected to bring up the fact his back-up plan—which also failed—turned out to be one of those loose ends. At least the fighter jets had blasted away any remaining evidence. That little incident had wound up depleting most of the allocated reserves, but the destruction of the yacht and everybody on board saved a great deal of clean-up effort on his part.

It was a pity that damn sniper didn't do his job and take care of Tyler Griffin on Ellis Island. Now that Griffin was in the White House, those kinds of opportunities were few and far between. Doing this by the constitutional route was a real pain in the ass. But this latest bit of news might finally force the rest of the deadbeats in congress to stand up and take notice.

The young congressman spoke up. "You think the president's advisors missed this? Anyway, what was in it for Griffin to negotiate with terrorists? Even without this new intel, he was already on shaky ground."

Constantine answered, "As usual, they're probably only thinking of the short-term benefits of looking patriotic. You know, never leave a man behind?

Especially any of our special operations guys. Jesus Christ. Three Navy SEALs. Think of the intel they gave up. They've probably spilled enough key information to have our intelligence community running for cover for the next ten years."

Senator Whitcome turned so fast he spilled his drink. Grabbing several napkins, he patted down his jacket. "Isn't that the excuse the president gave today? Not only do we bring our guys back home, but it was in the national interest to make sure they weren't left behind to be tortured and give up more intel." He tossed the soggy napkins aside. "Fifteen minutes before Griffin delivers his speech, my committee gets the notification that the exchanges had already taken place. But no specifics on when and where it all happened. Only that the SEALs had been stashed away somewhere on American soil and the damn detainees were back in sand land."

Constantine was getting tired of hearing this fool's persistent whining. Might be time to arrange for a little accident. It was a pleasant thought, but the old man still controlled important purse strings on the hill, not to mention the information he could leak from being on the Senate Intelligence Committee.

"Look," Constantine said using a placating voice, "once we get this latest information out… that these so-called brave Navy SEALs actually defected to a terrorist group in Afghanistan and have been spilling their guts for the last several months—Tyler Griffin will be finished once and for all. After he announced the hostage exchange details today, it's over. No way they can spin this thing or try to walk it back. By the time the names of those Navy SEALs are made public, the whole world will know they're traitors. And we got the evidence to show the nation that Griffin and his cohorts were all aware of the traitorous activities from the start. They thought they could bury those facts. You'd think they'd be smart enough to destroy the emails and other incriminating documents before going public. Not only that, but Griffin has also released four of the worst terrorist leaders back into the hands of our enemies. For the life of me, what the hell he's doing doesn't make a damn bit of sense. He's giving his opposition more than enough rope to hang him. You guys should be grateful for the president keeping congress in the dark. More fuel for the fire, and your hands are clean."

Even the senator begrudgingly agreed with that assessment.

Congressman Pranchard nodded. "I'm sure you got the timeline all set. Tell us what we need to do. It's about time we remove this self-righteous asshole from the White House."

Constantine did exactly that.

Afterwards, Constantine smiled. He watched the two men depart and picked up the phone.

* * * * * *

Leaving Arthur Constantine's hotel suite, Senator Henry Whitcome and Congressman Derrick Pranchard walked in silence and got on the elevator. As they reached the lobby and the door started to open, bony fingers clasped the congressman's shoulder.

The senator whispered, "We need to talk. I've got a committee meeting in forty minutes. But I can be at your apartment by three o'clock. You might want to keep an eye on the news reports. I'm holding a public session, and with the intel Arthur has given us, President Griffin is about to be cut in half." He turned away and left before the congressman could protest.

"Shit. The old turd can move fast when he wants to," the congressman muttered to himself. "Probably smells blood." Looking at his watch, he cursed again and headed home. He had other plans this afternoon. He shook his head, thinking somebody's going to be pissed.

* * * * * *

Arthur Constantine needed to iron out a few more details with the new attorney general. His smile grew wider as he considered the fortuitous timing for congress to finally come together and do something right. Once that was accomplished, it was only a matter of purchasing power and latching on to key private information about the new attorney general that placed him in the pockets of Constantine's nefarious group of associates.

The last mid-term elections did more than simply tilt the political scales further away from the RGA movement. The few carefully bought congressional seats did their part in making sure Griffin's effort to repeal ConnorCare was becoming less of a threat. And soon public opinion would probably drown away all remnants of opposition to the new healthcare law anyway. Nobody wanted the free stuff taken away. But the more important aspect of these elections was that for the first time in the history of our nation, a United States attorney general had been chosen by a general election.

Since the first congress established the office of the attorney general by the passing of the Judiciary Act of 1789, the attorney general was appointed by the president, with the advice and consent of the senate. For almost a century that position was a minor one with little power or appeal. In 1870, the Department of Justice was created and has steadily grown in size and power to become the behemoth structure that exists today.

Supposedly, it functioned as the executive branch's source of non-partisan legal advice, but due to the department's loyalty to only one elected official, the behavior of the department had been riddled with controversial decisions in regard to interpretation of executive powers, as well as its discretionary approaches as to how it selectively applied the law.

In theory, by independently electing the attorney general during the mid-term cycle, the individual would be isolated from those partisan issues, and thus serve as a balancing countermeasure to an untethered president.

The constitutional change required to strip the president of his power to appoint the attorney general is a rare event. This has been only the twenty-eighth time since 1789 that the constitution had been successfully amended, out of the over eleven thousand failed attempts.

Congress doesn't always do the right thing. In fact, they rarely do. And Constantine was doing his part to make sure this newly elected attorney general had his priorities straight. At least in terms of what role he would play in creating the necessary roadblocks to stymie Griffin.

Before the day ended, Constantine and his powerbrokers in Washington had made sure their version of the story reached the media outlets with the obvious intent of blindsiding the president's message of patriotism and honor.

The fanfare and joy of getting three decorated Navy SEALs released and brought safely home was abruptly overshadowed by the news that the president negotiated the return of three traitorous and disgraced Navy personnel who had willingly given the enemy vital intelligence information. And to top it off, four Al Qaeda terrorist leaders were now free to plan future attacks against us. This fueled the fire against a president already fighting a losing battle to accomplish anything, with both parties now squarely against him.

Congress, as well as the media, were gearing up to excoriate Tyler Griffin.

Al Qaeda and its growing list of affiliates were now emboldened by their ability to not only embarrass the United States in front of the entire world, but to have had the opportunity to gather important intelligence information from the three prisoners. The four returned terrorist leaders would be a strong motivator for terrorist groups all over the world. The message was that the United States could be brought to its knees.

CHAPTER 17

INSTEAD OF RELAXING HER HOLD, Edie clung to Steve, feeling his heart rate slow. Edie's lovemaking tonight had taken on an urgency that Steve had reacted to in kind. Enfolded in his strong embrace, the moist, warm flesh of Edie's body gradually turned cold and damp. She felt the shivering all the way to her heart, now beating at a steadier pace.

The long flight home had done little to calm her nerves after seeing the most powerful man in the world on the brink of collapse. Aside from the man she held onto now, Tyler Griffin was the most stable, committed, and direct person she knew. The haunted look in his eyes had scared the hell out of her. But he had drawn it in and gathered the strength to make this thing happen, and so would she.

After her flight landed in San Francisco, Edie rushed to the clinic to visit Catori. There she saw her young friend, sunken and withdrawn in a hospital bed. Edie left the clinic in a daze. When she walked through the door to her home, her emotional state teetered on the verge of collapse. She literally tore the clothes from Steve's body, and now with her entire being drained, no tears came.

At last Edie felt a different energy returning, and she stopped trembling. Her body restoring its resolve in Steve's arms. Although late, with the sun sinking across the Valley of the Moon, Edie knew neither of them would be getting much sleep tonight.

Steve's lips brushed lightly against her ear. "Hi. It's good to have you back."

Not to be outdone, Amber slip-slided up the covers and licked her other ear.

Edie sighed, enjoyed the needed attention for a few moments, and then slowly sat up. In a modest gesture, she pulled the covers over her breasts. Steve took advantage of her exposed back, and with a deliberate and painstaking pace, he nibbled the flesh until she turned, melting into his arms. This time they gently explored and soothed away the hurt and fear, readying themselves for whatever came next.

Giving up on sleep, Steve prepared scrambled eggs, bacon, and English muffins while Edie took a quick shower. Later, Amber munched down the leftovers, sticking to her own bowl while Greta, Sophie, and Max pushed their three bowls around the kitchen floor. Amber's puppies were proving to be quite a handful.

After much debate over the disposition of Amber's litter, Steve and Edie had decided to keep three of the puppies. Catori helped out with the brew whenever Steve and Edie weren't available. She had declined Steve's offer to pick out a puppy for herself, content to just be there when needed. Before Catori entered the clinic, she made arrangements for her roommate to assist Steve with the training classes and tend to the puppies.

Sophie was pure white and resembled Amber. Greta, as Catori had predicted, gradually transformed into a tri-color—black and tan with reddish overtones. Max, on the other hand, remained jet black, showing no signs of changing his colors.

Although Max continued on a course to be one big boy, he proved no match for his two female siblings. Sophie knew her place as well, as Greta's high drive and vigorous habits dominated the trio. Except for her outward colorations, Greta was a reincarnation of her mother. Steve had another girl he'd have to keep an eye on. Max and Steve were clearly outnumbered.

Steve and Edie sat in the vaulted family room with a large pot of coffee on the table. At this point, the events in D.C. and the far corners of the world were beyond her powers to change, so Edie focused her energies on the sight of her friend, describing to Steve how Catori lay helplessly alone in the hospital room. What had happened to the vibrant, beautiful girl, so full of life and spirit?

Neither knew where to start. Steve gave Edie the copy of Catori's admission papers. While she read them over, she said, "Learn anything interesting at the clinic?"

With a vivid image flashing in his head, Steve hesitated just long enough for Edie to look up.

"What? What's with the stupid grin?" she asked.

For the moment, Steve pushed the scenes with Tiffany Liebermann into the deeper recesses and took the easy route. "The clinic's security operations reminded me of a top-secret military installation."

Edie sat up a little straighter. "The clinic? You're kidding."

"Didn't you sense their security measures were over the top?"

Edie shrugged, shaking her head. "Not that I noticed. From the time they checked my ID at the gate and issued my guest pass, they treated me fine. Everybody seemed polite and helpful. When I was in Catori's room, Dr. Kessler stopped in and introduced himself. He said he was taking a personal interest in Catori's health problems."

"With you being the president's advisor, they might've wanted to go easy. I'm not saying *I* got treated badly, just got the impression their security department wasn't the typical mall cop police force."

Steve snapped his fingers. "Wait… you said Kessler showed up in Catori's room?"

"Yeah, so? He's one of her doctors."

"Okay, what did he do? Take Catori's pulse or study her chart or check… ah… whatever a gynecologist checks?"

Edie looked at him a little strangely.

"Well, I don't think Dr. Kessler is technically a gynecologist," she said with a weak shrug. "Now that you mention it, he didn't pay Catori much attention. He asked me a lot of questions. Guess he was surprised by the fact I knew Catori. That she was a close friend."

"How'd he react to that?"

"I don't know. Okay, I guess."

After uttering those words, Edie appeared to retreat inside herself. Steve knew she was an emotional wreck. Not seeing things straight, the way she normally picked stuff apart. Usually the other way around, he wasn't used to prodding her to analyze the details.

"Edie. Tell me. Did he look surprised to see you at the clinic?"

"Yes and no. I did have an invitation to attend that rally."

"You probably got the invitation weeks ago. I doubt he sent them out himself. And you didn't even go to the rally. Besides, the rally took place the day before."

"Yeah, but he did say he was sorry to see I missed it. He commented on how Tiffany Liebermann gave a terrific presentation. Said the audience was filled with mostly women though."

She would've been a lot busier if more men had attended.

"Sorry I pushed you into going."

Steve didn't believe that for a minute.

"Did you feel out of place? All that estrogen make you uncomfortable? Maybe you should've brought Max along."

Steve wasn't sure how to answer, but at least he saw a hint of the old Edie returning.

"From what I remember about Tiffany Liebermann," Edie said, "she's all talk—a political hack. Climbed on the bandwagon when this war on women hype got started. And the hard left jumped all over her."

At last, something he could agree with.

Edie smiled and leaned forward. "Hey. I hear she doesn't like men." She winked. "I mean in bed; not just as a political agenda."

That was true. The shiny surface of the conference room table popped into Steve's head.

"What? You're awfully quiet. Did something happen at the rally?"

Steve hesitated again, but only for a moment.

"In all the investigations for your stories on healthcare reform, did you ever come across the fact Ms. Liebermann doesn't like underwear?"

He gave an animated version of what transpired before, during, and after the rally. That seemed to do the trick. He watched as Edie sat up a little straighter, and the wheels began to turn.

"Derrick Pranchard," she repeated the congressman's name, nodding her head.

"You know him?" Steve asked.

"Apparently not as well as Tiffany Liebermann knows him. By the way. Nice job at keeping a low profile. Was I at least right about her earrings?"

Steve shook his head. "I guess your new political career has deadened your journalistic senses."

"Glad to see you so eager to help out."

"Did you know I helped get that little nerd Pranchard reelected once?"

"You jealous?"

"Nah. I'm beginning to think those two deserve each other."

Looking serious, Edie headed to her laptop. Steve followed and massaged her shoulders as she began reading a few old documents relating to her investigation into government healthcare programs.

"You still planning on going with me to the clinic tomorrow?" she said, and then looked out the window at the brightening sky. "Or I guess I should say later today."

Steve nodded.

She added, "How about we pop into Dr. Kessler's office and return the favor?"

CHAPTER 18

IT WAS CLOSER TO THREE thirty in the afternoon when Senator Henry Whitcome banged on the door to Derrick Pranchard's apartment. Pranchard was thankful the old pain in the ass had been tardy. Both men stood facing each other in the living room after Whitcome gave Pranchard an abbreviated account of his earlier meetings.

"Goddamn it, Pranchard. Are we on the same page or not?"

"Relax, Henry. I told you. We need this guy and his connections."

"Shit. I just don't trust that son of a bitch. He gives me the creeps. Always smiling and patting my back. Who the fuck does he think he is?"

"Look. The name Arthur Constantine pulls a lot of weight in this town. Most of it from behind the scenes. He's the guy you go to when you don't want to get your own hands dirty."

"Yeah? After listening to him at the hotel, I wanted to go home and take a shower." He shook his head while watching Pranchard press back strands of damp hair and tucking in his shirt. He then turned and looked down the hall.

"What's that noise?"

"Oh, I must've left the TV on in the bedroom."

Whitcome focused his eyes on the bar in the corner, already ignoring the sounds.

Pranchard knew that look but waited him out. Whitcome was anything but subtle.

"Like I said, I had to rush through my lunch. How about pouring me a little liquid refreshment?"

Pranchard smiled and feigned an apology. Mixing Whitcome his usual gin and tonic—with the cheap stuff—keeping the Tanqueray hidden below in the cabinet, Pranchard walked back and handed him his drink.

He accepted it without a word.

Henry Whitcome, the senior senator from Georgia, had his sights set on the White House. With today's news he more than likely considered himself one step closer to his dream. At lunch, he'd given instructions to his aides to push up the schedule to subpoena key officials from Griffin's administration for new hearings to look into inappropriate behavior regarding foreign policy decisions and a lack of leadership on the part of the president. Pranchard could visualize Whitcome salivating at the thought of cornering Griffin on abusing his executive powers to keep congress in the dark.

And with the information Constantine had presented to them today, they were poised to hammer the last nail into the president's coffin. Once they got rid of Griffin, things in Washington could finally get back to normal. Griffin was the RGA's last hope to make any real reforms. Nobody else would dare stand up against the traditional leadership ever again. The real power in Washington would be back in the proper hands.

Whitcome shook the ice in the empty glass. Pranchard got the hint and padded back to the bar to mix him a second.

"Aren't you having anything? I'm not used to drinking alone."

Pranchard presumed Whitcome did just fine on his own but splashed a little tonic water in another glass to be sociable.

A rare smile spread across the old senator's face. "You catch any of the reports from the Senate Intelligence Committee briefing this morning?"

"Ah… no Henry. I got kinda tied up in other business. How'd it go?"

"The press is going to be all over this thing. Griffin's days are numbered. His press secretary must be hiding under his desk. So far they haven't responded to any of our accusations. Hell, I don't think even Griffin can spin this. He can't fake ignorance about knowing the SEALs were traitors. We got the damn documents to prove he's been lying. Besides, he'd come off looking like an incompetent asshole if he pretended he hadn't seen the documents. The committee's already lining up the military officers to testify as to what information the Navy passed on to the administration. They had those SEALs pegged the minute they disappeared from base. Can't wait to see what tact the White House is going to take."

Wagging a finger in Pranchard's face, while managing to spill part of his drink, Whitcome said, "But just because we've caught a break on this hostage fiasco doesn't mean you should let up on what you're doing in the other house committee."

Pranchard nodded, watching the liquid spill onto his light beige carpet. Thankfully, Whitcome wasn't partial to red wine.

"You have got to keep the pressure on," Whitcome said, oblivious to the mess he was making. "Block everything Griffin's trying to do against ConnorCare.

Don't forget. That's why we got you on that damn committee to begin with. This would be a good time to start those public hearings too. Let's go after that bastard with everything we've got."

For an instant, Pranchard's mind focused on the TV sounds in the bedroom. "Sure, Henry. I'm all over that subject. Been working on it since we left Constantine."

"Good. Listen, Pranchard. I'm counting on you. Remember who made sure you got on both committees in the first place. Nobody gets to be a rising star in this town without the right backers. Don't forget who your friends are. And I won't forget mine. You're still my top choice for the number two position on the ticket."

Pranchard gave the expected thumbs up and nodded.

"Whitcome—Pranchard," Whitcome said. "That sounds damn good to me, son. What do you think?"

Pranchard's thumb was still up, and his head still bobbing. Behind his smile he thought, *This asshole doesn't stand a chance in hell to be nominated by the party, let alone elected president.*

That didn't matter to Pranchard. His career in D.C. was just getting started, while the old man's was just about over. But for now, he still needed to kiss the old senator's ass.

It took another gin and tonic before Pranchard finally steered Whitcome out the door. He drew a breath and double-checked the lock. He heard the bedroom door click.

"Jesus fucking Christ, Derrick. I was beginning to think you were more interested in that old man."

Tiffany Liebermann stood leaning against the doorway to the bedroom. She wasn't wearing anything at all over the underwear she didn't have on.

"Come on. Let's do it in your bed this time. I'm feeling all domesticated right now."

Pranchard figured that wouldn't last long. He knew she was partial to getting it on in elevators and conference rooms. Right now, his own personal elevator was taking him to the top of the city, along with Washington's most powerful wheelers and dealers.

God, he loved politics.

CHAPTER 19

THE TV DRONED IN THE background while Steve and Edie finished up a long and sleepless night. Although they found no answers, they tried to gather the strength to tackle the coming storms facing their friend, Catori, and the nation. The sun had risen, but hid behind a thickening blanket of ominous clouds, heralding in round one of the potential knockout punch of the century.

For now, they were more concerned for Catori's health and anxious to get to the clinic to see how she was doing. Although Steve had expressed an uneasiness regarding the clinic's overbearing security operations, and Edie disagreed with the political aspects of the clinic's ties to the new government healthcare programs, their concerns were softened by the fact that the Kessler Foundation was among the world's best female healthcare facilities in the world. At least Catori Torrence was in good hands.

Steve abruptly turned to the TV screen just as the camera pulled in for a tight shot on the sexily clad weather girl bobbing around in front of the large map, describing a weather alert for the entire Bay Area. Edie didn't recall Steve showing this much interest when Lloyd Lindsay Young yelled *Helloooooooo...... Sonoma.*

Steve grabbed the remote and punched up the volume. With his eyes glued to the screen, he said, "Wow, by the end of the week we'll be getting slapped with both barrels. Things could get hot around here."

He stole a quick glance at Edie who had her head tilted, her eyes darting back and forth between Steamy Knights, the name printed across the bottom of the screen, and trying to read the expression on Steve's face.

"What?" he said.

Edie just smiled and shrugged, remembering something Nana had said when she found out Edie was marrying a firefighter. She'd need every ounce of her estrogen to counter all his testosterone. Edie was giving it her best shot.

"What?" Steve repeated.

The San Francisco Bay Area represented a microcosm of the entire state of California; subject to the ever-present threat of earthquakes, not to mention some of the nation's most extreme weather conditions. Cyclic periods of extended droughts set the stage for not only severe wildfire danger, but the threat of mudslides brought on by the inevitable rains in the wake the surface-stripping devastation left behind after the scorching infernos did their job.

Building practices that allowed construction of entire communities on unstable hillsides only exaggerated the deadly consequences of moderate rainfalls and the ability to promote the heavily laden soil to rearrange itself beneath inadequate foundations.

Fortunately for the entire coast of California and the eastern portion of the Pacific Ocean, hurricanes, or tropical cyclones as they are referred to in this part of the world, are an extremely rare phenomenon. Usually, the worst result is the potential for an added dose of a few heavy downpours from the dissipating remnants of storms centered much farther out, over the central and western portions of the Pacific.

For any decent-sized tropical cyclone to form, several ingredients are necessary. The water which fuels the upper-level disturbances must be greater than eighty degrees. Even during a strong El Nino event, the cold waters of the Pacific fail to reach those temperature levels. On rare occasions, longer term cyclic changes coincide with an El Nino event and can raise the temperature of the water enough to provide the necessary conditions.

Global warming? Climate change? Perhaps it is simply the Almighty reminding the Hollywood elite, clinging to the precipitous California coastline, that they are in the business of fiction and not to take their scripts too seriously.

Regardless, even if somewhere out in the far Pacific, when the conditions are ripe for such tropical disturbances to take hold, the upper-level winds along the coastal waters of California tend to push storms in a northwesterly or westerly direction, steering the brunt force of the storms away from the coast and breaking up the vertical air patterns, weakening its intensity. The normal prevailing winds on the West Coast provide the added benefit of pushing the warmer water farther out into the Pacific, allowing the cooler waters to hug the shorelines and weaken even the most significant disturbances. Storm surges along the western coast do not present the same type of threat as they do on the eastern seaboard of the United States due to the high coastal cliffs along most of the state of California.

Of course there are always exceptions to the rule, but the only true tropical storm to make landfall in California in the twentieth century occurred in 1939, hitting the southern part of the state near Los Angeles. It resulted in widespread flooding and deaths.

Closer to home was the Columbus Day storm of 1962. Although it was one of the worst storms to hit the

San Francisco Bay Area, it was never recorded as a tropical cyclone. The cooling offshore water temperatures saved the area from an even greater catastrophe.

"You ready to go?" With a slight twinkle in his eyes, Steve hit the off button on the remote.

Returning to the task at hand, Stormy Knights forgotten, Edie looked at Steve. She strained to reconcile his first-hand description of the clinic with her own conflicted images of Catori. At this point, they might as well head over to the clinic and make sure Catori knew she was not alone.

As she tried to reassure herself that Catori couldn't be in better hands, she wondered why her gut wrenched and an acidy taste goaded her senses.

Chapter 20

Although growing accustomed to the security procedures at the Kessler Foundation, Steve couldn't help but feel he was heading into a war zone. He considered that the war on women might be taken more seriously here. More likely, it was probably the high stakes involved that hinged on the outcome of the clinical trials being run at the facility.

On the way to the clinic, Steve and Edie had gotten into their usual banter on government involvement in healthcare. Steve sensed Edie's heart wasn't into the fight today. He knew she was worried about Catori. He was too.

With the appropriate guest badges displayed, they headed across the clinic's parking lot toward the main building. Steve reached over, placing his hand gently on Edie's shoulder. "You're not thinking Catori's illness is in any way related to the government's involvement with this clinic, are you?"

"W-what?" Edie stuttered, and then stared at Steve. "Why would I think that? It's actually a good thing she's staying at this particular clinic. I told you, the Kessler Foundation is world renowned. That's most likely why the government selected them to promote this new research environment under ConnorCare."

"Good," Steve said with a crooked smile, "I was thinking you might be considering charging into Dr. Kessler's office and accusing him of a conspiracy."

Edie shrugged. "Those days are over, Steve. I'm a representative of the executive branch of our government now. I need to act accordingly."

Having arrived at the entrance, Steve didn't reply right away. He opened the door for Edie, and after she slipped by, he muttered, "I doubt that's why you got the job."

"I'm not deaf you know," Edie said, smiling. That remark sounded a little too close to Nana's tone for Steve's comfort.

Visiting Catori did little to ease their concerns about her failing health. The nurses insisted she was doing fine, but the procedures required heavy doses of sedatives and muscle relaxants. They swore she'd be back to her old self once the tests were completed. None of that allayed their fears.

They were waiting in the cafeteria for a chance to see Dr. Kessler while Catori was wheeled away for more tests. He had agreed to meet with them later in the day. Edie had been told by his administrative assistant that he was quite busy, and she'd call her the minute he had some free time.

Edie slammed her coffee cup on the table and got up. "Let's go, Steve. I'm not sitting around here waiting for Kessler while Catori's being probed and prodded. We'll just see how busy he is."

Steve looked at his watch as he ran to catch up with her. "Twenty-two minutes. You've shown a remarkable amount of restraint. I hope you're not getting soft, working in a government job."

That only stoked the flames. Edie hit the outer reception area and didn't break stride, heading straight for Kessler's office as his assistant jumped up in surprise.

"Wait. You can't—"

Too late.

Edie banged on the door, trying to turn the knob. Locked. Steve heard muffled cries and then a clearer voice.

"Emily!" Dr. Kessler's voice resounded through the closed door. "I told you not to disturb me. What the hell do you think you're doing?"

"I—I'm sorry, Dr. Kessler. She just barged right in here. It's that person I told you about. Edie Pauling. I'll call security right away."

Steve leaned against the outer doorway; arms folded. He had visions of Edie against the clinic's over-the-top security squad. This should test his theory.

"No, Emily. We don't need security. Just wait a minute. I'll take care of this. Tell her to be seated. I'll be there in a minute." Kessler sounded out of breath.

Edie and Steve sat down in the spacious waiting area. Steve picked through several magazines. He folded one open and handed it to Edie.

"Here. You might find this interesting. It's about coping with the stress of PMS."

Edie's mouth opened and her eyes stared hard at Steve when the door to Kessler's office swung open.

Dr. Kessler didn't emerge.

But Tiffany Liebermann did.

As she charged out of the office, Steve gave her a wide berth. Tiffany looked hassled: or jet-lagged? Those corporate jets could take you anywhere you needed; anytime you wanted; as many times as necessary.

"See," he whispered to Edie, "no earrings."

CHAPTER 21

CLARISSA MENDELSCHEIN HADN'T UNDERSTOOD THE complexities of what Dr. Dequain Johnson had tried to tell her over the phone. They were now sitting in a cozy restaurant in downtown Napa, overlooking the city docks, with the Napa River in the background. The setting sun reflected off the tranquil waters.

When Dequain had called her earlier today and invited her to dinner, she had expected a more romantic encounter. Clarissa rushed home from work and agonized over what to wear, parading countless outfits in front of her dresser mirror. Finally settling on a black embroidered halter dress with a plunging neckline, she was confident this outfit maximized her desirability and gave her the best opportunity to coax her perky breasts to work their magic on Dequain's sensibilities.

And now. *What the hell happened to his Jamaican lilt?* His damn voice sounded even more American than hers. It had taken her several minutes to realize something important was bothering him, and she had missed the key points in what he'd been saying. Trading a glass of ice water for her half empty glass of Merlot, Clarissa reached for her silky white shawl and wrapped it over her bare shoulders and swung it across her breasts.

Dequain blinked several times as if someone had just pulled down the shades. He pushed aside his empty water glass and took a healthy gulp from his untouched beer stein, shoving his half-eaten steak aside.

"Clarissa," he started, "I—I'm sorry. You look absolutely stunning tonight. But… but I didn't know who else to talk to…."

Clarissa discerned the lilt washing in and out of his words, as if caught in an inner storm. She relaxed with a tentative smile. The wine had begun to calm her and filled her with a warm glow that spread a pleasant blush across her previously exposed shoulders and down her chest. The moment lasted only until she noticed the painful expression on Dequain's face.

"Dequain," she said, at last burying her seductive thoughts and digging up her business persona, "I just got all those Uteroprost reports to you a couple of days ago. There were boxes and boxes of notebooks and data. You've already gone through everything?"

"Come on," Dequain said, signaling the waiter for the check. "Let's take a walk."

Although the sun had barely tucked itself behind the Mayacamas range, the air had taken on a chill. The mounting breeze caught the tips of Clarissa's blond hair as the glassy surface of the river started rippling in time to the prodding gentle gusts. A thick bank of clouds formed to the west. This wasn't the typical balmy evening normally seen this time of year in the Napa Valley.

Clarissa's dainty shawl did little to stop the goose bumps from breaking out on her neck and shoulders, so Dequain covered her with his tan cotton sports coat. His slender fingers lingered as they brushed her skin. His light touch sent chills through Clarissa's body.

Dequain began to speak as they strolled through Veteran's Memorial Park, along the edge of the Napa River. Without any trace of his Jamaican heritage, he painted a troubling picture for Clarissa, who for the first time began to question the company she had dedicated a good part of her career to promoting their numerous contributions to the healthcare profession.

Chapter 22

A PLACE LIKE THIS USED to be veiled in layers of dense smoke swirling about the heads of patrons too drunk to notice or care. But this was California in the age of smoke-free bars and even whole towns. Inside the packed tavern, the smell of stale beer and cheap alcohol escaped the senses of anyone in the dingy joint for more than a second round. If you hung on that long, you were probably there until last call.

Doug Tierney's close-set eyes scanned the crowded scene. "Kramer, my good man. You look about ready for a refill. I think we've got us a few more minutes."

Without waiting for a reply, he whistled to the hustling waitress, pointing his stubby finger to the empty glasses. Both hands busy balancing two heavy trays, she nodded and turned, giving her tight butt an added wiggle.

Eddie Kramer, sitting across from Doug Tierney in the back corner booth, wasn't in any position to argue the point. He gave a slight shrug, momentarily locking his bloodshot eyes with the clear, cutting eyes of his companion.

Tierney reached an arm across the table and playfully punched Kramer's shoulder. "This is gonna be the night, my friend. You up for it? Or you just been bullshitting me since we had our little talk?"

After a pronounced hesitation, Kramer sat up a little straighter and leaned forward. "You bet your ass I'm ready to do this. Those little fags need a real man to teach them a lesson." His voice cracked slightly as he spoke, but they both knew he couldn't back down now.

Kramer jumped as the two heavy mugs hit the table, frothy suds sliding down the sides. Ignoring him, the waitress focused on Tierney, for the moment preventing him from questioning Kramer's veracity. In a not-so-subtle move, she pushed her breast across Tierney's forearm.

"You certainly know what real men want and how to please them, Glenda." He wasn't looking at the mugs.

Dirty dish towel in one hand, she bent across to the far end of the table, wiping away unseen crumbs while the other hand reached under the counter. She cuffed Tierney's crotch, long fingernails scraping down his jeans. The same finger Tierney used to signal his refills now snaked under Glenda's obligingly short skirt and conveniently spread legs.

"We got us a little business tonight first, but if you're patient, I'll swing by when I'm done and see if we can knock that tin can off its cinder blocks again."

"Don't be too late, or I'll start without you."

"Yeah, maybe you can persuade that old geezer next door to finish the job."

Glenda smiled. "He's had two chances. The last time I thought I'd need the paramedics to pull his sweaty body off me. He did give it a good try though. The whole damn trailer park got a front row seat."

Tierney laughed and gave her a final pat on the ass. As she walked away, he turned his attention back to Kramer. "You better drink up. Show's about to start. Check those two fags out. They'll be moving out soon, or one of 'em will wind up with an ass job under the table."

Tierney slapped several bills down. "Tonight's drinks are on me and the Brotherhood. Let's don't forget you're going to be earning it later on. So make sure I get my money's worth."

Tierney and Kramer hit the street and picked up the pace to the back parking lot. Tierney grabbed a small leather case from the tool bin bolted across the bed on his pickup and they waited in the shadows. After a few minutes, they heard giggling and unsteady footsteps heading in their direction. The Hispanic boy had parked his car two down from Tierney's truck. Tierney had made the right call when he saw him earlier, heading into the bar. He told Kramer he could smell a fag a mile away. Even when mixed with burritos.

After handing one of the drug-saturated rags to Kramer, Tierney told him he could take the little beaner while he grabbed the nigger. Both of them together weighed less than Tierney alone. This should be pretty simple if Kramer kept up his end of the bargain. That's what tonight was all about. Tierney needed to find out if this guy had what it takes to join up with the big boys.

When the two fags got to the car, Tierney poked Kramer in the ribs and whispered, "Let's do it."

At first Kramer remained frozen in place, but then jumped into action a step behind Tierney. Tierney quickly dispensed with his victim and scraped the body across the gravel while Kramer struggled with the smaller Hispanic boy. Tierney shook his head but waited things out.

Kramer finally had the rag plastered squarely over the kid's mouth, stifling any screams. Eventually he completed the job and both boys were tied up, gagged, and blindfolded in the bed of Tierney's pickup. Gravel spattered the nearest parked cars as squealing tires dug in and the pickup crossed the four lanes of Santa Rosa Avenue heading north.

Kramer started to breathe again and looked over at Tierney for approval. Tierney's profile remained relaxed, and he casually started whistling a familiar tune.

"That was fun, Doug. We gonna dump 'em off at the fairgrounds in the horse shit behind the stables?" Kramer added a weak laugh to his question.

Tierney didn't say anything. After a quick glance at Kramer, he resumed whistling. Passing the turn to the fairgrounds, he swung the pickup onto State Hwy 12 and headed west.

"So, we're taking them out of town? Good idea. Let's dump them in the woods. Then the little fags'll have to hitch a ride back to their car. And we can strip 'em naked too." Kramer's neck turned clammy and sweat dripped down his back.

After those last words fell on deaf ears, he shut up and stopped grumbling. Tierney looked straight ahead and continued to drive.

Thirty minutes later, Tierney's whistling stopped. The kicking from the truck bed grew louder. "So, we got a plan, Doug?"

A smile spread across Tierney's face. "You might say that. It's time you got the chance to see the compound. If you're going to prove to me what you got, there's no better place to work."

Chapter 23

As the night air cooled and the breezes intensified, Clarissa opted to return to the restaurant's lounge to warm up. Dequain feared that the cozy atmosphere and the soothing glow of her Cosmopolitan were no match for his chilling tale.

"How could any of this be true?" Clarissa said, an unsteady hand lowering her glass to the table. "It's my understanding the clinical studies have substantiated the preclinical animal data."

Dequain tented his hands to support his chin as he gazed into Clarissa's absorbing blue eyes. He shrugged, trying to regain his focus. "So it would seem by reading the clinical reports and the media hype."

"And I've distributed at least a dozen company press releases supporting those conclusions."

"Sorry." Dequain shrugged. "I didn't mean to challenge you directly."

"But," Clarissa stammered, "the FDA and, more specifically, the PWA review board examined all that same data. If what you're suggesting is true, BioCoGen is about to unleash a treatment that not only doesn't work but could even be dangerous."

"Clarissa, I am not suggesting anything. I am simply analyzing the information you have provided me in those laboratory notebooks."

"You need to break this down for me. I'm not stupid; but I'm not a scientist. Help me understand what you're seeing in those numbers."

Dequain let out a long breath and clasped his hands together on the table. "We must start with the target. And how it was validated."

Clarissa shook her head, indicating those words meant nothing to her.

Dequain relaxed his body, but leaned forward to address Clarissa, his voice taking on a distinct professorial tone. "Ten years ago, the founders of BioCoGen purchased an extensive compound library from an outside source."

Clarissa's look remained blank, so Dequain backed up. "A compound library is a collection of proprietary chemical substances, usually organic molecules."

Clarissa nodded.

"Okay. So BioCoGen examined this particular library using a high-capacity screening process to identify a series of patentable prostaglandin analogues that had the potential to regulate key genes in the female reproductive cycle." He paused again to gage Clarissa's understanding. "You with me?"

"Yes, now I remember," she responded. "These methods are the mainstay of how fledgling start-up companies compete with the big boys."

With a reasonable start-up capital investment and a team of clever scientists with an innovative process invented, literally hundreds of thousands of molecules could be screened in a fraction of the time it once took to find a unique structure that possessed specific activity against a particular drug target. This was as close to a virtual approach to drug development as the technology allowed. BioCoGen was such a company striving to identify its one ticket into the major leagues.

In a painstaking fashion, Dequain guided Clarissa through an explanation of the primary screening procedures. He described how the cell-based functional assays, followed by *in vitro*, or test tube type studies, further identified key biological activities of a particular class of molecules. By the time a compound reached the stage of live animal testing, a great deal was already known regarding its specificity and selectivity for the given target.

In other words, they were close to identifying a potential new drug that helped interfere with the progression of a particular disease process, while exhibiting minimal side effects on normal tissues.

In another thirty minutes Dequain had completed his story of what had at first mystified him about his recent research findings, and now had him alarmed as to the validity of BioCoGen's soon-to-be-approved fertility treatment program.

Chapter 24

Closer to the coast, the intensity of the wind buffeted the pounding rains against the windshield of Doug Tierney's pickup truck. This little storm was only a sign of things to come before the main event crashed into the northern California coastline.

After Kramer's earlier questioning of Tierney's plans for their two captives secured in the truck's bed, he had remained silent, staring at the dark surroundings on the isolated final leg of the ride from Santa Rosa. Once they'd left the narrow country lane and passed through a locked gate, they drove by shadowed wood-framed buildings skirting the edges of a large, open field.

"Jump out and swing back those doors," Tierney said to Kramer, stopping his pickup in front of a large barn-like structure.

Kramer complied and slid back the metal bar, cringing as the rusted hinges cut through the night air. He fought the winds and pelting rain to push against the heavy doors.

Tierney pulled the truck inside and shouted to Kramer to shut the doors. After doing what he was told, Kramer swiped away the dripping water from his face and finally found his voice. "So, this is the Brotherhood's compound, Doug? This'll teach them a lesson, leaving them way the hell out here. But why'd you want the door closed?"

This was Kramer's first look at the headquarters of the Nordic Brotherhood.

Tierney stared at Kramer, expelling a rush of air and spitting on the ground. "Jesus, Kramer. I gotta walk you through every step? Want me to hold your hand like those two fags back there?" He arched a thumb over his shoulder at the two figures slumped in the truck's rain-soaked bed.

Tierney leaned against the truck's door and lit up another cigarette. He reached behind his back and pulled out a pistol. "They're probably pretty much awake by now. Cold rain and an open pickup will usually do that." He exhaled and blew smoke up toward the roof. "I'll keep the boys covered. Go cut them free. You see those cuffs bolted to the wall over there?" Tierney pointed with the barrel of his Glock. "Bring the fags over and shackle their hands and feet. Start with the little beaner."

Kramer's feet remained planted in place, and he stood staring dumbly at the wall. Tierney shouted out the commands again, and Kramer jumped into action. The task was made more difficult, not only by the constant blubbering and resistance of their two captives, but also by Kramer's sweating and shaking hands.

Tierney finished his third cigarette. The amusement on his face turned to annoyance at his friend's clumsy handling and apparent lack of enthusiasm for getting this done. Finally satisfied with Kramer's efforts at securing the two boys, Tierney walked up to them, shoved the Glock back in his waistband, and yanked the blindfolds off.

"Wh—what're you doing? Now they can see our faces," Kramer spat out, his face drenched in sweat. "Are you cra—" He stopped short of calling Tierney crazy.

"Still don't get it, do you?" Tierney said, sneering at Kramer, whose knees buckled.

Kramer grabbed on to a post to keep himself upright.

"This is your night to show me you're a man. All your talk about cleansing the world of the filth muddying the gene pools and dirtying up our planet? So now's your chance to prove to me you meant what you said. You wanna be part of the solution, you gotta stop talking and get the job done."

A strong waft of urine circled Tierney's face. He checked its source and laughed. "Well fuck, Kramer. For a second, I was worried it came from you."

Kramer checked his own pants and confirmed Tierney's observation. The Hispanic boy closed his eyes and cried.

"Just to move things along, I'll show you how this works. For old times' sake—I'll take the nigger." Tierney lifted up his pants leg and pulled out the six-inch hunting knife strapped to his calf. As both boys screamed and sobbed uncontrollably, he cut open the front of the boy's jeans and hacked away at his genitals.

Thankfully, the boy had passed out. Blood sprayed and torn flesh dropped to the dirt floor. The smell of urine and loosened bowels hung inside the barn. Outside, the winds and rains slammed against the building, taking the sharp edges off the last remaining screams inside.

Tierney wiped off the bloodied knife on the boy's shirt and turned to hand it to Kramer. He looked around to see him doubled over, vomiting up everything in his gut from at least the last two days. The heaving showed no signs of slowing down.

The door burst open and a large, older man walked in. Droplets of rain dripped down the side of his broad face. Without looking at Tierney, he strode up to the two figures slumped against the wall, arms held up only by the cuffs bolted into the timbers. Anguished screams no longer emanated from the barn. The young Hispanic boy had passed out at the sight of his friend's bloody member dropping into the dirt. The man drew the Colt 45 from its holster and put two rounds each into their heads. Only then did he speak.

"Tierney. What in the fuck is the matter with you? We're done with this kinda shit. Just because you weren't around for the fun in the fifties or sixties? We've got much more efficient ways of handling these things. The time is coming—real soon now. I can't let you young fellows muck up the works just for a few kicks."

"Sorry, boss. Didn't know you were in the farmhouse tonight. Didn't mean to disturb you."

"Shit. Here I was. In the middle of making love to my charming wife when the surveillance cameras bleep on. One minute I'm in the middle of a romantic encounter, the next I'm watching you holding this nigger's dick in your hand. Not exactly the foreplay Millie had in mind."

The man walked closer to Tierney and whispered something.

"You think that's necessary? He might come around."

"I'd do it myself, but you might want his help cleaning up this mess first."

Tierney took in the scene and then glanced over at Kramer rolled up in a ball in the corner of the barn. He grabbed his Glock and fired three shots into Kramer's head. "Don't think he'd be much help. And I'm tired of listening to him complain. It's getting harder to find decent white guys to work with nowadays."

The old man shook his head and walked away. "I'd help, but Mrs. Luntz is waiting inside. You know what to do. It's not the Hudson River, but there should be enough room in the Pacific for a couple more fags. And a useless white guy. Jesus H. Christ, Tierney. Where the fuck do you come up with these losers?"

After the thrill of blowing away those two fags, Karl Luntz was anxious to get back in the saddle and finish his business with the wife. Just like the good old days he'd just dismissed.

* * * * * *

The morning fog crushed the sun's bid to warm and brighten the day. Local residents savored the brief calm and waited for the next approaching storm to strike. The entire northern coast of California prepared to dig in for the big one. This one would be sweeping down from the heavens; not shaking and quaking from below.

Adolf Dinter, head of security at both the Kessler Foundation and BioCoGen, arrived at the Nordic Brotherhood compound for a scheduled training drill with the new recruits. Karl Luntz remained inside the farmhouse enjoying a hearty breakfast with his wife. Being late for the morning's training session usually meant he'd had a good night. Last night's distractions hadn't broken his stamina and may have even enhanced the experience.

After Luntz had intervened with Doug Tierney's little late-night party in the barn, Tierney had loaded up his pickup truck with the three bodies and took care of the trash. He now lay sound asleep in one of the bunkhouses. The retorts of automatic weapons and high-powered rifles from the Nordic Brotherhood's drill did nothing to disturb his erotic dreams of Glenda.

Adolf Dinter inspected the riddled targets which consisted of life-size human cutouts on sophisticated overhead tracks to mimic the potentially erratic movements of an adversary. To the Nordic Brotherhood, any minority group represented the enemy. They drew the line at children, but little else. While most of the civilized world focused on the more imminent threat from Islamic extremists, the Nordic Brotherhood guarded against a growing list of offenders to the pure race. They stood ready to take out any Muslim terrorist in the way, but they also enjoyed ridding the world of Blacks, Jews, Asians, Indians, Hispanics, etc.… etc.… etc.

According to their leader, Karl Luntz, times had changed and working piecemeal didn't cut it anymore. The good old days were gone and something larger loomed on the horizon. Exactly what that involved still remained a mystery to him. Regardless, he planned to be ready to face the conflict.

It all started for Luntz when the white limo had pulled up in front of his office in the Napa Valley. At first, Luntz thought the tall, bald man sitting in the back seat had chosen Moon Valley Air Rides to plan a large event, perhaps a company outing or a wedding for a granddaughter. He soon found out the visit had nothing to do with his company's picturesque hot-air balloon rides in the Napa Valley.

The man in the limo had possessed a great deal of knowledge about Luntz's past activities and the fact that he still embraced those same ideologies. The man persuaded Luntz to try a more organized approach to cleanse the world and had come forward with specific ideas and sufficient funding for Karl Luntz's bigoted transgressions to become a lucrative reality.

It had been over two years since this man first approached Luntz. The result had been the formation of the Nordic Brotherhood, and this secluded training compound near the Sonoma County coast. In addition, with the backing of the same man, Luntz had started a private security outfit that led to a beneficial working arrangement with the world-renowned Kessler Foundation and a new pharmaceutical company, BioCoGen. They paid Mr. Luntz and his fledgling security operations well. This new pact came under the stringent guidance and persuasion of the tall, bald man in the limousine.

The man Karl Luntz knew only as Mr. Clean.

Karl Luntz didn't think Mr. Clean was the least bit crazy. He enjoyed working with someone who grasped the problems facing the world and had the balls to do something about it. Most men who were involved with different aspects of Mr. Clean's vision didn't understand the scope of this undertaking. Karl Luntz always considered himself smarter than everyone else. Mr. Clean had provided him with just enough information to feed his overblown ego.

The influence brokers in D.C., such as Arthur Constantine, who had dealings with Mr. Clean, simply jumped on board for power and money. They didn't realize their little world might crumble as well. The time had come to restore order to a world about to implode. Every time Arthur Constantine met with the enigmatic Mr. Clean, he sensed an underlying danger, but the need for the man's money clouded his judgment.

Mr. Clean also worked to facilitate the collaborative efforts between the Kessler Foundation and BioCoGen. He funneled large portions of funding into both the company and the clinic. His input expedited the process to take advantage of the ConnorCare research and development incentives. The marriage between BioCoGen and the Kessler Foundation paved the way for pushing the new Uteroprost therapy to market. Having the might of the federal government at his back made things even easier. With his influence over the Nordic Brotherhood, Mr. Clean had greater confidence in the overall success of the project. He always looked at the bigger picture and envisioned a revolutionary purpose for treatment modalities such as Uteroprost.

Adolf Dinter had teamed up with Karl Luntz on the East Coast many years ago. Luntz had taken Dinter under his wing and mentored him. When local pressures had forced Luntz to disappear and head west, there was little doubt that Adolf Dinter would follow. Dinter became Luntz's natural choice to head his new private security company.

One night, not too long ago, history repeated itself outside a bar in Santa Rosa. Adolf Dinter watched a young man, Joseph Stock, beating the crap out of three Hispanics, each carrying knives and sporting brass knuckles. They didn't stand a chance against the burly and pissed-off Joseph Stock. When it was over, Dinter walked up to Stock, who'd barely worked up a sweat, and offered him a job.

CHAPTER 25

PRESIDENT TYLER GRIFFIN PLACED THE phone back in the cradle and spun the large leather chair around to the three south-facing windows. He ran his hands over his trimmed dark brown hair and rubbed the strain from his deep-set black eyes. The president stood and gazed out across the South Lawn. He observed the helicopter, formerly Marine One, which he had exited several minutes ago, flying away. The rattling of the White House windows subsided as the chopper banked over the Washington Monument and gradually disappeared.

Griffin checked his watch and allowed himself a rare fleeting smile. If things didn't go well over the next several days, he could soon be looking for a new place to live. One way or the other, tomorrow night would define his presidency, but more important for the nation, it could signal the turning tide on this damn war on terror.

The president's secretary escorted his next visitor into the Oval Office. As the door clicked shut, the president turned from the window. This time a genuine smile spread across his troubled face.

"Alice," President Griffin said and walked around his desk to greet the former president, Alice Andersen. They shared a welcome embrace.

"How're you doing, Alice? You look radiant, as usual."

President Andersen pulled back, still grasping both of Griffin's hands, and gave him a wistful appraisal.

"I'm doing just fine, but if I might say, you look like you've aged at least twenty years since your inauguration."

Griffin nodded. "You're being way too kind, Madam President. After the last several days, I'd consider that a compliment. Come on, Alice. Let's go sit by the fireplace."

Alice Andersen looped her forearm through Griffin's extended elbow and allowed herself to be led to the sofa. Griffin noted that while her gait appeared steady, there was considerable tentativeness in her movements.

Prior to the last presidential campaign cycle, President Alice Andersen had been diagnosed with early-stage Parkinson's disease. While she might have kept her condition a secret for the next several years with the appropriate treatment protocols, she opted to announce her illness to the people and head off any rumors from upsetting the delicate balance of the recovering political and economic climate in the nation.

President Andersen had made the decision to finish out her term, but not seek the party's nomination and run for reelection. She threw in support for her appointed vice president, Tyler Griffin.

Since Andersen and Griffin came from opposing political parties, the standard bearing party machines from both sides of the aisle spun out of control. Due to the bizarre circumstances of how both Andersen and Griffin wound up as the nation's top executives, the status quo of party politics became challenged to the limit. All Andersen's efforts to reunite the nation following the impeachment and subsequent prosecution of President John Connor crumbled to the current state of political dysfunction following the narrow victory of Tyler Griffin in a bitter presidential fight.

"How're things on your farm, Alice?"

"Not much going on since your last visit. Edie did make a beautiful bride."

That put a smile back on Griffin's face.

"And now here she is, right in the thick of things." She shook her head. "With you two teaming up again, can't say I'm surprised by all the attention you're getting."

Griffin's smile faded away.

"No telling what can happen when you double up on the Jersey attitude in the White House," Andersen said. "I can say that, even though I wasn't born in New Jersey. I sure lived in the Garden State long enough. And lord knows, I spent many years of my career dealing with you people. A poor southern black girl living in the heart of the union. And I'm not speaking about the New Jersey labor unions." The former president winked, leaned across the coffee table and patted Griffin's arm.

Andersen sat back and folded her arms. "If you care to enlighten a former colleague as to what you two have up your sleeve, I'd be more than happy to listen. But if for the sake of national security, you prefer not to confide in me, I'll not be offended."

President Griffin blew out a deep breath and stood. He walked over to the fireplace, stoked the burning logs and placed several more pieces on top.

"You know the secret service won't let me chop any firewood on the South Lawn?"

"I've seen your temper, Tyler, and I don't blame them."

Griffin placed the fireplace tools back in the stand and stretched. He turned to Andersen and gave her the long version of the story. She waited for him to finish before asking a few key questions. She nodded in response to his answers and, in an exaggerated effort, pushed herself off the sofa, waving off any assistance from Griffin.

Griffin watched the former president amble to the other end of the Oval Office. It appeared that her illness had intensified during today's short visit. He bore an overwhelming wave of guilt.

Andersen walked around the president's desk, tapping her fingers on the edge. She placed a hand on the leather chair and swung it back and forth several times. After a quick glance out the window, she faced the current resident of the Oval Office.

"Something has me worried about all this. And I don't mean the typical political fallout you're going to face. Don't get me wrong, I'm not belittling the battle you'll be up against with congress and the media."

She paused and tilted her head. "I think you'll handle that just fine. In fact, I might even feel a little sorry for anyone who is foolish enough to stand in your way."

Griffin was about to answer, but something in Andersen's eyes made him hesitate.

"Tyler. We all have enemies in Washington. Those you can deal with. I may be wrong, but there's something else going on here."

The former president stood up as straight as her failing body allowed. She glanced around the familiar office one more time, and her next words sounded hollow. "So many papers to read. Too much smoke and mirrors." She closed her eyes for a moment. "This topic always seemed too far-fetched to warrant any serious consideration. Reminiscent of urban legends and lies.

That's why I never shared it with you." She drew in a deep breath. "Now it's all coming back, like a cold wave."

Staring at Griffin, she said, "I'm afraid. For you and our nation. Be careful, Tyler." She reached into her purse and pulled out the folded documents, dropping them on the president's desk.

"From what I've been told, eventually every occupant of this office gets to see some version of these papers. This information may give you a head start. Then again," her eyes focused on the raging fire, "you might be better off forgetting you ever saw this."

Andersen grabbed the back of the president's chair, but her hands still shook. Griffin didn't think it was any manifestation of her Parkinson's disease.

CHAPTER 26

ON THE FAR SIDE OF the limo seat from Arthur Constantine, the tall, bald man made a finicky gesture of straightening out his tie. He had listened to what Constantine had been saying for the last ten minutes without interruption. His face remained unreadable, but his eyes looked right through the usually imperturbable Constantine.

They sat alone. The limo driver had left, having walked in a discreet manner away from the car to the top of the knoll, passing the temporarily deactivated surveillance cameras. The local authorities were aware of another malfunction in the system, but it wasn't a high priority for them to check it out. This sort of thing had happened before, and usually got straightened out on its own. No need to drive all the way out to such a remote location at this stage of the game. There weren't a whole lot of things that could sustain damage anyway. Graffiti artists had long since found more visible targets to show off their handiwork.

Earlier, Arthur Constantine had been ushered onto one of the man's corporate jets and flown out of a small airport in the D.C. area. The jet landed at a private airfield about thirty miles north of their present location. The limo picked him up at a nearby truck stop after a local taxi had dropped him off. These atypical travel arrangements had become the norm whenever Constantine was summoned by the man seated to his side, although the particulars of the itinerary and the destination varied.

The man had asked Constantine to remain quiet until they reached the current destination, and then motioned for him to begin his update on the latest activities in D.C. The silent ride had given Constantine the creeps, and by the time he finished his little speech, a sheen of perspiration had formed on his forehead and the moisture from his armpits had soaked through his crisp white shirt. He was more used to causing such a response than being the one experiencing this discomfort. He should at least be thankful that direct encounters with this individual were rare.

The advanced age of the tall, bald gentleman should have highlighted his frail appearance, but somehow an inner strength pushed the physical shortcomings aside. Not for the first time, Constantine wondered if the man was insane, a total psycho. If that were the case, it made him even more dangerous.

Did the old man believe all this crap?

Here they were standing in the middle of a damn cow pasture looking at a bunch of granite stones. What were his real motives? Not that it would've mattered, his money provided for the bulk of this fight, so Constantine supposed the man could think whatever the hell he wanted. No harm in that.

Then why did this guy make his skin crawl whenever they met?

Right now, Constantine would give just about anything to instead be dealing with that pain-in-the-ass senator, Henry Whitcome, and that twerpy little congressman, Derrick Pranchard. He thought of his last meeting at the Willard Intercontinental Hotel, within reach of the White House. Obsessions of importance, like those exhibited by Senator Whitcome, were far easier to deal with.

Before the return trip, the man, known only as Mr. Clean, motioned for Constantine to join him in a short stroll around the knoll and clustered granite structures. He had told Constantine it was just to remind him of what was really at stake.

Chapter 27

As Clarissa Mendelschein slipped the key card into the security lock to the research laboratory suite at the Kessler Foundation, Dr. Dequain Johnson repeated the same question he'd been asking since he'd gotten into her car in front of his condo.

"Clarissa," he said, "do you think this is a good idea?"

She responded with the same exasperated sigh. "If this is what you need to find out the answers, I don't know of anybody else who can get you in here."

Thirty minutes later, Dequain relaxed a bit, thinking things were going smoothly. Clarissa had no problem gaining access to the lab and the freezers where they stored the archived samples. She printed out copies of the documents Dequain had requested as he packed up the selected specimens for testing in his own laboratory back on the BioCoGen campus. They were in the small administrative office in the back of one of the labs when they heard footsteps.

Clarissa signaled Dequain to shove everything underneath the desk. Her voice sounded so urgent he did so without question. Once he completed the task, he turned back to Clarissa and the next words out of his mouth were accented in the thickest Jamaican lilt he'd ever uttered.

"Cl… Clar… Clarissa? What are you—"

He never finished as his eyes bulged at the sight of Clarissa peeling away her clothing right in front of him. Before he registered what was happening, Clarissa's hands worked in a flash. She unzipped his pants and yanked them to his ankles. Her fingers flew to his shirt and before he could protest, she popped open the buttons and ripped back the material.

Next thing he knew, Clarissa pulled him down to the floor on top of her naked body, her legs spread-eagled beneath him. She then vice-gripped her legs around his buttocks and wrapped her arms onto his shoulders, drawing him into a tight embrace, just as the office door sprang open and two security guards, guns drawn, flanked the entrance.

Clarissa spoke first, taking the offensive. "What the hell do you think you're doing barging in here like this? If I wanted your help—I would've called you myself. Now, if you don't mind, I'm kinda busy here."

The two guards, new to the job, looked so stunned, at first their guns remained aimed at the couple glued to the carpet. After Clarissa restated her suggestions in even stronger terms, they backed out the door and re-holstered their weapons. But not before Clarissa's final command for them to close the door echoed in their heads.

They belatedly recognized the naked blond lady on the carpet with a black man on top as they retraced their steps out of the lab and headed back down the corridor. Apparently, it was Clarissa Mendelschein's thick black-rimmed glasses that helped them identify her. Somehow the glasses had stayed in place, although had begun to fog up as the result of Dequain's heavy breathing.

Clarissa solved that problem by tossing them aside. She didn't lessen her grip on Dequain, but at this point it wasn't necessary since Dequain was a quick learner and got with the program. He stared into Clarissa's unobstructed blue eyes and finished the job she had started.

They held their embrace long after the unexpected passions subsided. Dequain attempted to speak several times, but Clarissa placed her index finger over his lips and pulled him tight to her chest. He listened to the slowing of her heart and drank in the rhythmic heaving of her breasts.

At last, Dequain whispered in Clarissa's ear. "You are right, Clarissa, I know of no one else who could have made this work."

His voice had Clarissa gasping, but they both knew they needed to get the hell out of the clinic before those two morons had a chance to spread the word and get somebody a little higher up on the food chain involved.

CHAPTER 28

A SHORT TIME AFTER CONFRONTING Clarissa Mendelschein and Dequain Johnson at the Kessler Foundation, the two befuddled security guards got off duty and headed to their favorite bar in one of the rowdier sections of Santa Rosa. They were not only relative newcomers to their positions at the Kessler Foundation, but were also new members of the Nordic Brotherhood, the group that formed the essential backbone to the security operations at the clinic.

The head of the Kessler Foundation, Dr. Rudi Kessler, was a stickler for protocol and tradition, and that mindset had been the impetus for him to hire this particular security company. He had learned of this outfit through his associates in Washington, D.C. At the request of his good friend, Arthur Constantine, a behind the scenes D.C. powerbroker, Kessler met up with an individual whose true identity to this day remained a mystery. He knew of him only as Mr. Clean. Constantine had told Kessler that Mr. Clean was not someone to be ignored. So far, Kessler had no problems with the way things had worked out.

The Nordic Brotherhood had its roots in Santa Rosa and nearby Sebastopol under the oversight of a local businessman, Karl Luntz. The group held strict beliefs regarding racial and ethnic compositions, and their tactics fit in well with Dr. Kessler's own ideology.

A lot rode on the Uteroprost clinical trials, and he didn't believe in taking chances. He needed a level of security that left nothing to chance.

Still laughing about the shocked expression on Dequain Johnson's face, the two young security guards swaggered through the door, casting glances around the crowded bar. "I'll be damned. Look who's sitting in the corner booth."

"You think I'm an idiot? It's the boss and his overgrown sidekick. But who's the other guy across from Dinter and Stock?"

"Fer chrissakes, I don't think you're an idiot, I know damn well you are. It's the big boss. Karl Luntz. The head of the Nordic Brotherhood himself."

"Well, shit. Why don't we find a stool at the far end of the bar and melt into the background before they see us?"

"You see. That's why you'll never get anywhere in this organization. Come on. Let's go over and pay our respects."

"You think that's a good idea?"

After an awkward exchange with their bosses, the two men then went on to join a more boisterous group at one of the tables in the center of the noisy room. Before moving on they relayed the humorous story of finding Clarissa Mendelschein being ridden by a black dude on the floor in the restricted research area of the clinic.

When pressed for details, they had come to the unfortunate conclusion that none of their superiors had found any of it amusing. At least they had the foresight to check out the security cameras and had identified the second person involved as Dr. Dequain Johnson.

After dismissing the two rookies, Karl Luntz took a long draw from his beer and smacked the empty mug back on the table. Wiping the suds from his lips, he placed his beefy elbows on the table and stared hard at

Adolf Dinter. "How in the hell are we getting these useless cretins into the Brotherhood?"

Dinter's blue eyes blinked several times before answering. The dim light in the bar hid most of the coloring rising over his shaved face and scalp. He leaned back and tented his fingers, exaggerating the slender, almost feminine profile of his hands.

"Karl," Dinter said, trying to sound stern. "I'll make sure those two understand the seriousness of their jobs and—"

Luntz leaned across the table. "You can do whatever the hell you want with those two fools, but you need to find out what Mendelschein and that nigger she was with were doing in a restricted area. If she wants to fuck a monkey—that's fine with me—but not after hours in the clinic. Something's not right about this."

"Of course, Karl," Dinter responded, untangling his fingers and raising his arms. "I was just about to say we'll look into this matter first thing in the morning." He glanced at Stock and added, "We'll personally keep an eye on both Mendelschein and this Dr. Johnson too. I never trusted that nosy little bitch in the first place. Always thought Dr. Kessler gave her too much latitude. Not only at the clinic, but also her unfettered access at BioCoGen."

Joseph Stock kept his head down, looking for answers hidden in his empty beer mug. Interacting with the bosses wasn't one of his strongpoints, and this conversation only made him more nervous. He'd much rather use his muscular six-foot-four-inch frame to knock a few heads around. That was when his talents came to the forefront. He was already looking forward to kicking the living shit out of that stupid black schmuck. The fucking nerve of him, dipping his wick into a fine white girl of Nordic descent. She needed a few lessons taught to her as well. Stock had given her the chance several times, but he'd been blown off. The uppity bitch needed to be straightened out. He'd make her forget that sweaty black pig.

"Hey, Joe." Dinter smacked him on the arm for the second time. "You listening to me? We gotta go. What's so interesting in your glass anyway? There're only suds left."

CHAPTER 29

THE DRIVE HOME FROM THE clinic had dragged on forever. Neither Steve nor Edie felt like any small talk, so they made the ride in relative silence. Edie now lay in bed staring at the ceiling. She turned to Steve and saw he had already fallen asleep.

Their earlier visit to the Kessler Foundation had failed to calm Edie's concerns for Catori's health. In fact, their encounters with Dr. Kessler and her old friend, Tiffany Liebermann, stirred up memories about her previous investigations into government healthcare programs.

Edie had interviewed Liebermann on several occasions. The sight of the woman always reminded Edie of how the government used people to spread their message to an unsuspecting population and manipulate ideologies to push forward political agendas.

The lofty attitude and condescending nature of the activist had frustrated Edie's attempts to debate the serious issues relating to women's rights and healthcare on a fact-based platform. Liebermann's narrative of fearmongering and demonizations allowed little room for an honest discussion.

After Ms. Liebermann's hasty departure, Steve and Edie had been let in to see Dr. Kessler. His patronizing demeanor did little to appease her. He promised to oversee every step of Catori's diagnosis and subsequent treatment protocols, stating unequivocally that they would get to the bottom of her worsening condition. He assured Edie that no other clinic in the world matched the Kessler Foundation at any level, but he refused to give specific details on Catori's health, citing patient confidentiality.

While sitting in Dr. Kessler's office, all Edie could see was red. Her eyes fixed on the smudged lipstick stains imprinted on Kessler's neck, only half-hidden by his collar. She could only imagine the other spots where Liebermann's lips had nibbled. When her gaze turned to Kessler's hands, she wanted to scream at the thought of those same fingers touching Catori. What the hell had they just been doing to Liebermann?

In the darkness, Edie remained alone with her thoughts. As the night slowly slipped away, she continued listening to Steve's rhythmic breathing and occasional quiet snores. After what seemed like hours, she felt her eyes grow heavy.

And then Steve's phone rang.

He answered it, fully awake and moving before Edie's head cleared enough to grasp the intrusion. The brunt of the storm was about to make a direct hit on the Bay Area. All station shifts were being called on duty. He needed to report to work immediately.

Edie's flight to D.C didn't leave for quite a few hours, but she gave up any further attempts to sleep. She decided to take a quick shower and then begin to work on figuring out what, if anything, she could do to help Catori.

* * * * * *

Steve had long since reported to work, and Edie's notes remained scattered on the kitchen table. After gulping down two cups of coffee, she hadn't uncovered anything useful. Only her usual skepticism with anything the government attempted to regulate. With a lack of sleep and multiple caffeine fixes, her body was wound up, ready to spring loose.

The taxi arrived to take Edie to the airport before she had the chance to come to any new conclusions. She wasn't even sure what she was looking for. At this point, there was no specific reason to link the clinic with any questionable activities. Maybe she was simply overreacting. She had told Steve that the clinic was above suspicion. That was probably true. Right now, she was feeling a bit foolish for barging into Kessler's office and making a scene.

Settling into her seat as the jumbo jet prepared to depart from SFO, Edie decided to use the opportunity to get a few hours rest before joining the president in the Situation Room. She mouthed a silent prayer, not only for Catori, but for the safe conclusion to a dangerous mission about to start halfway around the world, and then fell into a fitful sleep.

Chapter 30

WITH A BRIEFCASE DANGLING FROM his arm, Dr. Dequain Johnson inserted the key card into the slot and walked through the main entrance to the animal facility building at BioCoGen. Although Dequain preferred biking whenever possible, due to today's deteriorating weather conditions, he drove his brand-new white Ford Explorer to work.

He waved at the familiar face of the security guard who looked up from his magazine and smiled back. Although the guards had the right to check whatever he brought in or took out, they had never bothered to do so. Security at the research facility was supposedly good, but nowhere near as stringent as the clinic. Today, Dequain was grateful for this.

He ran the standard battery of genetic profiling tests on the stolen biopsy samples from the clinic. There were no names or other identifying information, only clinical trial participant numbers and the usual generic patient profiles found in such a study. That was it.

The results from these tests confused him. They suggested that the samples came from, not a diversified population base, but were more consistent with everyone having a similar ethnic background. That made no sense, given the stated subject profiles.

What struck him as being even more curious was that based on his own research work, he was very familiar with the genetic profiles now sitting in front of him. He grabbed his keys, opened the locked file cabinet behind his desk, and pulled out the laboratory notebooks of the original studies at BioCoGen. Those used to validate the targeted basis for the Uteroprost project.

After last night's incident at the clinic, he struggled to maintain focus. Clarissa's alabaster image kept flashing across his mind. The guns pointed at him should've made a bigger impression, but that wasn't the case. Shaking his head, but not wiping the smile from his face, he dug into the information spread over his desk.

Suppressing Clarissa's naked body from his brain, the impact of what stared back at him took over. How could the clinical trial progress to this stage with no one coming forward? Even if the company ignored or falsified data, the regulatory agencies should have picked up on this.

CHAPTER 31

CATORI TORRENCE'S BODY APPEARED ANCHORED to the hospital bed in her private room at the Kessler Foundation. Until now, all vital signs confirmed her resting under the influence of a regimen of sedatives following the last round of procedures.

Inside Catori's mind, everything changed.

Soaring high above her body, she only got a brief glimpse of her physical self before her psyche made the abrupt shift to a picture of her grandmother, Lomasi. Catori watched with great curiosity as she witnessed herself three years earlier. She was holding Lomasi's hand while the dying matriarch of the Torrence family chanted ancient verses to a perceived mythical creature poised at the foot of her bed.

Catori was convinced Lomasi's words were somehow now different than she had remembered, but no matter how hard she strained to listen, the meaning of these new words escaped her grasp. But the urgency in Lomasi's voice couldn't be denied.

In the next instant, Catori's attention turned to the image of the rising sun, and a much younger Lomasi materialized, sitting on her porch and rocking in her favorite chair while cuddling an infant in her arms. Soothing words floated up to Catori, but nevertheless sounded disturbing.

Catori knew that she was the infant in her grandmother's arms. Rationally, she didn't think she could have remembered that particular moment, but in her heart, she sensed those words had long ago been planted in her soul.

As long as Catori recalled, she had known she'd been chosen to carry on the legends of her tribal ancestors, just as Lomasi had done before her.

Catori blinked. Her eyes next gazed at a new rising sun, and now Lomasi had transitioned into a young girl, a few years younger than Catori's present age. Catori was captivated by the beautiful and sensuous image.

The naked body of the girl who was to be her grandmother lay at the edge of a virgin stream pouring out of a rocky formation atop the ancient mountains of her native lands far to the north. Although no winds created any turbulence, the waters ebbed and flowed about the languid body nestled in the sacred mountain soil along the banks of the stream. A reddish hue emerged as the icy waters diluted the virgin effluent from the girl's womb.

A band of young braves stood motionless around the beautiful young maiden, but none dared touch her, lest they disturb the unfolding fertility ceremony taking place. To do so would have ended in their death. This evolving female in their midst was a symbol of the tribe's creation and protection.

They watched in awe as the torrent waters gained energy and penetrated the young woman. This was followed by blazing rays from the sun mimicking the same routine. Lomasi's body trembled from the icy fingers of the waters and shimmered from the heat of the sun.

As the ritual persisted, Lomasi moaned. Her eyes opened in a fixed stare, and she began rubbing the skin from first her right breast; and then her left. This repeated over different parts of her body, and the birth of the ancestral tribes commenced. Lomasi's image had been altered into the nurturing symbols of the earth, assuring the continuance of her people.

Catori was just coming to comprehend that the persona of the fertile woman was no longer Lomasi, but herself, when a bright light and a worried voice brought her crashing down to reenter her sleeping body on the hospital bed.

"Ms. Torrence? Are you okay?"

Catori's eyes fluttered and then attempted to focus on the sounds assaulting her head and intruding on her vision.

When the elderly nurse checked Catori's pulse and recorded her other vital signs, she breathed a sigh of relief. Looking at the helpless girl in her charge, she smiled.

"The monitors must've malfunctioned," she said shrugging her broad shoulders. "The alarms sounded at the station and there appeared to be no pulse. No electrical activity in your heart. But now everything looks normal."

Catori's senses edged her toward the present, and she recognized the person leaning over the bed. It was that nice lady who'd been taking care of her. The nurse. Martha. That's right. On the day shift. That meant it was morning already.

Did I sleep the whole night?

Had I slept at all?

The last thing she remembered was seeing the faces of Edie and Steve.

When was that?

The only thing she recalled from their visit, if they were really here, were the frightened looks on their faces.

Something must be wrong.

She needed to get out of here and warn them before it was too late. A light pressure on her shoulder startled Catori.

"Ms. Torrence," Martha said, "you mustn't try to sit up. The medicines you're taking will make you dizzy. For now, you need to rest. From what I've read on your chart, you've also lost quite a bit of blood during one of the procedures."

Martha pointed at one of the plastic bags hanging from the rod attached to the side of the bed. "See here? This is a transfusion unit. When this is empty, you're scheduled for one more unit. So, you're not going to go anywhere for a while."

Martha smiled, her voice sympathetic, easing Catori's tension. As Martha checked the intravenous line on Catori's arm, she glanced at the unusual transformations to her skin. She reached out and ran her fingers along the subtle lesions. Her perplexed look confirmed Catori's fears that the changes she'd sensed were real.

Catori nodded and tried to talk but found it difficult to speak; her throat parched and on fire. "Do you know if the doctor will be here soon? I can't seem to recall what they've been doing. Have they found out what's causing all this?" Catori placed her hands over her abdomen to reassure herself she was still whole.

Martha's expression became troubled, her eyes scanning the charts. "I'm afraid you'll have to ask Dr. Kessler those questions. I'm sure he'll put your mind at ease."

As Martha finished speaking, they were interrupted by a knock on the door. She patted Catori on the arm, walked to the door, and listened to the other nurse.

For the moment, Catori's senses became stronger, and the voices registered with an almost normal clarity in her ears.

The two nurses discussed routine questions regarding doctors' orders for several patients, as well as a little juicy gossip about one of the doctors and a particular nurse's aide. It turned out to be three nurse's aides and the same doctor—at the same time.

Catori began to tune out the droning voices when something caught her attention. She sensed the younger nurse staring in her direction. Before shutting her eyes, she saw Martha, still holding on to the chart, pointing emphatically at one of the pages.

"Are you telling me, Doreen," Martha said, "that you don't see any similarities?"

Doreen, the nurse in charge, placed an arm about Martha's shoulder and guided her further into the corridor. The loud click of the closing door accented Catori's impression of being alone and trying to swim back to the surface of the icy stream in her vision.

She could still feel the swirls of blood flowing menacingly around her naked body. She gazed at the faces and listened to the chanting of the braves peering through the waters, and no longer heard Martha's concerned voice.

* * * * * *

"Don't you remember?" Martha said while staring at the closed door to Catori's room.

"Please, Martha. Keep your voice down." Doreen had taken the chart and held it up against her chest.

"The same symptoms. On those other girls. And last month. The girl who died." Martha looked around. "And what about those others? Whatever happened to them? Nobody ever said. One day they were just—gone. Let me show you the results of Ms. Torrence's kidney function test." She tried to grab the chart back, but Doreen pulled it away and stared at her.

"And did you see her skin?"

"Martha. Are you aware that Dr. Kessler himself is taking care of Ms. Torrence? You're not questioning his ability to handle this, are you?"

"But—"

"Look, Martha. I know you're just doing your job and are worried about the patient. We all are. I'll tell you what. When Dr. Kessler makes his rounds this afternoon, I'll bring up your concerns."

Martha nodded absently, but said, "Now I remember. The other girls? They were Native Americans too. Weren't they?"

"Now, let's go, Martha. You've got other patients to look in on, don't you? There's no need for you to worry. I'll be sure to bring this to Dr. Kessler's attention. And I don't want you talking about this to anyone else. We wouldn't want to cause any problems with the Uteroprost trial going on. You know how the media can blow things out of proportion."

Martha looked confused. "But Ms. Torrence isn't part of the clinical trial."

"That's exactly right. So don't rock the boat."

As Martha walked down the hall, Doreen stood motionless until the older nurse disappeared around the corner. She then grabbed her cell phone and punched in a number.

CHAPTER 32

EDIE PAULING GLANCED AT THE haunted face on President Tyler Griffin. A group of select individuals sat in the secure conference center within the White House Situation Room watching a parade of images dance across banks of high-resolution monitors. The sounds of disembodied voices crackled from the sophisticated audio system. For the moment, no one in the room talked. Their eyes and ears absorbing the unfolding drama taking place in the darkness on the other side of the world.

"Copy that Golf-Lima Com. Give a holler when Leprechaun clicks his heels and delivers the thumbs up. This is Golf-Lima One standing by."

"For the record, Golf-Lima One—we're live and rolling in the cement mixer."

Capt. Fergusen leaned back against the rocky outcropping. Several guys in his squad looked on, nodding their approval, feigning a knife slash across their throats. Never hurt to break the tension that had been building since they'd completed the recon mission earlier today and waited for the go ahead from D.C.

Fergusen knew damn well that from this point on all satellite communication uplinks were not only fed to command centers at McDill Air Force Base in Florida and the Naval Special Warfare Group in Virginia but were at the moment being monitored by the top brass in the White House Situation Room.

He always wondered why they called it the cement mixer. And if rattling the brass bothered him—he needed to change his line of work. From an early age, his mom had harped on his compulsion to constantly one-up his dad's kick-ass attitude. Things certainly weren't going to change at this juncture in his life.

While he waited for the nod from the president, Fergusen's mind relaxed and drifted to stories of his father's military career in Vietnam. That's what prompted his own enlistment into the Navy and working through the arduous training to become a SEAL just like his dad.

Green Faces.

That's what they called them back then. His father's stories so vividly told, as a child he always imagined himself in one of the Chinook slick-configured choppers riding gunner on hit and run assault missions in the Mekong Delta. His dad died, not as one of the forty-six SEALs killed in action over fifty years ago in Vietnam, but of a sudden coronary attack watching a Raiders game with a can of Coors at his side two years ago.

Fergusen was willing to forgo the wait. If his time was now, he'd take as many of the bastards along with him as possible. He was confident that Leprechaun, the secret service's designated code name for Tyler Griffin, wouldn't back out of the mission. Fergusen prayed that D.C. had finally gotten the memo. The war on terror was alive and well.

He hoped this president did the right thing. Tonight should at least jump-start the troops. Payback time had arrived. His mind flashed on the remaining hostages and prayed he didn't fuck-up and get any of them killed tonight. Glancing at his comrades reminded him of their high level of commitment and expertise to pull off this op. The limits of their comfort zone constantly shifted, pushing the envelope and redefining the boundaries.

President Tyler Griffin didn't keep them guessing. A curt nod got the secretary of defense relaying orders to the linked-in command centers and an explosion of activity blasted from the speakers and flashed across the monitors. On the pad in front of him, the president wrote down a few notes, underlining the name Fergusen. This was one of the guys he wanted to shake hands with at the first opportunity.

From across the table came the familiar caustic words from Senator Henry Whitcome, the chairman of the Senate Intelligence Committee. "Do you think you're going to get away with this? How dare you blindside congress again. Your pitiful last-minute attempt to satisfy oversight requirements is the last straw."

Whitcome looked at the attorney general who had his head buried in a pile of documents. Even he hadn't been consulted on the legality of how this was going down. But so far, he was coming up blank on a way out. The one thing the attorney general knew for sure was that his relationship with Arthur Constantine had just taken a bad turn.

He had assured Constantine that when the president had announced to the nation about freeing those Navy SEALs, he had the documentation to back up the fact that the administration was hiding key information regarding the treasonous acts they had committed. Now reading these classified documents and listening to the unfolding drama, the attorney general knew his own credibility, and with it his usefulness to Constantine, was evaporating before his eyes. His only chance at redemption was that the mission would fail, and they'd have the president painted back into the corner. Spin this as a desperate act to distract from all the accusations being thrown at the president. Other presidents had tried similar scenarios in the past to deflect their deceptions from the spotlight.

Agent Mike Finley helped the civilian personnel seated in the Situation Room to translate and digest the cacophony of seemingly discordant activity flowing in from the newly discovered terrorist training camps scattered within the borders of Syria, Afghanistan, and Pakistan. The mission briefs in front of all the attendees, including the attorney general and the committee chairman, detailed Operation Guiding Light, from its inception over a year ago to the dramatic concluding events today.

Edie Pauling's hands rested on top of the closed documents on the table. She didn't have to read them again. Her eyes took in the action on the myriad of monitors surrounding her, but the only thing registering in her brain was the confident looks on the faces of the three Navy SEALs when they had approached her last year after one of her TV appearances. They knew Edie's father had been a Navy SEAL and had died saving the lives of Americans. They knew of her history with President Tyler Griffin and that she would be the only one to convince him of their plan.

Far from being traitors, they had volunteered to walk straight into the hands of the devil and deliver secrets that were in reality lies and misdirection. Enduring unspeakable acts of torture, they convinced the enemy they hated America and its values. To this day, Edie could not fathom how they survived the physical and mental anguish to maintain their cover and pull this mission off.

The face of the one female in the group, Angela, remained branded in Edie's head. She had only a brief moment to visit with her in the hospital room after she was released from captivity in exchange for the return of four top Al Qaeda leaders. On the surface, she looked the same, but she knew it was impossible for Angela not to have been transformed by what she had endured. Edie certainly didn't diminish the atrocities faced by the two men involved in the plan, but she had read about the special training program Angela insisted on going through at the hands of our own people.

That's what Edie saw when she looked into Angela's eyes.

Somewhere in the distance, Edie picked up the background sounds in the Situation Room. Now this part of the mission was over. Prior to their release, the Al Qaeda leaders had been implanted with transponders and unwittingly guided U.S. Special Forces troops to the far corners of the earth.

Their guiding light had lit up a path and several of the more important terrorist training camps had been exposed; and now decimated. It would take weeks, even months, to sort through all the intelligence gathered from these raids. But for now, the remaining hostages had been saved, and while our troops experienced minor injuries, there were no reported casualties on our side.

Edie's eyes shifted back to the president. They stared at each other silently, but neither one found it possible to force even a small smile.

CHAPTER 33

FORBIDDING CLOUDS CHASED ACROSS THE sky. Gusting winds pelted raindrops onto the large glass panels leaving a dark and somber sentiment reflected on the face of the woman seated alone near the doorway. Only a few patrons remained in the cafeteria adjacent to the glassed-in atrium lobby of the Kessler Foundation's administrative building. The staff in the kitchen prepared for the evening rush that always accompanied the end of the daytime shift.

The woman glanced up from the untouched coffee mug and waved her arm, catching Clarissa Mendelschein's attention as she strode through the entrance.

Clarissa smiled and walked over. "Hi, Martha. Don't usually see you still here at this time of day. Especially sitting in the cafeteria by yourself. You pulling overtime tonight?" She sat across from the woman.

Martha pushed her cup aside while her eyes darted around the quiet room. "Ah, no. I was waiting to see you. Spoke to your mom earlier today. She told me you'd be dropping by the clinic before heading home." She reached under the table and opened a large carryall, placing a wrapped package on the table and sliding it across to Clarissa. "This is for you, dear. Just a little something for putting in a good word and getting my interview set up."

"Thank you, but I think you've already done that—several times, if I'm not mistaken. And I told you, the Kessler Foundation is fortunate to have a dedicated nurse like you on their staff."

"Well, I do need to talk to you about one other thing," Martha said, her eyes again scanning the room.

"Would it be alright if we took a walk through the lobby?"

Clarissa nodded. "What's wrong?"

As they got up to leave, Martha leaned in toward Clarissa and said, "The last thing I want to do is to get you in trouble. So, let me get this out right away. I think there's something suspicious going on here at the clinic. And I'm certain there's something terribly wrong with the Uteroprost trial. Patients are dying."

As they left the cafeteria, the man seated at the table behind Martha lowered his newspaper and spoke into his phone. After a quick conversation, Adolf Dinter folded up the paper and headed back to the security office.

* * * * * *

"Just the old lady? What about the bitch? Mendelschein," the man said to his partner who just got off the phone. "After what she and the nigger pulled on us last night, I'd like to fix her ass. They made us look like fools. Did you see the look on Dinter's face when we told him what happened?"

"Just telling you what Dinter said. He's got other plans for Mendelschein. Says if we can take care of the meddling old bag, it might redeem us." Dinter had threatened to not only fire them both, but to string their sorry asses up on the old apple tree in front of Luntz's farmhouse if they happened to fuck up this little job.

"What's the plan?"

"We're supposed to pick up the old lady's trail after she and Mendelschein split up. Follow her home and make sure she's no longer a problem. Dinter told me she lives up in the hills. Nobody around. The boss is leaving it for us to work out the rest."

"Do we need to check in at the main office first?"

"Nope. It's time to head over to the lobby before the old lady leaves."

"Better not get too close to Mendelschein. She sees us again, she might start thinking."

"I don't think she paid too much attention to us. Her eyes were fixed on the nigger's gun; not ours."

CHAPTER 34

CLARISSA SAT ALONE IN HER car and watched Martha drive away. She didn't notice Martha's car being followed out of the parking lot. She'd never seen her mother's friend so spooked before and had trouble making sense out of Martha's words.

Earlier, as they had walked through the greenhouse-styled lobby and atrium at the Kessler Foundation, Clarissa struggled to understand Martha's description of what she had seen, and the potential implications of what it all meant. Outside, the increasing winds kept the glass walls and sloped glass ceiling of the imposing lobby rattling, but the storm forming inside Clarissa's head had grown far stronger as she listened to Martha's frightened explanation.

Clarissa got the part about a group of patients, apparently all Native Americans, manifesting similar symptoms, and no one wanting to discuss their diagnoses or whatever happened to a number of them. She had no idea what convinced Martha this had something to do with the Uteroprost trials. They weren't even subjects in the study to begin with. She watched Martha getting frustrated with her inability to grasp the situation.

Martha had promised to dig a little deeper and talk to her the next day. She wanted to make a copy of Ms. Torrence's chart and check out the list of procedures that had been performed on the young Native American girl. Something struck Martha a little odd about what tests had been either already performed or had been scheduled. None of the procedures or the treatment protocols matched Catori Torrence's symptoms.

The ringing phone almost made Clarissa jump through the roof of her car. She grabbed the steering wheel to steady herself. The sound of Dequain's voice had a momentary calming effect on her nerves until she realized what he was saying. She immediately agreed to meet him at his condo.

* * * * * *

Dequain Johnson opened his condo door and Clarissa Mendelschein fell into his arms.

"What the hell is happening?" Clarissa blurted out after releasing Dequain from an urgent embrace.

He guided her to the sofa in his sparsely decorated living room and gave her a questioning look.

"Maybe if I listen to a rational explanation for what's going on at the clinic, I won't freak out," she said. "Because right now I don't think I can handle any of this."

Dequain, about to offer her a glass of wine, sensed the tension in her body. Instead, he poured two generous portions of Meyers dark rum over several ice cubes. For a moment, they both listened to the crackling sounds of the ice as the smooth liquor tempered in the glasses.

"Stop me if I sound too technical," Dequain started.

Clarissa nodded and reached for her glass, not caring if the spirits hadn't reached the proper temperature. The first slug made her eyes water, and she imagined swallowing caramelized turpentine as her throat burned from the assaulting liquid. Any hints of molasses in her nasal passages disappeared as her throat clenched in protest. She watched Dequain imbibing in small, metered sips. She mimicked his technique, satisfied with the results.

Dequain settled on the coffee table in front of Clarissa and began his story. "You know the Uteroprost program is based on the substance called transuteroglobin, a protein which modulates the gene expression of key components of the prostaglandin pathway."

It wasn't a question.

"The company has used the abbreviation, TUG, when referring to this protein. This is all spelled out in the brochures you distributed to us new employees during your orientation speech. The background on BioCoGen's screening program and how they searched out a number of patentable small molecular agents to modify the activity of TUG on different parts of the prostaglandin pathway was also described in one of the brochures."

Clarissa opened her mouth to confirm her understanding, but a loud burp emerged instead.

Dequain never thought it sounded sexy when his mother did the same thing. To keep from being distracted, he stood up and increased the distance between them. Clarissa's face started to glow, and he envisioned it radiating over her chest. He reached for his glass and gulped down a healthy portion. That elicited a waving finger and another burp from Clarissa.

He coughed, in part, from the acrid taste of the liquid, but mostly to redirect his thoughts back to his story. "As you know, your scientists have found a way to link these agents to specific antibodies which target certain cells."

Dequain watched Clarissa's body listing to one side and grabbed her half empty glass. He headed into the kitchen to fire up the coffee maker. While he liked the dreamy vibes coming from her intense blue eyes, he knew he needed to keep her brain sober enough to comprehend his message.

"Go ahead, Dequain," Clarissa said, the delicate muscles on her face set, forming a rigid frame for her eyes. The glass of rum had been traded for her first steaming hot cup of coffee.

Dequain's scientifically precise presentation of the facts only made Clarissa more nervous. She shook her head and stretched a hand across the table, grabbing his wrist. They were now seated at the bar table in the kitchen area.

"Just tell me what it all means. I don't need you to prove your hypothesis. I trust you. I trust you with my life." She had pulled those last words from the recesses of her soul, and they had driven a stake into Dequain's heart. Clarissa's face burned, but her hand held tight to his wrist.

Placing his own hand over hers, he swallowed and said, "I didn't put it together at first. But the initial studies—when they validated the target? I thought the codes looked familiar but brushed it off." He paused, keeping his hand in place. "Remember, I told you about the cell lines they used? I'd seen those designated codes before. In my own work."

Clarissa's eyes blinked in confusion. "But you were doing genetic studies on specific ethnic populations. Weren't you investigating gene pools in Native American tribes?"

"Right. I examined the exaggerated incidences of scleroderma in those populations. And the role of prostaglandins in either predisposing them to the disease or the potential use of those agents in treating it. This was why the cell line was made available to me. My research focused on helping the tribes."

Dequain paused again. "At the offer of great sums of money to aid struggling tribes, their leaders sometimes allowed scientists to take advantage of the privacy of the members. Under the guise of helping them understand how specific gene pools related to tribal health issues, they were allowed indiscriminate access to Native American patient records and specimens. Then unethical scientists sold many of these harvested cell lines to the highest bidder. They gave uncontrolled access of personal data to companies who could care less about doing research to help the tribes as the original scientists had promised."

Clarissa's blue eyes narrowed. "Okay, so you're saying BioCoGen used a similar cell line for their original screening program. I can understand why Native Americans would be reluctant to sell these specific cell lines to researchers not focused on tribal health issues. So, it's possible that BioCoGen exerted pressure to buy those samples. I guess that's probably not the most ethical way to run a research facility, but I'm sure it's not out of line for the way a number of start-up companies compete with the larger pharmaceutical corporations."

Shaking her head, Clarissa added, "Those practices definitely need to be stopped, I agree. It's unethical, and private companies shouldn't have access to medical samples without complete disclosure. But why would this matter to the integrity of the drug development program. To the Uteroprost project specifically? As far as I can understand all this, that first step just identified a bunch of compounds that…." She struggled to make sure she got this right. Dequain patiently waited for her to think it through.

"So, they patented selected compounds based on their chemical structures and activity on specific aspects of the prostaglandin pathway. And then they confirmed everything in—what you refer to as *in vitro* experiments— or isolated animal tissues. And then all those animal studies to prove the compounds worked and were safe before jumping into the clinical trial."

Dequain nodded. "Yes. All that is correct. But the prostaglandin pathway is complex. The specific activities are unique in different species. Not only that, but there are distinct variations within the human population."

"I'm still not sure I understand what this has to do with the Uteroprost data. The results look promising. The safety data hasn't shown any problems."

"Are there any Native Americans in the study?"

"Would that make a difference?" The words came out slow and deliberate. A shadow crossed her face and flitted across her gut.

"According to the genetic profile tests I ran on the samples we took from the clinic, they *all* came from Native American females. I based this on specific markers identified from my previous work. I'd never used uterine tissue before, but the same markers are present."

"I don't understand," Clarissa said, and thinking out loud, she relayed the conversation she had with her mother's friend.

The frantic words from Martha now took on a whole new meaning.

Dequain stood up, pacing back and forth in the small kitchen. He leaned against the sink cabinet and folded his arms. Like looking at unexpected results from one of his experiments, a light bulb flashed on in Dequain's head. He moved closer to Clarissa, grabbing her shoulders. He nudged her out of the chair and turned her body around to face him.

"They must be switching the samples."

CHAPTER 35

MARTHA NEEDED TO RELAX. SHE thought she had reasoned it all out, but the conversation with Clarissa left her less convinced. Tomorrow she would follow up by trying to access those patient records. Getting into the clinical trial data could be more challenging. She knew they stored the data in a different file server that was off limits. But she had a few tricks she'd learned from her grandkids about overriding computer passcodes. Hacking into the system they'd called it.

For now, instead of heading home, she decided to do what she normally did when upset by something. She drove past the turn-off that led to her house and headed into downtown Napa to go shopping. That always cleared her mind and helped her think better.

The two rookie security guards from the Kessler Foundation looked puzzled when the old lady drove into town instead of heading straight home, but they kept up the surveillance at a safe distance. She didn't appear to be paying much attention to her surroundings, so they weren't concerned about being observed.

After floating in and out of several downtown shops, she entered a restaurant and was seated at a narrow table by the window. The guards jumped at the chance to take up a position at the far end of the large horseshoe-shaped bar in the center of the restaurant.

Over a few beers, they kept an eye on the old lady and formulated the finer points of their plan. At one point their arguing reached a level that drew unwanted consideration from nearby patrons, but Martha didn't appear to notice the small commotion as she enjoyed a light dinner and a single glass of red wine.

She had almost reached the door before the two security guards looked up from their bickering and realized her table was empty. Scrambling to pay the bill, they approached their car just as Martha pulled onto Main Street and drove away. Luckily for them, she was headed home, and they knew where she lived.

They picked up her trail again when she'd turned onto the isolated road leading to the hillside location of her house. They killed the headlights and followed at a safe distance. When they saw her brake lights come on and her car making a left turn at a barn-shaped mailbox, they slowed at the first clearing and pulled onto the side of the road.

Martha fumbled with her keys to get the front door to her house open, struggling with the packages in her arms. Just as she flipped on the light switch, something slammed her body from behind. Packages flew across the living room, and her body smacked face down onto the beige carpet. She lay there stunned, spitting out threads of carpet.

Before she responded, a rough hand grabbed hold of her collar and pulled her up. One bag remained clutched in her hand against her stomach. Landing on it had taken her breath away, but she stubbornly kept her fingers wrapped around the slender glass neck.

In a reflex action as the man yanked her up, she swung her arm and smashed the merlot onto the head of her assailant. Glass shattered and a chocolatey, plummy fragrance filled her nostrils as the deep purplish vintage burst over the man's skull. It mixed with the blood from the nasty cut the broken bottle carved in his temple.

A fist smashed into Martha's jaw. She heard the sickening crunch, and at first didn't connect it with the blossoming pain radiating to every crevice in her brain. Before her eyes rolled upwards, she watched the beige carpet absorbing a stain that could never be removed. As she lost consciousness, a picture of her late husband materialized, and she heard herself asking him to be careful not to let the salsa drip onto the carpet.

"Fucking bitch," the guy screamed, flailing for the blanket folded across the upholstered arm of the sofa. He pressed it against the bloody gash on his temple. "And I think I broke a couple fingers on her fucking face."

His partner, still standing by the open door, allowed his jaw to drop at the site of the blood dripping down his buddy's cheek. He took a few steps forward and bent over the old lady. He pressed an index finger to her neck, checking for a pulse from a heart that had stopped the instant the back of her head cracked against the corner of the slate fireplace hearth.

"Nice work, asshole. You forget about the plan to question her first? Remember? We needed to find out what she knew and what the hell she was up to. Show the boss how we can think on our feet. Make ourselves more useful?"

"Well, fuck you. Why the hell didn't you get your lazy ass over here and grab the old bitch before she hit me with the goddamn bottle?" He dabbed the blanket against his wounded scalp. Drops of blood pooled in his ear.

"Hey, if you can't outmaneuver an old lady—" The other man shrugged and helped his partner to his feet. "Shit. You'll live. Your head's so callused from being wacked with beer bottles, I'm surprised you even noticed it."

He pulled the blanket from his head and threw it at his partner. "Here, go fill this up with some valuables around the house while I head to the bathroom and check out this cut. We need to convince the cops they're looking at a robbery gone bad."

"Oh, so that was your plan? Being overpowered by the old lady to make it look real? Nice work."

"Fuck you."

Chapter 36

The airport terminal bustled with travelers frustrated by the mushrooming list of delays and flight cancellations due to the storm battering the California coast. Hordes of travelers rushed to find ground transportation before conditions grew worse, while others prepared to honker down and ride it out in the overcrowded waiting areas at the airport. Few were quick enough to find accommodations at one of the nearby overbooked hotels.

"I guess that's the smart thing to do," Edie said into her cell phone, wheeling her overnight bag down the ramp into the main terminal of Sacramento International Airport.

"Yeah, the weather's getting nasty here at the coast. Never seen anything like it," Steve said.

"Right," she responded, thinking isn't it just a hurricane dying out as it reaches land? Growing up in New Jersey, Edie had become hardened to these kinds of storms. Then she remembered Hurricane Sandy.

As she walked, her eyes checked the long lines at every kiosk.

"From what I understand," Steve said, "there won't be any flights into the Bay Area until sometime tomorrow morning. So you might as well relax out there where the weather problems aren't so bad. As I said, I got you a room at the Four Points Sheraton. Right close to the airport. I called in the reservation as soon as I heard your flight was going to be diverted to Sacramento. All you have to do is pick up the courtesy phone in the terminal, and a shuttle will come get you."

"Thanks, Steve. That was thoughtful."

"Sure, no sense hanging out in the airport lounge or trying to sleep in the waiting area. And it's not safe driving in this weather. The room's got a large, jetted tub, so you might as well relax and keep warm. I also ordered a bottle of your favorite champagne. It'll be waiting for you in the room."

"Ahhh… that's sweet of you."

"Yeah, just think of me out here in this storm while you're relaxing in a nice hot bath. And think of what I have in mind for us the next time I lay eyes on you."

"I can always count on you to come up with a plan. Should I be worried?"

"Edie, I'll have you falling right into my arms."

"Can't wait to see you too, honey. Please be careful out there in the storm. And tell the guys in your squad the same thing. At least the weather will probably keep the criminal element off the streets for a while. So you won't have to shoot at any of the bad guys."

"Funny… but that's a job for the cops anyway. Our weapons are only brought out in unusual circumstances. Remember, I'm primarily hazmat, not dirty Harry."

Edie slowed her pace. "Well, let me get going. I'll give you a call after I settle in."

Edie placed the phone back in her pocket as she stepped up to the Hertz rental counter, showing her VIP pass and reservation number.

The first thing Edie had done after finding out her flight was headed for Sacramento instead of San Francisco was to call ahead and reserve a vehicle.

There was no way she'd be staying put in Sacramento tonight. She was still worried about Catori and didn't want to delay seeing her any longer. She felt guilty enough about her frequent journeys to D.C. Thank God she had Steve to step up and be there for Catori.

She finished adjusting the seat of the Ford Expedition to allow her small frame to peer over the hood and her legs to reach the pedals of the large SUV. Even this far inland, the weather wasn't all that great. As she pulled onto the freeway her wipers struggled with the heavy rains as strong winds shook the bulky SUV. In places, she had difficulty differentiating the rain covered causeway from the increasing tidal surges and flooding inundating the delta wetlands.

Alone in the SUV, with few other drivers on the freeway braving the torrential rains and high winds, Edie's mind drifted to the earlier events of the day.

Was it over? Or was the fight just beginning? The long flight back from D.C. did nothing to answer those questions for Edie.

She imagined herself still locked in the Situation Room listening to the matter-of-fact chatter communicating the progress of one of the most daring special ops missions taking place on the other side of the world.

Everyone had deemed the operation a success. Nine key terrorist camps raided. All the remaining hostages rescued, and none of our military personnel had suffered anything more than minor injuries. The extractions went off without a hitch, and ground forces and intelligence officers were now flooding into the terrorist camps to begin combing through mountains of documents and computer files. Prisoners taken during the raids would soon be whisked from the primary staging area at the military base in Kandahar to the aircraft carrier, the Ronald Reagan, for interrogation.

No telling how long before all the information got sorted out. The next several days would see the president carefully outlining to the nation the true scope of what had started over a year ago. Edie had wanted another chance to talk to the female Navy SEAL, Angela, in private, but was told in no uncertain terms that that wouldn't happen anytime soon. It left Edie with the worst images possible. She had problems celebrating the success of this twisted plan but had no trouble laying any blame or the potential consequences on her own shoulders. Even if she had just been the messenger.

One look at President Tyler Griffin told her he bore the same burden.

* * * * * *

The drive had been a lot more strenuous than anticipated, but eventually Edie pulled the Expedition into the Kessler Foundation's parking lot. When she got to Catori's room, the young girl appeared to be struggling, lost in a restless sleep. After holding Catori's hand until the sight of her poor friend etched a chasm in her heart, Edie stepped into the adjoining bathroom and slapped fistfuls of water on her face.

Her clothes remained damp from the earlier mad dash from the SUV into the lobby, but a greater coldness radiated from deep inside, clammy fingers chilling every inch of her consciousness. Edie's eyes had become swollen from the tears she fought back. The soaked washcloth she'd pressed to her brow soothed away only a small part of the hurt.

Edie returned to Catori's bedside and stared at the scribbled note waiting on top of the folded comforter at the foot of the bed. She took a final look at Catori, whose lips moved in silent tremors, her fingers twitching in time to a hidden vision. Edie gave her a kiss on the forehead.

"I'll be right back, sweetie."

Edie picked up her purse and headed to the office number circled in the note.

CHAPTER 37

EDIE HADN'T SEEN WHO LEFT the note on Catori's bed, but the scene was witnessed by Doreen, the head nurse on the floor. She had a clear view of the person sneaking into Catori Torrence's room from the nurses' station just down the corridor.

The head of security at the Kessler Foundation, Adolf Dinter, responded to Doreen's call. She had snuck in and read the note before Edie returned from the bathroom. Sitting in his private office in the clinic's main security suite, Dinter placed the headphones on and fiddled with the controls. Earlier today he'd had the foresight to instruct Joseph Stock to plant a listening device in Clarissa Mendelschein's office.

Edie knocked, and a soft, feminine voice told her to come in. Entering, she found herself staring at an attractive woman about her own age. She recognized her beauty in spite of the plainly distorted features on the woman's face. At once drawn to her blue eyes, Edie perceived them as being watery and bloodshot, not unlike her own.

"Thank you for coming, Ms. Pauling. My name is Clarissa Mendelschein. I'm the public relations liaison for BioCoGen and the Kessler Foundation."

Puzzled, Edie took a step forward and shook the woman's hand. The brief contact with the damp, tremoring hand reinforced Edie's belief that Clarissa Mendelschein was nervous; perhaps frightened would be a better term. Both women remained standing. Edie waited her out.

"I saw your name on the visitor list, Ms. Pauling," Clarissa Mendelschein started, but abruptly stopped.

"Edie. Please, call me Edie."

Clarissa reciprocated the offer, but still didn't seem to focus any better.

"Ms. Torrence is a friend of yours?" Clarissa asked, but Edie could see even Clarissa considered it an inane question. She sensed this woman was not used to being out of control in any situation.

Edie nodded. She opted to sit down, hoping to get Clarissa to relax. It worked. Clarissa moved around her desk, pulling a second chair closer to Edie. She sat down, turning it to face her guest.

"I—I stopped by the ward to see Martha. She's a nurse. My mom's best friend." Clarissa's head dropped as she rambled. When she looked back up to face Edie, tears were streaming down her face. "I was supposed to meet her in the cafeteria today, but she never showed up."

There was a long pause. "She tried to tell me. And now… she's dead." The last words came out with an agonizing burst of sobs. Her hands shot to her face.

Edie's mind raced, trying to unravel the situation. She leaned forward and gently pried Clarissa's hands from her face, and in a quiet voice said, "I'm sorry, Clarissa."

Edie looked around the office, seeing a small refrigerator. She walked over and brought back a bottled water. Pulling a handkerchief from her purse, she splashed water from the bottle on it and pressed it to Clarissa's tear-filled eyes.

"I want to help, Clarissa, but I need to know what's going on." Edie, afraid to ask the next question, swallowed hard and continued, "Does this have something to do with Catori Torrence?"

At first Clarissa's shoulders hiked. When Edie removed the handkerchief from Clarissa's eyes, she saw that for the moment, the tears had stopped. She detected a growing clarity in Clarissa's eyes. They turned a deeper blue. The redness retracted.

Edie again leaned forward, her voice more forceful. An image of Catori's stricken body flashed in her mind. "Clarissa. Just spill it out. Tell me what you think is going on."

"I'm not sure myself," Clarissa said, "but I'm afraid they might be doing things to your friend. I think they're giving her the same drugs being used in the clinical trial."

"The Uteroprost study?" Edie asked. "What are you talking about? She's not even a participant in the trial. She's supposed to be here for tests. To see why her menstrual cycle is causing so many problems."

"You're right. And that's what it says on her chart. But my mom's friend told me her symptoms were telling a different story. Similar to the others she talked about. All the Native Americans previously admitted to the clinic."

"You're losing me. What do you mean? Which symptoms? And what does being a Native American have to do with any of this?"

Clarissa's words now formed more rapidly. "Okay. One of the scientists who works at BioCoGen—Dr. Johnson—before coming here, his research focused on investigating how a unique genetic profile in Native Americans predisposes them to a disease called scleroderma."

"Scleroderma?" Edie interrupted, brow scrunching. "What does that have to do with Catori, let alone the Uteroprost trial?"

Clarissa sighed. "Bear with me, Edie. I'm not a scientist, so maybe I'm not making myself clear. The way Dequain—Dr. Johnson—explained it, there's an abnormality—no, not an abnormality—a gene variance, I think he called it. Anyway, those same prostaglandins that are important to the Uteroprost study cause different effects in certain Native Americans. Actions that are not seen in the general population. For some reason, they're also responsible for Native Americans having a higher incidence of scleroderma."

Clarissa looked at Edie, biting her lower lip. "I don't think I'm explaining this the right way. But the *real* data suggests Uteroprost is ineffective in the general population. And Dr. Johnson has proof somebody has been switching the biopsy samples. He thinks they've been secretly treating Native American patients who are not a part of the study to make it appear that the treatment is efficacious."

Edie's mind raced to process this. If true, how did this slip through all the government oversight involved in this flagship study under the new ConnorCare guidelines? She shook her head. What better way to stick an ineffective treatment on an unsuspecting population. Right under their noses. And these new regulations allow for limited approval without the need to perform the rigorous double-blind clinical studies.

"And it gets even worse," Clarissa said. "In the general population, the treatment doesn't work but there doesn't appear to be any significant side effects—at least in the short term. On the other hand, in select Native

American patients, it can be deadly. Dr. Johnson says because of this so-called genetic variance, it precipitates severe, sometimes fatal forms of scleroderma."

"You said other Native Americans have been given this same treatment?"

Clarissa eyes opened wide. "Yes. That's what my mom's friend was trying to tell me. I've just checked through the records, and since the start of the Uteroprost trial there has been an unusually high number of Native American patients at the clinic. None of them were part of the Uteroprost trial. Many have either died here at the clinic or shortly after being released. And several have… just vanished."

"Nobody saw this pattern?"

"Well, if they're not part of the clinical trial, we don't track patients by ethnicity. And the admissions were spread out over time. All the scrutiny has been on the Uteroprost trial. And, as I said, none of the Native American patients were ever designated as subjects in the trial. Besides, if all this is true, I'm convinced that some very important people at the clinic know exactly what's going on."

"Clarissa, I should talk to this Dr. Johnson. But first, I need to get Catori out of here."

"I think that's a good idea. I'm heading down to the labs at BioCoGen where Dr. Johnson works. We're trying to gather enough evidence to put a stop to this before anybody else dies. Let me know when you get your friend to someplace safe. I'm sure we could use your help and influence to go to the authorities."

Edie rose to leave. Before she got to the door, she turned. "Clarissa. This nurse you talked about? Your mom's friend. How did she die?"

"It happened last night, in her home. The police said she apparently walked into her house and interrupted a burglary in progress. It looked like she got into a struggle with one of the intruders. Martha's jaw was broken. Then either she fell or was pushed onto the fireplace hearth, hitting her head. She died instantly."

"Do you believe in coincidences?" Edie stared hard at Clarissa. "Make sure you're careful who you talk to. I'd keep quiet about all this until I can meet with Dr. Johnson. Once Catori's out of here, I'll make a few calls. No sense you taking any more chances. We don't know who we can trust."

Clarissa grabbed the phone as Edie rushed out the door. She caught Clarissa's first frantic words.

"Dequain, this is Clarissa. I need to talk to you right away."

In his office, Adolf Dinter removed his headset after listening to the entire conversation between Clarissa Mendelschein and Edie Pauling. And then Mendelschein's phone call to Dequain Johnson.

He called Joseph Stock and gave him the order to follow Mendelschein to Dr. Johnson's lab. He instructed Stock to take care of that part of the problem. Dinter headed out the door, ready to deal with the immediate issue at the clinic. He wasn't about to give Edie Pauling any opportunity to screw up their plans.

Chapter 38

EDIE SIGHED AND GAVE UP her struggle to dress Catori. Catori was by no means heavy, but her almost comatose state worked against all Edie's efforts, so Edie left her in the flimsy hospital gown. She planned to wheel her right out the front door. Focused on the task of sliding Catori into the wheelchair, she didn't catch the intrusion until it was too late.

Adolf Dinter had already determined a course of action. With no time for a delicate handling of the situation, he crashed through the door, the resolve fixed in the shadows on his face. His hand pulled back out from underneath his jacket, carrying his Glock.

Edie reacted, making a desperate attempt to dive for her purse at the foot of the bed.

Quicker to respond, Dinter blocked the action by connecting the butt end of the Glock with the back of Edie's head. Her body dropped to the floor, now less of a threat than the semi-conscious girl she was trying to save.

Dinter kicked the door closed and engaged the lock. He pulled out his phone and called for assistance.

Outside, the intensity of the rain pounding the area for the last several hours picked up and the gusting winds hammered against the windows. The cascading rain blotted out most of the parking lot below.

For the briefest of seconds, the lights flickered off and the droning background noises hiccupped. The back-up generators kicked in so quickly most people wouldn't have noticed anything, except for the multitude of alarms erupting up and down the corridor as sensitive monitoring systems reacted to the transient power shift.

Curiosity got the better of him. Dinter walked over to the bed and examined the purse Edie had attempted to grab. Confirming his suspicions, he found the weapon concealed inside.

"Well, well," he said, shaking his head and running his eyes over the powerless body on the floor, watching the shallow heaves of Edie's chest. "Saves me the trouble of frisking you. Usually, I'm not comfortable putting my hands on the black ones, but in your case, I might've been tempted to see what a little fresh dark meat feels like."

Dinter ran his tongue over his lower lip and took a step toward Edie. "In fact, I'll just see—"

A sharp knock reverberated from the door. It startled Dinter enough for him to swing the Glock around and almost pull the trigger. Recovering, he swallowed and asked who was at the door. A distinct voice answered using a short phrase in German.

Dinter gave a final look at Edie and shrugged. Holstering his Glock, he unlocked the door and stood aside as the men pushed two transport gurneys into the room. After a quick glance up and down the corridor, he closed the door and barked instructions to his men. They got to work lifting both women and securing them in place on the gurneys.

Dinter noticed they were paying a little bit too much attention to not only Edie Pauling, but the younger girl as well. He cursed them half-heartedly but questioned himself on how he had missed the titillating image of the half-naked Indian squaw. Jesus Christ, he thought. It's getting harder and harder to find any decent white girls around here. Goddamned gene pools are getting all fucked up.

"Sure is tempting though," he muttered, taking one final look before both girls were covered with the blankets.

"Let's move it guys. Bring them down to the Jeep and then ditch the gurneys. I want to take these two out to the compound in Sebastopol before things get worse. Then, if I'm feeling generous, you can choose which one to go at first before we make them both disappear for good."

The two men glanced at each other, but kept their mouths shut. Dinter would find out soon enough.

CHAPTER 39

THE RAIN POUNDED AGAINST THE roof of his car. Due to the deteriorating weather conditions, few vehicles braved the treacherous roads in the Napa Valley. Knowing Clarissa Mendelschein's intended destination allowed Joseph Stock to hang back at a safe distance. Mendelschein drove up to the locked guard gate, swiping her ID badge over the access panel and waited for the gate to lift. She pulled into the employee parking lot for BioCoGen and sped across the empty pavement, her spinning tires sending sprays of water over the slickened surface. Stock gave her thirty seconds and repeated the process but parked away from the main complex.

"Yeah, she just got to the BioCoGen campus," Stock said into his cell phone, answering Dinter's question. He watched Mendelschein exit her car and dart across the flooded parking lot as his windshield wipers struggled against the driving rain.

"I know. I know. I'll see what she's up to. And if she's meeting with Dr. Johnson, my job will be even easier. What do you mean I can't bring them out to— really? No shit. Okay. Right. I know what to do. Don't worry, I'll come up with something. It'll look like an accident. Then we don't have to deal with ditching the bodies. I'm going to enjoy taking care of that stuck-up little bitch. Did I ever tell you I asked her out a couple of times? The snotty little cunt gave me the cold shoulder. Right. Ya don't gotta tell me. Yeah, I couldn't believe it when those fools we just hired told us they found miss too-good-for-us white boys getting her brains fucked out by that Jamaican mutt. Hey. She just went into the animal facility building. What? His lab's in the west wing? Okay. I'm right on her ass."

Stock waited for Mendelschein to disappear inside the building. He had parked at the far end of the lot to make sure she didn't spot him. As he ran through the relentless downpour and gusting winds, he cursed himself for not pulling his car closer before chasing after the bitch. His shoes sucked up the pooling water and made squishing sounds as he approached the building.

Under the relative safety of the overhang, he waved his ID card across the panel, punched in the security code, and slipped into the building. Reaching under his jacket, he patted his Sig but left it in the shoulder holster. The vestibule and reception area were deserted. Stock checked his watch and smiled, noting that the normal work shift had ended at least thirty minutes ago. Most of the employees had probably taken advantage of the management's offer to head home early anyway.

He had received the email late this morning advising workers to leave as soon as possible before the storm's impact made the roads too dangerous to travel. It looked as though even the hardcore research fanatics had heeded the warning. Dr. Johnson should've taken the company's advice.

Stock checked the facility map on the wall and tracked down the room number of Johnson's lab given to him by Dinter. To access the research wing, he had to first go through the secured animal facility. That always gave him the creeps. After entering the locker room, which served as a partition and barrier to the main animal holding area, Stock neglected to follow procedure, not bothering to switch out his street clothes before entering the restricted facility.

Peering through the small window on the door, he noticed Clarissa had taken the time in the female locker room to don lab scrubs. She headed down the corridor inside the facility. He gave her a decent enough head start and then pushed open the door. The muffled animal sounds mixed with the insipient smells of the housed creatures. The disinfecting agents assaulted his senses but lost the battle to mask the underlying character of the environment. He had never been comfortable inside this part of the building.

His footsteps clicked off the polished surface of the sealed epoxy-covered floors, leaving small puddles in his wake. The constant hum of the massive ventilators droned around him. The confines of this tomb-like structure veiled any evidence of the violent storm brewing outside. Just before reaching the entrance to the main laboratory wing, Stock glanced at one of the signs above a wide stainless steel door on his right.

A small smile spread across his face as an idea formed in his head.

After passing through the double entry sealed door lock and exiting the animal housing area, Stock turned left into the far corridor and headed toward Room 144, Dr. Johnson's lab. As he approached, he noted the outer door had been propped open, a clear violation of the company's safety policies. That made him smile, giving him confidence his plan would go off without a hitch.

With his back pressed flat against the wall, Stock stopped just short of the open doorway. Animated voices resounded from somewhere inside. It seemed like only two people were involved in the discussion, but he wanted to be sure no one else was in either the lab or the attached office. The conversation sounded muted enough for him to conclude that Clarissa and whoever she was talking to were probably inside the office which adjoined the lab in the left rear corner of the room.

Stock peered his head inside the opening and scanned the room. From his position, the lab appeared empty. He crouched down and swung himself inside and squatted behind one of the base cabinets in the first row of counters.

The large state-of-the-art molecular biology lab was approximately forty feet wide and twenty-five feet deep. One of the shorter walls was filled with centrifuges, biosafety cabinets, and a bank of large freezer and refrigerator units. Four specialized laboratory hoods, including one class three laminar flow station, lined the other short wall.

The sight of all this high-tech equipment made Stock's blood run cold. He instinctively pulled his hands away from any of the surfaces. He wondered what kinds of invisible microscopic nightmarish creatures lurked around him. Even taking short, shallow gulps of air he imagined the strong pickle-like odor of formaldehyde disguising the minute creatures dancing along his nose hairs.

These fool scientists might think it cool to breathe in God knows what, but he didn't want to get used to this environment anytime soon. His eyes began to sting in response to the pungent chemicals permeating the lab. He needed to take care of business and get the hell out of here as fast as possible.

He finally had no choice but to exhale and take in a large slug of the germ-infested air. A tingling sensation already hung in his throat. He attempted to calm himself and tried for a better look at the back section of the lab.

At this point he was confident the room was empty, except for Clarissa Mendelschein and presumably Dr. Dequain Johnson. From the direction of their voices, Stock was positive they were holed up in the office.

As he crept to the edge of the line of cabinets, he got a much better look at the entire back wall. Most of it was fitted with kneehole benches and lined with computer stations and an array of microscopes. The left quarter of the wall jutted out into the lab and separated the office from the rest of the room. The long wall of the office had windows cut into the upper half, and Stock could now clearly see the profiles of Clarissa Mendelschein and Dequain Johnson. They sat across the desk from each other, engrossed in an intense conversation. He watched as the doctor opened a briefcase on his desk and stuffed papers and several glass vials inside.

The door, located on the short wall of the office, stood ajar. Stock listened and didn't like what he heard. He especially didn't like what the two assholes planned to do with their new-found information.

Stock reached inside his jacket, pulling out his Sig as he stood up. He closed the distance to the office in several quick steps. At the last second, Dequain looked up and Clarissa turned around. They gazed at the weapon aimed directly at their heads.

"Mr. Stock?" Clarissa said. "What are you doing here?"

Dequain glanced at Clarissa but focused most of his attention on the gun pointing right at them. "You know this guy, Clarissa?"

If Clarissa was trying to turn her trembling lips into a smile, she fell short.

"Yes, Dequain." The words came out weak and shaky. "This is Joseph Stock. He's one of our security guards. Ah… Joe… please put your gun away. You know who I am. What's going on?"

For the moment, Stock ignored Clarissa and stared at Dequain.

"So, *doctor*," Stock spit out, "I was kind of hoping for another command performance."

"I—I do not understand," Dequain stammered. "What are you talking about?"

"What's the matter, *boy*?" Stock said through tight lips. "Can't get it up? The story is you were sticking the big one in this little bitch the other night. Putting on quite a show. How'd you persuade this little iceberg to spread those long, frigid legs?"

Dequain lunged at Stock who reacted more quickly by kicking Clarissa's chair aside, knocking her to the floor. His left forearm chopped into Dequain's neck, sending him arching backwards. Landing in his chair, Dequain choked and gasped for air. The chair spun around from the impact, and his head slammed into one of the metal filing cabinets.

"That was your only warning, doctor. Next time I'll be putting a slug into your head," Stock said as he stepped around Clarissa and eased his way toward the door. Waving the Sig at Dequain, he continued, "Time to go. Grab hold of your little whore. NOW!" Stock added for emphasis when Dequain didn't move fast enough.

Dequain complied and helped Clarissa to her feet. He had to hold her with one arm around her waist. Her whole body shook, and small sobs poured from her lips.

Stock pointed toward the door at the front of the lab. "Okay you two—start walking. Don't worry, we're not going far." He laughed. "I'm looking forward to see how hot she is doctor. I got an idea to help her out. What do you think it is that turns her on to the dark meat? Guess she's not into the lean, mean white meat."

Out of nowhere, between sobs, the words rushed from Clarissa's mouth. "You got that right you pathetic little prick."

Dequain almost dropped Clarissa, but discovered she was now capable of standing up on her own. Stock didn't take the bait but came up behind Dequain and lodged the muzzle against his bare scalp. "Oh yeah, I'm gonna enjoy this."

Stock turned back to grab the briefcase off the desk and then prodded Clarissa and Dequain all the way to the other end of the lab wing and back into the animal housing area of the facility. He could see the doctor's movements becoming more directed, getting over his initial shock of staring down the barrel of the Sig, probably searching for something to turn the tables.

Since Stock's earlier reckless actions of getting a little too close to his prisoners, his professionalism took over, and he maintained a safe distance to avoid further confrontations or opportunities for any offensive moves by the gangly Jamaican.

They arrived at the wide stainless steel door Stock noted when he'd followed Clarissa into the animal facility. Stock punched his fist against the plate on the wall to activate the automatic mechanism, and the door swung open. A loud rumbling from the room's powerful ventilating system filled their ears and a wall of foul odors from the soiled animal cages hit their senses. Stock stifled a gagging sensation as he ordered Dequain and Clarissa to enter. He tried to ignore the smells and followed them into the area housing the state-of-the-art cage cleaning apparatus for the facility.

They stood in the designated dirty zone. This was where the staff brought the soiled animal cages. The room contained about a half dozen dirty double-height wheeled dog cages lined against the side wall. Stacks of dirty plastic rodent cages with metal barred lids sat in storage racks.

Stock had an overactive sense of smell and had reacted the same way when he, along with several other new employees to the company's security department, had been brought to this room as part of their training orientation class. As a safety precaution, all security personnel were required to learn and understand the operating procedures for this cleaning system in case an emergency situation arose and one of the workers became trapped inside the apparatus.

The design for this sanitizing process provided a one-way path to avoid any possibility of contamination of the sterilized cages. The dirty cages started in this room and passed through the heavy-duty cleaning and sanitizing procedures. When the previously soiled cages were removed from the other side of the cleaning apparatus, they were sterilized and ready to be returned to the animal housing rooms again.

The highly efficient steam and chemical sterilization processes exacted a heavy toll on any pathogens hiding on the surfaces of the stainless steel and plastic equipment. No living creature, large or small, could survive this ordeal. Clarissa still looked confused, but Dequain's eyes bulged in recognition of their fate.

Before Dequain reacted, Stock moved in on Clarissa, grabbing her by the hair while keeping a safe distance from Dequain. Still grasping a fist full of Clarissa's hair in one hand, the muzzle of the Sig all but penetrating her right ear, Stock began to bark orders at Dequain.

Dequain had no choice but to comply with what Stock commanded. He impotently watched Stock manhandle Clarissa. He couldn't make out what Stock was saying to her but saw the man's tongue flicking in her ear. He propped open the large stainless steel entry door to BioCoGen's newest automated large-animal cage cleaning module with an equipment dolly. Several smaller automated conveyor type cleaning systems for the plastic rodent cages flanked this unit.

The large-animal cage cleaning module could handle four of the standardized double height canine cage units used in the facility's dog housing rooms. The interior of this cleaning chamber was constructed of stainless steel. Steam and chemical jet ports lined all surfaces. Small monitoring panels were mounted inside the unit, near the entry and exit doors. The main exterior control panel was mounted on the right side of the entry door. The dimensions of the unit were approximately eighteen feet long and five feet wide.

Once the four canine cage units were placed inside, there was less than six inches of clearance on either side. There was about twenty inches of headspace between the tops of the cages and the ceiling of the cleaning chamber.

Dequain had just finished wheeling the second of two cages into the cleaning module and was emerging back out of the entry door. Stock had been watching carefully to make sure Dequain positioned them as ordered and had securely locked both units into the safety track on the floor. The locked and sealed door at the other end of the chamber led to the clean side of the cage washing area and could only be opened after the sterilization process had been completed. This avoided any possibility of contamination. As directed, Dequain then positioned a third cage unit several feet outside the entry door to the cleaning module and turned to glare at Stock.

"Now, good doctor," Stock said. "It's time for you to shed those scrubs you're wearing. I sense a tragic accident is about to take place. Wouldn't you agree, Clarissa?"

Repeating something along the same lines as she had said earlier, Stock responded, "My, my, Clarissa, you don't have much of an imagination, do you? What do you think, doctor? Or don't you care?"

Stock looked at Dequain's naked body. "Doctor. As I see it, it sure doesn't look like you're up to taking care of business. Get into the chamber and we'll see what we can do about it."

Instead, Dequain took a step toward Stock. Stock reacted by tightening his grip on Clarissa's hair enough to make her screech out in pain.

Dequain did as he was told.

"Move as far back as you can, doctor," Stock ordered. "That's right. Now keep your skinny black ass against the cage."

Stock shoved Clarissa to the side while he kept an eye on Dequain. "Now, take off *your* clothes. Let's see if the good doctor is interested in anything you've got to offer. By the way. I'm in no hurry; what with the crappy weather outside. And I'm getting used to the stinking shit in this damn room. First time for everything. So, you can take it slow. We've got plenty of time."

In a mocking tone to Dequain, Stock added, "Isn't that right, doctor? Maybe something will pop up after all."

Clarissa's arms hugged her shoulders as she glanced at Dequain. With an insolent look in her eyes, she stared right at Stock and ripped off her clothing and flung everything in Stock's face. Her lacy bra dangled from his shoulder.

Looking at Clarissa, who stood defiantly with hands on hips, Stock stole a quick peek at her bra before tossing it on the floor and then stared at her bared breasts.

"Humph," he said. "A bit smaller than I imagined. I'd have guessed they'd be a little plumper. Kind of disappointing to see from anyone with a good German background."

"Must be from my grandmother's side. More typical of my Jewish heritage."

Stock flinched and took two steps back, shaking his head. "I should've known. Well, at least you spared me the humiliation of fucking a Jew. That would've been problematic to say the least. Thank you for turning me down. I don't date Jews."

"I don't doubt that," Clarissa said, raising her chin for him to take the bait. "Must be why you have such strong hands."

"Go join the doctor," Stock said through tight lips. He took several breaths and continued, "This makes it even better—a black pig and a Jew—all in one clean sweep, so to speak. I'd say I've done my fair share of cleansing humanity today."

Once Clarissa had joined Dequain in the chamber, Stock said, "Turn around and face the back, both of you."

Stock commenced wheeling the third and final cage inside the cleaning module. The reverberating clang indicated it was locked in place, as close as possible to the entry door. This left about four feet of space for Clarissa and Dequain between the locked cage units. He commented, "It's a toss-up, but I'd say Clarissa's ass is a tad bit cuter."

"Some latent tendencies, asshole?" Dequain said over his shoulder.

"Good one, doctor," Stock said. A slight smile forming. "But let's not get too cocky, or I won't be so nice and give you time for one last fuck with your little Jew girl. I'd stay to watch, but I don't think there'll be much to see."

Stock slammed the entry door shut and got to work punching keys on the control panel.

"Is this as bad as it seems?" Clarissa said.

Dequain stared through the bars of the third cage at the monitor next to the entry door. He saw the sterilization mode light up and the start time countdown sequence begin. The wash system consisted of three separate cycles. The first was fifteen minutes of high-pressure steam. This was followed by a thirty-minute spraying of sterilizing chemicals. The last phase was a repeat of the first steam cycle. No human could survive more than several minutes into the first cycle.

Clarissa kept talking while her eyes remained fixated on the entry door's viewing port. "Dequain, I just saw Stock walk out of the room and close the door. Do you think there's a way out of here? Can't these cages be moved? This thing must have safety features, doesn't it?"

Dequain pointed at the panic lever on the floor adjacent to the entry door. It might just as well have been located on the moon. His hands were already grabbing the bars on the cage unit that separated them from the door. He pulled slowly at first, then grabbed the bars more forcefully and started shaking it as hard as he could. The unit didn't budge.

"It's locked in place," Dequain gasped, "and the release mechanism is located below the control panel by the entry door."

Dequain glanced up at the monitor and saw the countdown timer closing in on their fate. He leaned back against the other two cage units that were also locked in place. He sprang forward against the single unit locked between them and the entry door, bashing his shoulder again and again into the immovable object. Clarissa, for what good it did, added to his efforts, but the cage would not budge.

The countdown timer continued down.

Dequain slipped to the floor, breathing hard, blood dripping down his battered shoulder. "I've been told… the locking mechanism…." The words came out in spurts. "Is one of the newer safety features… to help avoid being crushed… from a rolling cage."

"That's good to know."

Clarissa sat down beside him. Dequain stared up at the ceiling. He shook his head. "There might be enough space for me to climb to the top of the cage unit and shimmy over to the door, but that son of a bitch locked the unit so close to the door, there's no way I can reach the release lever or the mechanism to unlock it."

The countdown timer continued down.

Clarissa leaned in as close as possible, closing her eyes. Dequain closed his eyes as well.

But then—they popped open wide.

He grasped Clarissa's shoulders and pulled her up. Clarissa blinked her eyes open but remained silent.

"Clarissa! I just remembered—a story Dr. McBride told everyone when I first started working in his lab." He lunged for the front cage unit and began climbing up. "Come Clarissa, we need to do this together. I'll explain, but we need to move now."

There were only seconds remaining on the timer.

Dequain pulled Clarissa up to him as he squeezed into the narrow space between the top of the cage and the chamber's ceiling.

The timer reached zero and the steam valves snapped open, followed by a few distinct gurgling sounds and then a steady hissing noise building in strength. Dequain had to shout over escalating blasts of the jetted steam. In a matter of seconds, the temperature would become unbearable, then deadly.

CHAPTER 40

THE WEATHER FORECASTERS GOT THIS one right. The Bay Area was experiencing the full extent of the rare tropical storm even as the bulk of the storm's fury diminished after making landfall. Although it would fall short of reaching hurricane status, the pounding winds would still provide sufficient punishment to the infrastructure of a large part of the region. The rains alone had already brought the populated area to its knees. Major roadways flooded, stranding motorists and causing massive traffic jams.

Normally languid streams and riverbeds at this time of year turned into raging rivers. Clogged with debris, they threatened the structural integrity and overran many of the secondary bridges in the rural areas, cutting off residents from any routes of escape. People living in expensive hillside locations were not without their own problems as mudslides threatened the most exclusive communities. Power outages grew exponentially, adding to the emergency response crews' problems in handling the crisis.

The latest weather bulletins reported that the storm would be short-lived. Upper-level patterns had started to tame the storm's impact and would soon drive the gale force winds back out to sea and reduce the tidal surges along the coast. For once, the area's coastal geography worked in its favor.

During the peak impact of the storm, while motorists struggled with deteriorating and dangerous road conditions, the Bay Area's mass transit rail systems provided a stable alternative to moving harried commuters with relative safety and minimal delays. The stellar performance of the mass transit system was welcomed by the commissioners and supporters of the long-awaited opening ceremonies for the first phase of the futuristic Transbay Transit Center.

For years, the city administrators fought with state and federal agencies to find the necessary funding to demolish the original terminal. It had long ago become obsolete. Visionaries foresaw that modernization and coordination of the mass transit systems were critical aspects for the revitalization of the impoverished downtown district of San Francisco. The dream to funnel all major forms of mass transit, including buses, high-speed rail, and the area's subway system, BART, to a central location in the city was poised to become a reality.

The long-range goal would tie San Francisco to the entire Bay Area and other major cities throughout the state. With links to the major Bay Area airports, this ultra-modern transportation hub would set an example for the rest of the nation. Surrounding this new transit center, soaring skyscrapers and spacious rooftop parks and gardens would spark a rebirth to a part of the city that had been in a long, spiraling state of decline.

* * * * * *

Along with every other emergency responder in the area, Steve Casella's crew from the Dogpatch fire station worked at a feverish pace since reporting to duty just prior to the arrival of the devastating storm. Navigating the city's streets became more treacherous as downed power lines added to the dangerous conditions. Police and fire crews coordinated their efforts with teams of utility workers to minimize the dangers and keep the public clear from the most hazardous situations. Even with the latest encouraging news that the main force of the storm would soon be over, Steve knew the aftermath would leave them busy for days.

Edie's flight had been diverted to Sacramento. Steve hoped she would've not boarded the flight in the first place and just stayed in D.C. for the night. Next, he tried to convince her to wait things out in Sacramento instead of fighting the storm. He even reserved a hotel room for her at one of the airport hotels.

She had agreed too easily to his plan. Later he found out she had plans of her own. He had been absently stroking Amber's ears when   Edie called to tell him she had rented an SUV and driven to the Kessler Foundation. She planned to wait out the rest of the storm visiting with Catori.

After his initial response to her stubbornness, Steve breathed a sigh of relief, thinking she at least had the good sense to stay at the clinic, and he would have two less people to worry about. Now all he had to do was concentrate on his job of keeping the rest of the city safe.

CHAPTER 41

NOT TAKING ANYBODY'S WORD FOR it, Adolf Dinter had to see for himself. It didn't take long for him to confirm the impossibility of getting anywhere close to the Nordic Brotherhood's compound today. In fact, he had been forced to backtrack at least a half dozen times before realizing that the flooding of the valley's roads had all but blocked travel in any direction. Getting out of the Napa Valley with his two prisoners wasn't going to happen anytime soon. He had immediately relayed that information to Joseph Stock who had been poised to grab Clarissa Mendelschein and Dequain Johnson from the animal facility at BioCoGen.

Dinter gave his guys a new command and they headed the short distance to Moon Valley Air Rides. Despite the fact his boss's company was only a short distance from where they had started, getting there proved to be quite a feat due to the degrading road conditions.

As they pulled the Jeep into one of the utility buildings, they were met by Karl Luntz, leader of the Nordic Brotherhood and owner of Moon Valley Air Rides. Dinter had called ahead, but the look on his boss's face still had him worried.

Dinter stuck his head out the Jeep's window. "Karl, we needed to take Pauling and Torrence as far away from the clinic as possible. I was thinking to stick them out at the compound, but there's no way to drive to Sebastopol with this damn storm."

Luntz had been furious after receiving Dinter's call but had told him to come here anyway. Having just listened to the latest weather report, he decided on a new course of action. He didn't like it, but he needed Pauling and Torrence out of here now.

"Drive to the training building," Luntz shouted, opening the rear door of the Jeep and climbing in. "Come on, move it."

After backing out into the raging storm again, they headed around the utility building and negotiated the muddy track across the open field to the back of the property where Luntz had pointed. The going got more difficult, and the four-wheel drive kicked in, straining to pull them through pooling water and muddy ruts.

Luntz ordered the man sitting next to the driver to jump out and open the huge sliding doors. Before they were fully opened, he snapped again at the driver, who gunned the engine and drove the vehicle out of the deluge and into the relative safety of the building. The spinning tires spattered mud over the helpless cohort whose shoe had been sucked down into the mud as he jumped aside to avoid being hit by the Jeep. By the time he'd extricated himself, the others were already pouring out of the vehicle and responding to Luntz's next commands.

"You want us to do what?" Dinter said. After listening to what Luntz repeated even more rapidly the second time, a smile formed on Dinter's face, and he nodded his head.

Luntz walked over to where more of his men were busy getting things ready. He stood watching them follow the procedures and moving the apparatus into position. Luntz gazed up and into the monstrous silo surrounding the men and the equipment. The howling winds and the torrential rains pounded down on the canopy that covered the silo, providing a dry work area for the final assembly.

Turning to the driver and his mud-encrusted partner, Dinter said, "You heard the man. Grab 'em out of the back. I guess there won't be any play time today."

One of the men opened the rear cargo hatch and grabbed the semi-conscious Catori, lifting her out of the Jeep. She offered no resistance. Probably hadn't even realized she'd gotten her wish and was out of the clinic. Not that she was in any condition to be of any help to Edie.

Edie had started to come around as the Jeep bounced and skidded the final hundred yards of the journey. As one of the men reached in to grab her, she mumbled several curses and said she could get out by herself. The last thing Edie wanted was for any of them groping their filthy hands over any parts of her body. That wasn't because she was being shy, but a few moments ago she'd touched a familiar object in her pocket and didn't want to give these creeps an opportunity to make the same discovery.

The last thing Edie remembered was her obvious failed effort to reach the pistol hidden in her purse. Then everything went black. Apparently no one had checked any further. Either that or they'd been more interested in other parts of her body. That told her they could be a little sloppy. But as she looked around at the situation, that thought alone didn't give her a whole lot of encouragement.

She had been tempted to thrust her foot into the guy's crotch but instead just let her legs drop to the floor. That wouldn't have gotten her much more than the slight satisfaction of humiliating the bastard. She took a few steps and almost keeled over, but stubbornly kept her balance. Her head hurt like hell from the smack of the first guy's weapon.

Before lifting Catori into the wicker basket, they bound her hands and feet together. Once dropping her inside, they shackled her to a large metal ring on the outer perimeter of the basket's floor. They repeated the same process for Edie. Looking around at what was going on and listening to what was being said, Edie doubted the usefulness of the object still hidden in her pocket.

It was clear to Edie that the men made no attempt to hide their identities or to keep her from overhearing the plan. Those thoughts sent a cold chill down her spine.

After their wedding, Steve and Edie had taken time off from their busy schedules, but instead of traveling off to the more exotic parts of the world, they chose to nestle themselves away in Steve's A-frame home in the beautiful hills of Sonoma. On one of the rare occasions during those intimate ten days when they emerged into the outside world, they had taken a hot-air balloon ride, coupled with an all-day wine tasting tour and a picnic lunch.

Edie recalled the romantic sensations of floating above the unending rows of vines dotting the rolling hills of the Napa Valley, punctuated by an array of wineries presenting a range of grand and stately, to quaint and modest.

Their pilot and tour guide had been gracious and informative on the day-long journey skirting over the stunning landmarks of this world-renowned wine growing region. Just because Steve lived in the Sonoma Valley, didn't mean he couldn't enjoy what the competition had to offer.

Although the company logo on the wall of the building was familiar to Edie, Moon Valley Air Rides was not the outfit Steve had chosen for their romantic adventure. Right now, this was a small consolation to Edie's predicament.

Edie tried repositioning herself to get a better look at Catori, who appeared oblivious to her surroundings. Edie then focused her energies on checking out the remaining parts of the basket. On her previous endeavor she had asked the pilot dozens of questions as to how these damn things flew, and how you could control where you went.

As she remembered, it was all pretty simple. Since hot air rises and gets trapped in the huge fabric envelope above them, the more the propane burners heated the air, the higher the balloon would rise. A flap called a parachute valve at the top of the envelope allowed the hot air to escape, thus helping to control the rate of ascent or descent.

For lateral movements, the balloon depended on the direction of the winds. Since wind directions usually varied with altitude, the pilot adjusted the altitude of the balloon to catch the appropriate wind direction for where he wanted to travel. All-in-all, the whole thing was remarkably simple.

Edie looked up and watched the burners cycling on and off, presumably to keep the envelope expanded and provide the necessary buoyancy to stabilize the apparatus on the ground inside this weird looking structure. While the burner assembly itself looked familiar, there appeared to be an additional complement of instruments attached to the control platform.

She listened to the incessant rains pounding on the metal roof. The metal siding of the building rattled and groaned in time to the cascading rains and damaging winds. She did not like the picture that formed in her head.

She remembered something else the pilot had told her on their honeymoon ride: you never want to be up in one of these balloons in the rain, let alone a hurricane or typhoon or whatever the hell they called these stupid storms in California. You didn't need to be a rocket scientist to figure out why.

But Edie had asked the question anyway, since she liked to know all the little details. His answer had surprised her. The pilot told her the cold rain hitting the heated surfaces of the envelope destroyed the integrity of the standard fabric materials used in constructing the balloon. He had laughed at this explanation. Right about now, Edie didn't think any of this was at all funny.

As if the person read her mind, one of the men leaned into the basket and smiled at Edie.

Nodding his head, Karl Luntz said, "I almost wish I'd be joining you for the ride. There is nothing like this rig anywhere in the Napa Valley." He spread his hands wide. "Or most likely anywhere else, at least not for the general public's entertainment."

Luntz leaned over and nudged Catori's shoulder. She barely reacted. "Pity. It seems your friend will miss all the fun."

"Get your filthy hands off her," Edie spit out. She tried twisting herself around and leveraged her feet against the restraints.

Luntz shook his head. "They said you were an important person. They neglected to tell me you could also be annoying. I will make sure the clinic adequately compensates my company for this little ride. This is an expensive prototype. The envelope is made of a heat-resistant Teflon blended fabric. We've also incorporated a state-of-the-art navigation device. And my technicians have tied it into the military's latest satellite weather system. Which, by the way, gives us real-time updates on the stratified wind conditions."

Luntz interrupted himself to shout more orders to several of his men while he checked the information on the touch screen notebook in his hand.

"Now, where was I?" he said, redirecting his attention back to Edie. "As you might imagine, this gives us the capability to fly this primitive aircraft, pretty much wherever and whenever we like. Of course, so far we've only tested it out in rather benign weather conditions. This is exciting, don't you think?"

Luntz took in a deep breath. "It's a shame Moon Valley Air Rides won't get any publicity from this next trial run. You see, this particular rig has none of the usual company logos or markings on it. So, this will be our little secret."

"Ready to go, boss," one of the men shouted. "The coordinates have finished downloading, and we're ready to open up the canopy."

"I understand," Luntz said to Edie, "this storm bypassed Hawaii. The view flying in from the east is quite breathtaking from what I hear. Unfortunately, if my calculations are correct, your fuel supply will run out well before you get anywhere close to the islands. More likely this whole rig will probably disintegrate before that can happen. But anyway, ladies, enjoy the ride."

Luntz turned back to his men. "Let's do it, guys."

The next scene only took several seconds, but to Edie it appeared to play out in slow motion. The pounding rain on the top of the envelope became deafening as the canopy slid back. The flames on the propane burners brightened, accompanied by a loud whooshing sound. Edie got a whiff of the rotten egg smell from the odorant added to the otherwise odorless gas.

The wicker basket shook as the men severed the last of the moorings. The floor of the building disappeared as the red and white balloon rose up and out of the silo and into the treacherous storm. The heavy rains drenched Edie and Catori before the basket cleared the roof of the silo. Edie shivered from the soaked clothes clinging to her skin. In Catori's state, she showed only slight signs of awareness of their predicament.

Edie hadn't bothered to answer any of Luntz's last remarks. She needed all her energy for what needed to be done next. Although she didn't have a great deal of confidence in even the first step, she'd never been one to quit this early in the game.

CHAPTER 42

IT DIDN'T TAKE LONG BEFORE Edie realized that no matter how much she twisted, turned, or contorted her body, she couldn't insert her hand into the front pocket of her jeans. The added factor of the wicker basket bouncing and swaying as the hot-air balloon whipped along, driven by the fierce winds, made the task all but impossible.

From where her restraints were anchored into the floor of the basket, she had no chance to reach the control panel. She wasn't sure what good it would do anyway. Pulling the plug might not be the answer, because whenever the basket tilted enough for her to glimpse the passing scenery, all she could see were angry parades of white-capped waves swirling hundreds of feet below the bobbing balloon.

* * * * * *

The absolute darkness mixed with a faint grayish curtain of shadows. An icy coldness embraced Catori Torrence, but not from within. She tried to move but was unable to pull from her restraints. The winds and rain slapped against her face, bringing her back to the real world. What she saw made her want to shut her eyes again. She was still wearing her hospital gown… well sort of. But obviously, she was no longer at the clinic. Unless this was another diagnostic test they were putting her through.

Something bumped against Catori's side. She turned her head and saw Edie bent forward and twisting her body around in an odd manner. Her memory returned in miniscule threads of understanding, and the sight of Edie jolted her into remembering the last thing she had been trying to do. She needed to warn Edie. But warn her about what?

Catori at last found her voice, but the first weak attempt failed to get Edie's attention. In desperation, she butted her head against Edie's ribs, finally getting her friend to react.

* * * * * *

Edie, although glad Catori appeared responsive again, was concerned about how her friend would deal with this new situation. She could see Catori was trying to tell her something, so she leaned in closer.

"Edie," Catori said, "I've been trying to find you. You need to be careful. You are in great danger. I have seen it. In my vision."

"W-w-what?" Edie said. Her brows arched. She thought Catori's words were quite an understatement.

"Catori. I need to make a phone call. Can you reach into my pocket and grab my phone?" She prayed the device was still in one piece and functional.

It took a considerable effort, but between the persistent movements of both girls, Catori pulled the phone from Edie's pocket. After more wiggling and shifting, she positioned the phone in front of Edie's face.

With an exaggerated effort, one of them hit the right button.

* * * * * *

Steve rode in the passenger seat of his command vehicle playing catch-up with the mounting paperwork from the myriad of incidents they'd responded to since the storm slammed into the Bay Area. Parkinson drove.

Steve's crew had just finished helping coordinate emergency repairs of a dangerous gas line break in the midst of a jumble of downed power lines.

The crew's rigs sloshed along the Embarcadero, and the men craved a brief respite to grab a quick bite to eat before heading out again.

Steve's phone buzzed. He took the call from Edie, thinking by now she'd be settled in at the clinic and enjoying a quiet meal in Catori's room. Recognizing the ringtone, Parkinson leaned over to Steve, set to call out a 'hello' to Edie, when he saw the stunned expression on Steve's face.

Steve had trouble figuring out what the hell Edie was saying. He grabbed Parkinson's arm and shouted, "Parky—turn us around and head out onto Pier 39."

Without hesitating, Parkinson maneuvered a tricky U-turn and within moments they skirted around the main entrance to the aquarium and tore down the delivery concourse toward the end of the pier. To the right they could see the ongoing havoc the storm played on the moored boats in the basin next to the pier.

In between Amber's barking in response to the anxiety in his voice, he tried to bring Parky up to date on Edie's situation. Before Parkinson stopped the rig, Steve jumped out and ran down to the pier's edge with Amber right at his side. He had the phone in one hand, making sure he was still in contact with Edie. He brought a pair of binoculars up to his face as he reached the railing.

Edie described a few landmarks while Steve tried to get a fix on the balloon. At last he spotted a small, bright red and white object out to the northeast. It appeared to be east of the Richmond-San Rafael Bridge. He barely made out the wicker basket swirling below the envelope.

"Steve," Parkinson said, coming up next to him. "I've contacted the coast guard and the marine police. They're gearing up, but they've got stand down orders to wait for an opening in the storm. Right now, they're looking at no sooner than forty to fifty minutes, best-case scenario. The commander said it would be suicide at this point."

Without taking his eyes off the balloon, Steve nodded, took a deep breath, and spoke as calmly as possible into the phone. "Edie, take a look at what's in front of you. Tell me what you see."

The next time the basket swung back, Edie peered out. "Alcatraz. We're heading toward the island."

"Okay, good. Now look farther out. Can you line up anything with Alcatraz. You know, pretend you're sighting in with your rifle. What do you see?"

"Gimme a minute, while we dip back. Yeah—I got it. I'm looking at the Golden Gate Bridge... wait... lost sight... here we go again."

Steve held his breath, picturing Edie spitting the driving rain from her lungs, as he strained to catch her words.

"It's the tower on the San Francisco side of the bridge. We're lined up right on it."

"Can you tell how high off the water you are?" Steve asked.

"That's an easy one," Edie said, without much enthusiasm. "I'm looking at a digital altimeter, and we're riding at about a thousand feet. Even with all these winds, that's what it's been sticking to this whole time."

After a few seconds, Edie added, "Pretty remarkable technology when you think about it. I understand it's expensive too."

Steve knew she was rambling now. Wracking his brain, he tried to come up with a plan. He'd probably need more than one option but would likely only get one shot at this.

"Hang on a second, Edie," Steve blurted out, cringing at his choice of words. Away from the phone, he shouted out orders for Parkinson, who got on his hand-held and relayed Steve's requests.

Steve closed his eyes for a second and then trained the binoculars back on the balloon.

"Edie," he said with as much calmness as he could muster. "Do you trust me?"

Edie never hesitated with her answer. "You're damn right I do, Mr. firefighter. Even when you're lying to me. Whatcha got in mind?"

His voice sounded like a whisper, but she heard him loud and clear. "I'm gonna bring you home. Right into my arms. Like I promised. Nothing to worry about."

"I know you're lying. Guess that's why I trust you. Besides, whaddaya think Amber would do if you didn't?"

"I think even Amber would be wondering why you chose to take a cold, wet balloon ride instead of sipping champagne in a steamy, bubbling bath."

Steve turned and charged back to the rig.

Right behind him, Parkinson shouted, "Everything will be in place like you wanted. Care to fill me in on what you got up your sleeve?"

CHAPTER 43

"I'M GLAD I'M NOT MARRIED TO YOU," Parkinson said after listening to Steve's plan. "Because if I were, I sure as hell wouldn't trust you."

Steve elected to drive. Parkinson called in a few additional orders. They were just getting put in place as Steve swung onto the last onramp to the Golden Gate Bridge. Minutes ago, traffic on Hwy 101 had been stopped in both directions.

It was an eerie sight, seeing nothing but flashing lights and at least a dozen police, emergency, and fire rigs scattered along the span. Steve skidded to a halt next to the large ladder truck parked opposite the San Francisco tower of the bridge.

He jumped out and ran to the back of the rig, yanking open the rear doors. He unlocked the container and worked on assembling what he needed. Amber barked frantically, spinning around and nudging his arm.

"You're gonna have to trust me on this one, girl. I want her back just as much as you do," Steve said as one of the crew members from the ladder company ran over to him.

"Casella," the man said, "we got her in sight. Spotted her over Alcatraz. But the balloon's way too high. Damn. They'll go right over the top and—"

He looked down at what Steve was doing, his eyes bulging.

"What the fuck are you gonna do with that?"

Steve stared back at the man for a second, then picked up his gear and hurried over to the ladder truck.

The man called after Steve. "Are you outta your fuckin' mind?"

Steve joined the men huddled by the massive vehicle. They were trying to keep out of the main brunt of the storm's gusting winds.

"Parky," Steve said, "you tell our guys in the tankers what to do? Only if necessary. But they gotta be ready to move—and move fast."

Parkinson nodded. "We're lined up every which way we can. Don't worry, we got your back on this." He put a hand on Steve's shoulder and then gave him a thumbs up. "Just don't make her mad. You know you can be a real pain in the ass when your bride's not happy."

Steve gave Parkinson a quick nod and went over the final details with the crew running the ladder truck.

One of the men said, "Okay, Casella. We've made a few last-minute adjustments to our position. Whenever you're ready, climb on board and we'll take you up. Ziggy's at the controls. He'll get you where you need to go. I understand you've worked several tours with one of the ladder companies before, so you know you can fine tune things from up top on the platform. But remember—don't be cute. Ziggy's kinda sensitive about his equipment."

Steve gave him a tight smile.

He hesitated as Steve placed the gear onto the platform and then watched as he started to climb in. "Casella?" he said. "They tell me if anybody knows what to do… you'd be the one?"

It was a question, but then again, maybe it wasn't.

Ziggy glanced over as Steve settled in but didn't say a word. He fiddled with the controls, and the ladder assembly began arcing upwards and extending out. Steve grabbed on to the railing and thought he heard Ziggy whistling to himself while maneuvering the platform into position. The driving rains made it hard to focus on anything, but Steve detected a slight easing up on the storm's intensity.

On the other hand, the winds still buffeted the tiny platform around like one of his dad's old tinker toys. Steve looked down as the truck and the road deck got smaller and the shaking of the platform steadily increased. His eyes drifted toward Ziggy.

Ziggy stopped whistling long enough to smile. He picked up his handheld and said to Steve, "I've seen worse, Casella. Of course that was in a training video." He started whistling again. Steve supposed that was how he calmed his nerves. Or maybe he was just insane. A lot of that going around these days.

Before climbing onto the platform, Steve had given Edie a heads-up on what he planned to do. When the platform was almost in position, he wedged the cell phone onto the tiny ledge, close to his chin, and punched up the volume on the speaker. He barely made out Edie's voice as she discussed something with Catori. She then told him Catori didn't think this balloon ride had anything to do with why she needed to warn her.

What the hell was that about?

He tried to keep his own voice steady. "I can clearly see you now without the binoculars. You're still coming in way too high. So, you know what that means. Right?"

"Jeeze, Steve. That's quite a party you guys got going on the bridge. We'd love to come and see your friends." In a more serious tone she added, "Catori's in real bad shape. She needs to get to a hospital as soon as possible. Maybe I was wrong in trying to yank her from the clinic. No matter how bad it seemed, this whole mess has only made things worse."

Steve closed his eyes one last time and prayed.

Below, Ziggy kept whistling.

Shouldering the Remington Wingmaster, Steve rested the barrel of the 12-gauge deer gun on the rail of the platform. It was loaded with five, full choke 00 shots. Ziggy stopped whistling and worked his magic in an all-out effort to stabilize Steve's position.

It was a difficult shot with the balloon bobbing erratically in front of him. Steve waited as long as he dared, hoping the balloon would catch a steady wind gust so he could take a clean shot.

Finally, he muttered to himself. "This is about as good as it gets."

Steve squeezed the trigger, aiming high on purpose. With each shot he gradually lowered his aim. The balloon began to pick up speed as it approached. He had to make the next shot, or it would sail right over his head.

He aimed right at the fat part of the envelope and squeezed the trigger one last time.

Then a chilling thought came to him. He didn't know what to expect. His head spun with images of the balloon dropping like a rock into the bay, or a huge fireball exploding right before his eyes.

What the hell was I thinking?

He saw a large circular gap appear in the envelope close to where he had aimed his last shot.

But nothing happened.

Steve began to panic. The balloon was about to sail right over the bridge.

Slowly at first, and then more rapidly, it began to lose altitude. Then a sudden wind gust buffeted the balloon and lifted it higher.

It was going to be close.

Steve looked on helplessly, lips moving in silent prayer.

CHAPTER 44

EXCEPT FOR DEQUAIN JOHNSON AND Clarissa Mendelschein, the animal facility building in BioCoGen's research center was completely deserted.

As soon as the countdown timer reached zero, the steam jets lining the interior of the automated cage sanitizing chamber sputtered to life, and spits of air and water cleared the lines. Working hard, the powerful steam generators quickly heated the water.

Snake-like hissing sounds reverberated around them, making Clarissa's and Dequain's eyes bulge in terror. In a matter of seconds Clarissa's skin flushed, her entire body turning a vivid red in response to the building heat. Not evident on Dequain's ebony skin, but the intruding jets of steam stung just the same. Following Dequain's frantic instructions, they worked their way to the top of the cage that stood between them and the entry door. The brunt of the intense heat was much more pronounced so close to the ceiling.

"Clarissa." Dequain's voice sounded raspy, all traces of Jamaican lilt long gone. His lungs burning from the intense vapors. "Don't breathe deep. Take shallow breaths."

"What are we doing up here?" It hurt worse than she'd thought just to inhale between those few short words. With every breath, a metallic burning etched into her throat.

"I think there's another safety cut-off built into the door's viewing glass. Dr. McBride pointed it out when I worked in his lab. The university had a similar unit. We need to reach it. It's supposed to be a final fail-safe mechanism. Responds to impact. From this angle, I don't think I can hit it with enough force."

Clarissa looked down through the bars of the cage at the tiny window.

"The space is too narrow. Neither of us can squeeze in front of this cage. How can we reach it?"

"Follow what I'm doing." Dequain inched forward while turning over on his back, squeezing and scraping between the ceiling and the cage. Every part of his body that came in contact with the hot metal screamed out in pain. The encroaching steam filled the cavity, making it almost impossible to see anything but surreal, misting shadows. Dequain could no longer see the blinking lights on the control panel but didn't need to read the gauges to know they would soon run out of time.

Clarissa mimicked the same body maneuvers as Dequain, desperately trying to ignore the biting heat assaulting her flesh. Multiple sear marks started forming wherever her exposed skin came in contact with the heated bars on the cage. They both contorted their bodies, trying to steer clear of the steam jets.

Approaching the edge of the cage, Dequain swung his body around, so his legs were now closest to the entry door. He bent his knees and began twisting his legs down into the narrow space between the side of the cage and the door, pressing against the hot surfaces. Clarissa picked up on his actions and followed suit. A tight squeeze—not much room for any leverage.

"If we can hit the glass with enough force—the vibrations might—"

Clarissa had already joined in with Dequain's kicking, but still asked, "What could this possibly do to get us out of here in time?"

Dequain didn't bother answering. He kept his lips tight as the heated air assailed his lungs. They kicked their bare feet against the glass, ignoring the pain and blood dripping from cut and bruised toes.

Clarissa got her answer when a deafening blast occurred, sending a violent shockwave across the interior of the cage washer. The door flew outward, its hinges snapping free from their moorings. With a frightening thud, the heavy door crashed to the floor.

Clarissa and Dequain first slammed against the scorching hot bars of the cage, then slid down the side and spilled to the floor, landing on top of the door. They hurried from the hot surface to the cold floor and collapsed.

CHAPTER 45

Northern California

Mendocino County

(three days ago)

THE TIME HAD COME. ALL the delays and waiting had frustrated Farid beyond belief. To be so close to realizing his personal jihad consumed his entire being. But the last pieces now fell into place. They could not wait for this upcoming storm to blow itself out. The leaders ordered him to travel to his final destination and complete the preparations for the greater jihad—a massive attack against the infidels.

The timing of the storm at first concerned his leaders, but they could do nothing to change the scheduled events. The storm must be a sign from Allah.

Farid could not have cared less about this. He had only one goal in mind. They had used his hatred for the person who killed his father as the bait to convince him to participate in the larger jihad against the land of the Great Satan. Farid needed to feign his support for this part of the mission. But his ultimate goal stared him in the face. Nothing else mattered. He did not care if he lived long enough to complete the group's primary mission. Primary for his leaders and handlers, but not at all critical for Farid. When the time came, only Allah could give him the correct answer. He would depend on Allah to guide him in making his ultimate decision.

Earlier, when Farid's initial journey to the southern border in California had been accomplished, he was met by a member of an embedded terrorist cell who whisked him to this compound in an isolated region in the northern part of the state. These jihadists hid in plain sight, near the coast, in the heart of one of the last redwood forests in Mendocino County.

He had grown sick of the endless rehashing of the details of what they required him to do. Time after time he had been forced to demonstrate the necessary skills to perform their mission. The maps, the diagrams, and the schedules became second nature to Farid.

Since his arrival in the United States, the one thing that surprised Farid the most was the openness in which his compatriots lived and carried out their activities. He did not believe his eyes as the car he had ridden in approached the location of the training camp after his long, arduous trip.

An ornate sign announced the presence of an Americanized Islamic community. Once inside the gates, they had taken Farid to the mosque. While waiting to be introduced to the imam, he spent the time looking over brochures testifying to the fact that all Muslims in this community lived by Sharia law. It also surprised him that this was only one of many such Muslim communities throughout the United States allowed to do so without any real oversight or intrusions from the government. This occurred right before the eyes of the authorities.

As long as the inhabitants espoused the peaceful virtues and teachings of Islam, they remained free to train a whole new generation of jihadists. They would soon infiltrate all important aspects of the Great Satan while politically correct politicians and the media kowtowed to their so-called peaceful beliefs.

To be sure, a small, but growing trend in the younger, Americanized Muslims to reform the timeless traditions of the Prophet had sprouted, but this movement would never develop fast enough to alter the ultimate triumph of the coming world-wide Islamic state. The radicalized leaders were more than willing to slaughter those Muslims who questioned the teachings of Mohammed.

A few minutes ago, they announced the plan to take Farid to his base of operations in the San Francisco Bay Area to prepare for the final details of his mission. The impending storm could make things difficult, but they needed to seize upon this opportunity. It was critical to strike at a time to maximize the death toll of the unsuspecting infidels.

And that time was imminent.

Before leaving, Farid's handler gave him the list of instructions, which included the latest known activities and whereabouts of his personal quarry. He would receive a final update just prior to his mission.

The closeness of his personal jihad brought Farid's hatred for the person who killed his father back with a vengeance. He would never forget the day he learned the horrid details of his father's death. Farid's fury became unimaginable at the news his father had been cut down by a mere woman. This had only brought shame and loathing to the family name. Such an indignity could never go unavenged.

While the young Farid had trained in the terrorist camps in Syria with the other brave jihadists, he became fueled with the dream of exacting revenge on the infidel whore. He kept her picture taped to his locker door, a reminder of the face who destroyed his family. Written next to the picture, Farid had chronicled her achievements since killing his father. His handlers kept a keen eye on him and stoked the flames of his hatred by feeding him news of the whore's activities.

At the training camp in Mendocino, Farid had been given the task of unleashing a mighty blow to the people of San Francisco in exchange for the opportunity to achieve his ultimate goal.

Farid made the long ride from Mendocino County to the San Francisco Bay Area in complete silence. At first the driver attempted to converse with Farid, but quickly learned it was going to be one-sided. If he assumed Farid used the silence to communicate his love and faith to Allah: He was wrong.

The vision had become clear in Farid's mind as he sat and watched the scenery change from redwood forests to picturesque hillsides and vineyards, to crowded freeways, and the final exit just south of the Oakland Coliseum.

When the car stopped in front of the deteriorating wood-sided structure, Farid grabbed his bag and exited. Without looking back, he walked up the crumbling concrete path to the house.

Although it gave him no great pleasure to spare the residents of this decadent country another dose of destruction, he would neglect the commands of his handlers and focus on avenging the death of his father. In doing so he would at last join him in Paradise at the same time the worthless whore died in terror. He would end his life along with the female and be a direct witness to her descending into Hell.

Farid entered the house and tossed his bag on a frayed upholstered chair in the dining room. His eyes stared at the supplies waiting on the sturdy old table. He examined several packages and smiled. Everything here was easily obtainable. This land of plenty unknowingly provided him with the tools of his trade.

Most of the items would evade suspicion. His handlers had been generous in gathering more than enough materials to complete both missions. But at this point his mind was made up. Farid separated out the exact items needed for his chosen task. He would be long dead before his handlers discovered this decision.

Farid had been a good student and an eager learner. In his bag he carried several pieces of unique equipment that *would* cause the authorities to be suspicious. If things went well, he would not need these. He put those items aside and got to work assembling his personal instrument of death.

CHAPTER 46

ABOUT TWENTY YARDS FROM THE San Francisco tower of the Golden Gate Bridge, the deflating red and white envelope started to drop more rapidly. The lower portion, just above the skirt, caught onto the downward angling main suspension cable of the bridge. The basket holding Edie and Catori leveraged up and looped around the cable from the force of the impact, snagging itself along with the collapsed envelope.

For a brief moment, Steve watched Edie and Catori dangling from the inverted basket, their shackles the only thing keeping them from plunging into the churning bay waters—or smacking down onto the deck of the bridge. Then the basket righted itself but flopped about in a perilous dance high above the bridge.

The crew stood ready with the hoses, but the safety cut-off on the propane burners did their job, and with the help of the driving rains, the flames had extinguished themselves.

Edie's phone fell into the bay when they'd first hit the bridge. Strong winds battered the basket against one of the vertical suspender cables. Steve was frantic. He could no longer see inside the basket to determine if Edie and Catori were okay. And nothing about the position of the basket looked stable. It hung out of reach from Steve's location on the extended ladder and platform.

"Ziggy!" Steve shouted into his handheld. "I can't reach them. You need to retract this ladder so we can move the truck closer to the basket."

Ziggy responded to him and someone else, but Steve never grasped what he'd said. The platform remained fixed in the same position. At the proper height, but about ten yards away from the basket. Steve extended an arm to hit the override button and lower himself down so they could move the ladder truck closer to the basket. He wasn't going to wait to see what the hell Ziggy was shouting about below. He needed to get into position to reach Edie and Catori in the damn basket. No guarantees the thing would stay in place for any length of time. Plus, he didn't know the extent of the injuries to Edie and Catori.

All of a sudden, the entire extended ladder tipped precariously, and Steve needed to grab onto the railing as the platform bounced from side-to-side; up and down. Peering over the railing, Steve didn't process what he saw. The ladder truck began crawling along the deck of the bridge with the partially raised outriggers scraping and crunching along the pavement. The entire rig jerked with every movement.

His handheld crackled and Ziggy's voice burst from the tiny speaker. "Hang tight, Casella. Don't think we got the time to reel you the hell back down here. Just don't puke on my rig. As you might've guessed, the guys made a few modifications to the truck. Always thought those safety lock-out mechanisms were a nuisance. Never tried it out before though."

Ziggy started whistling a few bars of a song Steve couldn't quite recognize. Then he saw the basket, almost within his grasp. If the ladder truck didn't flip over, he'd get to the girls in a few seconds.

The platform jolted violently, and Steve's body slammed to the floor. He heard a screeching sound and watched the shotgun clamoring over the edge of the platform. He prayed it didn't land on Ziggy's head. Although that would've stopped the incessant whistling.

The platform stabilized.

He looked down and saw Ziggy working the controls to maneuver the ladder into position so Steve could tether the basket to the platform.

Steve secured the basket and lifted the girls out after using heavy duty cable cutters to cut them free from their shackles. He then severed the ropes holding the basket to the platform. From below, Ziggy began retracting and lowering the ladder.

Paramedics took over as soon as they'd gotten to the ground. Edie's head was still bleeding, but she was conscious and talking. Catori slipped into unconsciousness again. They secured both girls in the ambulance. Edie filled the paramedics in on what Catori had suffered through at the clinic. Amber took the last place in the ambulance, but no one argued. Edie and the paramedics convinced Steve they had everything under control, and he reluctantly agreed to meet them at the hospital.

Steve watched the doors slam shut and listened to the fading sirens as the ambulance sped off north over the bridge toward Marin County. The glimmering, spinning lights cast stark images on the rain splattered roadway. He grabbed a towel from his rig and wiped off his drenched face and hair. His helmet had been lost somewhere between Ziggy's tunes and grasping Edie and Catori from the basket.

The ladder crew busied themselves securing their equipment as Steve jogged over and tapped Ziggy on the shoulder, interrupting the chorus from Frank Sinatra's 'My Way'. A tune Steve might get used to. Maybe the Casella family had a few Sinatra genes as well.

The two men stood eyeing each other, while the rest of the guys in Ziggy's crew wrapped things up.

"You try and hug me, I'll kick you right in the nuts," Ziggy said, trying to hide a smile.

Steve shrugged. "You that desperate for a soprano in your two-bit blues group?"

"Heard you got connections in the Garden State. You know that's where *Ol' Blue Eyes* got his start."

"So I've been told. You must be older than you look to remember an old-time crooner like Sinatra."

They continued to stare at each other. Steve broke the macho awkward silence. "Ah… nice work and quick thinking. The basket wouldn't've hung on much longer." He paused, giving Ziggy a funny look. "How in the hell did you convince the captain to okay those modifications to the truck? Thought it was impossible to override the safety checks."

"Captain's pretty flexible. And forgiving too. He did look a bit surprised when we started cat walking the truck across the bridge. Guess he didn't get the memo. I might've sent it to the wrong email address."

Steve smiled and shook Ziggy's hand, turning to go.

"Hey, Casella. Just wanted to thank you for something myself."

Stopping, Steve looked over his shoulder, raising his eyebrows.

"Yeah," Ziggy said, "the captain just gave us the okay to put a gun turret on the platform—thanks to you."

While Steve stood there puzzling that one out, Ziggy reached inside one of the truck's compartments and came out with Steve's Remington.

"Here you go, Casella. The captain reckoned if the damn thing had been attached to the platform it wouldn't a come crashing through the windshield of his brand-new Suburban."

Steve took the damaged shotgun, shaking a few crystals of auto safety glass from the barrel.

He nodded and headed back to his own rig. This time he let Parkinson drive. They took off with Parkinson betting him he'd make it to the hospital before Edie's gurney crossed the threshold of the E.R.

Steve expected Edie would be at least two steps ahead of that same gurney, running alongside Catori as they wheeled her into the hospital.

Chapter 47

The menacing sounds of the cage sanitizing system disappeared. As had the echoes from the blast of the safety release mechanism. Most of the fragments of shattered glass from the broken window lay hidden under the flattened door.

Clarissa Mendelschein and Dequain Johnson pulled themselves up and looked at the heavy steel door lying on the floor. They gazed into the interior of the cage washing module. The inside air began to clear, and droplets of cooling steam particles cascaded down the slick surfaces. After a brief embrace, they scrambled back into their scrubs.

"My phone's gone," Clarissa said. "The son of a bitch must've grabbed it."

Dequain checked his pockets. "Mine's gone too. Let's go to my office."

They sprinted down the deserted corridor, but when they got to Dequain's office, the phone was dead. They tried several other phones in nearby labs with the same results.

"Come on," Dequain said, "let's get the hell out of here before your friend returns and finds out we're still alive."

"Did you drive in today?"

"Yeah," Dequain said.

"Good. I think your Explorer is better equipped to handle the flooding than my car."

They took a moment to hit the locker rooms to shed the scrubs and change back into their street clothing. By the time they reached Dequain's SUV, their clothes had soaked through from the continuing rains. Starting the engine, Dequain shifted into drive and gunned it. The tires screeched against the wet pavement, and he headed through the empty parking lot toward the guard gate.

He slowed as they approached the locked gate and looked at Clarissa. "Think we should tell these guys what happened?"

"Let's just get out of here. At this point, I'm not sure who we can trust. We should head to police headquarters in Napa. And I need to give Edie Pauling a call. Remember what I told you? She promised to listen to what you've pieced together. I'm sure she'll know who to contact to put an end to all this."

Dequain stopped at the automated card reader and went to reach for his badge. "Oh-oh. I don't have my ID badge."

"Mine's gone too. Pull up to the guard house. Guess we've got no choice."

Before Dequain responded, the door to the guard house opened and two security guards in glistening black rain gear ambled toward the Explorer. One stopped in front, resting his boot on the Explorer's bumper, while the other shuffled around to the driver's side and rapped a gloved hand on Dequain's window.

As soon as Dequain lowered his window, Clarissa leaned over and spoke.

The guard cut her off in mid-sentence. "Good day, Ms. Mendelschein, Dr. Johnson. This is not the kind of weather you should be driving in. Creeks are overflowing with widespread flooding. Power lines are down everywhere. And trees are blocking many of the roadways."

Clarissa tried again. "Thanks for the advice, but we need to drive into town as soon as possible. With this vehicle, I'm sure we'll have no problems."

The guard leaned in closer. "I'm afraid it's just too dangerous, Ms. Mendelschein. And I do have my orders."

"That's okay, sir. I'll be sure to tell your boss you did your job, but we insisted. It's important for us to drive into town."

Both men reached under their raincoats and withdrew their service revolvers. The guard standing next to Dequain's window said, "Sorry if I didn't make myself clear. You two are not going to leave. This is not a suggestion or advice. Now, I need you to get out of the vehicle and join us inside the guard house. Someone will be along to take you to your next destination. You might as well make yourselves comfortable though. From what I understand, the roads *are* pretty dangerous, and it could be quite a while before your driver can take you to where you're going."

Chapter 48

The attorney general completed his remarks and cast a wary eye at President Tyler Griffin.

"So now the sonsofbitches want to shut down the interrogations before the prisoners have even settled into their cells? Instead, why don't we just transfer them to a Caribbean Cruise Line ship in the Bahamas?" the president said.

They were seated alone in the Oval Office.

"Look, Crutchfield, you were elected by the same people who elected me. Not a secret consortium fixated on undermining the executive branch. And me, in particular."

With a tight smile, the president added, "If I wanted to discuss the long-term legal arguments of whether or not we're dealing with the Geneva Convention, the Military Commissions Act, or the civilian court system, I'd apply to law school and spend the next ten years trying to sort through all this red tape. Oh, wait. Perhaps I'll leave that to the Supreme Court. I trust they may have an interest in the constitution."

He stopped and stared hard at the attorney general. "So unless you got something to bring to the table, I suggest you stop with all the bullshit. And for now, I don't want to hear another word about separation of powers and intent to keep congress in the dark in regard to special ops missions. Understand? We're in the middle of a real war here. Whether or not anybody wants to admit it. I know damn well my political enemies are still trying to nail me to the wall on this, one way or the other."

The president slammed a fist on the table. "For the love of God, Crutchfield, can you for once put the politics aside and do your damn job?"

Before the attorney general answered, the president waved him off and stood, indicating the meeting was over. "Think about it, Crutchfield."

The president headed for an important briefing in the Situation Room concerning the recent raids on the terrorist camps in the Middle East. One which the attorney general's name had been deliberately omitted from the list of attendees.

* * * * * *

The president was the last to enter the Situation Room. Taking his customary seat at the head of the table in the secure conference room, he glanced at the empty seat to his left. And turned to Agent Mike Finley.

"What's the latest, Mike?"

"Edie's doing fine, Mr. President. She's got a nasty bruise on her head, but the doctors think she'll be going home tomorrow or the next day at the latest."

"And that brave little girl—Catori Torrence? I heard it was touch and go for a while."

Finley shook his head. "Steve tells me they got the situation under control. Another day in the clinic and things would've been a whole lot worse."

"Why didn't Edie just sign the papers to get her released? A goddamn hot-air balloon ride? And Steve's got a lot more guts than me. A shotgun?"

Finley shrugged.

"But seriously, Mike. Do we have a handle on what the hell's going on in that clinic?"

"I've initiated inquiries with the PWA. For now, they say they're letting the local authorities complete their investigation. Officially, the company line is there is no possible connection to the Uteroprost trials."

President Griffin stared at Finley and waited.

"Ah, unofficially, I've heard another incident occurred involving one of the clinic's employees. They found a nurse murdered in her home. Right now, the authorities believe she surprised a would-be burglar. No evidence of any links to the clinic. But it also appears that two BioCoGen employees have disappeared."

The president interrupted. "Doesn't BioCoGen own Uteroprost? And don't they have close ties to the clinic?"

"Yes sir, and there's more. Edie's the one who put us onto Clarissa Mendelschein, who is one of the missing employees. She came to Edie claiming to have uncovered major irregularities with the clinical trial."

"Irregularities? What the hell does that mean?"

"Apparently, incentive enough for Edie to try and get Catori out of the damn place. And listen to this. Edie said Mendelschein got her information from the other employee who's now gone missing. A Dr. Dequain Johnson. From what I gather, there's a lot of nasty stuff going on out there."

Finley paused and raised his eyebrows. "I think it's about time congress takes a long, hard look at ConnorCare."

"Now why didn't I think of that?" He stared intently at Finley. "It's possible the local authorities could also use a little help."

The president turned to the rest of the people seated around the table. "Sorry folks, but I'm sure you all heard about this unfortunate incident in San Francisco and why Edie Pauling won't be joining us today. So, let's get to work. Mike and I will return to that subject when we've finished with today's agenda."

"If I may, Mr. President?" the secretary of defense said, looking down at his notes, avoiding any direct eye contact with the president. "Something I just learned might convince you to stay on the topic of Edie Pauling a little longer."

"What do you mean?" The president sat up a little straighter.

The secretary of defense pulled a folder out of his briefcase. He glanced at both the president and Finley and pushed the papers toward the president. He looked back at Finley. "Mike. I didn't get the chance to call you either. This information just came in. The credit goes to Capt. Fergusen. You remember? The special ops team leader at site AB1? You know there're tons of documents and computer files that still need to be examined. But one of Fergusen's men saw this, and it kind of creeped him out. So Fergusen checked into it right away."

The president opened the folder, and his eyes burned into the photos as he spread them out on the table.

Finley, looking over the president's shoulder, spoke first. "What the hell is Edie Pauling's picture doing in a terrorist training camp on the other side of the world?"

"Well, they found the picture you're looking at taped on the inside of a locker door. If you check out the other photos, you can see some particularly negative information scribbled on the door in regard to Ms. Pauling."

"Motherfucking—sonofabitch," Finley muttered. "Ah, sorry, Mr. President."

Looking at the secretary of defense, the president said, "Do we happen to know the identification or the whereabouts of the owner of this particular locker?"

"Not exactly, Mr. President. But all the survivors of the camp are currently being interrogated. As you know, by tomorrow they're scheduled to be transferred to the Ronald Reagan, where they can be processed and undergo further questioning."

"And where are they being held now?"

"They're at our facility in Kandahar, Afghanistan, as per normal protocol, Mr. President."

President Griffin glanced at Finley, who gave a quick nod. "Mike, you have orders to keep all those prisoners from this particular camp right where they are. I don't want them anywhere near the Ronald Reagan. There's about to be a firestorm of attorneys filing a slew of legal documents to block any further interrogations from occurring. And right now, they're taking aim at the Ronald Reagan. Some genius in the Senate Intelligence Committee leaked classified information as to the carrier's location, and the shit hit the fan. I'm not about to let the courts decide when and how we find out who the hell this is and what's going on. Let's hope to God the son of a bitch who owns this locker is either dead or we've got him in custody."

He tapped his finger on Edie's photo. "How soon can you get Finley to Kandahar?"

The secretary of defense looked at his watch. "I thought you might ask me that. On my way over, I ordered a special transport to be fueled and ready." He addressed Finley. "Unless you need time to go home and pack your bags, there's a chopper waiting on the South Lawn to take you to Andrews. The minute you land, the transport's cleared to fly you to Kandahar."

An hour after the door closed behind Finley, the president completed his meeting and dismissed the remaining attendees. He sat alone for a long time, looking over his notes. He wondered and, not for the first time after this mission had been completed, if this was a win, what the hell would it feel like to lose?

Before getting up, he jotted down a few more notes. As he headed out the door, he came to the unwelcome conclusion that if his political enemies just left him alone, he'd probably be close enough to making his own case for impeachment all by himself.

He remembered a conversation with his wife— must've been eons ago—at the breakfast table in his home in Morristown, New Jersey. Long before he got into politics. She had chided him into thinking he'd be the one to straighten out all the local problems, not to mention putting the state and the entire nation back on track. Today, for the first time ever, he contemplated whether or not she was just being facetious.

"Gotta love that woman," he mumbled as he pulled open the conference room door.

"Yes? Mr. President?" asked the secret service agent seated outside the door, jumping to his feet.

"You're married, aren't you, Frank?"

"Ah, yes sir, I am."

The president smiled and slapped the agent lightly on the back. "It's time I head upstairs and visit with the first lady."

CHAPTER 49

ARTHUR CONSTANTINE WAS SITTING ALONE. Ever since learning of the successful raids on the terrorist camps, he'd stayed secluded in his private beach house. That couldn't last forever, so today he started taking and returning the more urgent of his calls.

He'd been staring at the phone long after placing it back in the cradle. Earlier, he'd listened to the annoying tirades from Senator Henry Whitcome. Constantine's eyes turned to the walnut bar cabinet tucked at one end of the great room.

The phone call from Whitcome had put him back over the edge. Things were coming apart and the last thing he needed was to listen to the constant complaints of the old windbag. Unfortunately, this time Whitcome hadn't overstated the problem, as he was known to do. Constantine could only imagine the scene that took place in the Situation Room as the raids unfolded.

They'd all been blindsided by the president.

Too late, Constantine now saw everything clearly. Tyler Griffin had played them from the start. It had been too tempting not to jump all over what appeared to be gross negligence on the part of the administration. The leaked information had come from the president's staff.

Whitcome threatened congressional investigations into the president's abuse of power and overstepping his bounds in neglecting to follow the necessary laws to notify congress of the covert operations. But once the president announced the details of this operation in his upcoming address to the nation, public opinion would sway to his side.

All the efforts to demonize the administration for orchestrating the release of four key Al Qaeda leaders in exchange for three treasonous Navy SEALs would crumble. They had been led into the trap as easily as the terrorists had taken the bait.

Whitcome could argue his case on technical and legal grounds, but once the entire plan and the details of the successful raid on the terrorist training camps became headlines, he'd be better off keeping a low profile and pick another battle. Constantine doubted Whitcome could do anything in a restrained manner.

Constantine needed to concentrate on regrouping before things got too far out of hand. Instead of sinking Griffin's administration, the president could come out of this stronger than ever. At this point, the repeal vote on ConnorCare might gain enough traction to succeed. In a way, Constantine admired Tyler Griffin's tactics.

He'd need a way to attack from a different angle.

It was a fine line for the leader of the free world to be seen as strong and decisive, rather than overpowering and despotic. If the American people could be convinced into thinking the president's actions somehow threatened their own freedoms, they would view his behavior as dangerous and repressive.

Time to design a new media campaign.

The American people would never tolerate an out-of-control government suppressing the civil rights of American citizens. He'd convince his cronies in the White House press corps to start digging into this from a new point of view. He'd plant a few seeds to get things started, but now was not the time to be subtle.

After succumbing to his immediate needs, Arthur Constantine stood glancing out through the floor-to-ceiling windows facing the outer banks along the North Carolina coast. He downed the clear liquid, but it did little to calm his nerves. Outside, the crisp blue sky appeared to go on forever, and the tranquil sea lapped rhythmically against the sandy shores. A maddening contrast to the events now threatening the plans of his benefactors.

For the first time in quite a while, Arthur Constantine felt vulnerable. He held the empty glass in his hand. The afternoon had barely begun, and his first martini was already history. He was desperate to work on a second one. But the phone call after he'd finished with the pesky old senator put a screeching halt to that idea.

Whitcome was merely a pain in the ass; Constantine had never been comfortable dealing with this other man. In his mind he pictured an insane old man with too much money. Constantine had been more than willing to take his fair share and put it to work feeding the fantasies of his power-grabbing colleagues inside the beltway.

Still, something behind the old man's eyes scared the hell out of him. Although he'd made many attempts, he'd never succeeded in finding out the man's true identity. Only the name, Mr. Clean. Despite all his digging, the man's past was a black hole.

Mr. Clean had left a message for Constantine to remain where he was until certain arrangements were finalized. They were about to embark on a little journey.

Chapter 50

THE STORM HAD BLOWN ITSELF OUT of the Bay Area and the morning promised to be more tranquil. Steve looked forward to the possibility of Edie coming home from the hospital today.

The non-stop emergency calls during the storm and the harrowing episode with Edie and Catori had left him completely drained, and his aching muscles screamed for a little rest and relaxation.

Once he got Edie home, playing nursemaid and pampering his wife would be just what the doctor ordered.

"Hey, Mike." Steve had just pulled the Tahoe into the parking lot of the Sausalito Trauma Center when his phone rang. The number was unfamiliar, but he had no trouble recognizing the voice.

"How's Edie doing?" Agent Mike Finley asked.

"Not bad, considering."

"Considering you fired several rounds at her with a Winchester shotgun?"

"Check your sources, Mike. It was a Remington Wingmaster. Standard department issue."

"And whose standard might that be? Clint Eastwood's?"

"I'm just heading in to see Edie now. If you hang on long enough, you can ask her if she's considered filing an official claim against my department." Steve smiled as he pushed the door open to the trauma center's lobby, juggling a box of candy and flowers, while cradling the phone to his ear.

"Is she sharing a room with Catori?"

"No. Last night they transferred Catori to Saint Francis Memorial Hospital in San Francisco. They got her stabilized but wanted to do a thorough work-up after her experience at the Kessler Foundation. Compared to the ordeal at that clinic, the trauma she suffered from the balloon ride was minor."

"Yeah. Guess she was lucky you didn't shoot her. I don't know, Steve; two unarmed female minorities… but anyway, why don't you take a seat. We need to talk before you go to Edie's room. You might want to digest what I'm about to tell you before seeing her."

Steve cringed at how Finley transitioned from small talk to business in an instant. He'd seen it happen before, and always with good reason. He detoured to the back of the reception area, dumping the gifts on the nearest chair.

"What's going on, Mike?"

For several minutes Steve stood motionless, phone glued to his ear, listening to Finley outline the unfolding scenario from the intelligence gathered in Kandahar.

Steve responded to Finley while trying to process the frightening story. "This is about the guy Edie shot in San Francisco a couple of years ago? He has a son? Farid Khan?"

Finley added a few more particulars. Steve didn't think to question the veracity of what he heard. He took a long look out the window. His next words sounded hollow, almost pleading.

"Tell me you know where this Farid Khan is located."

"We're still working on it, Steve. So far, all we've got is that he was training for an important mission in the United States. And this fixation on revenging his father's death. Give us a little time, and one of these guys we've been interrogating might be coaxed into giving us more specific info. But for now, the bastards haven't been too cooperative. Most of what I just told you came from the intel uncovered at the training camp."

He stopped and cleared his throat. "We got one major problem though. We're at a military installation and under pressure to complete the processing of the prisoners. We may not have much time left. I've been trying to move them off base before they get transferred to the Ronald Reagan because there's a welcoming party of lawyers on board the carrier waving Miranda cards all over the place. The president doesn't want that to happen. If one of these assholes knows something, I promise you we'll make him talk."

Steve didn't trust that Finley would get the chance to make that happen. The media had latched onto the story about the raids on the terrorist camps, but instead of focusing on the administration's success, they kept looking for abuses of power and infringements of civil liberties at the hands of an overreaching president.

A lot of that paranoia stemmed from the nasty scandals uncovered in John Connor's administration, but Steve also understood that President Griffin had substantial enemies, and they appeared to have unlimited funding and influence.

Steve ended the call, picked up the gifts, and hurried down the hall to Edie's room. The door was shut. He raised a hand to knock, when the door burst open and a startled nurse bumped into him. He dropped the candy and flowers. Helping him pick up the items, she apologized and explained that several minutes ago a technician took Edie away for a CT scan.

"I thought she was being released today," Steve said. "Is there a problem?"

The woman shook her head. "No. Not that I'm aware of. A few hours ago her doctor phoned in a last-minute order for this scan. It's just a precaution. No need to worry. She'll be back in less than thirty minutes." She smiled and left Steve standing alone in the room.

The empty hospital bed looked damn inviting. Whatever remaining strength Steve had been harboring in his tired muscles just got zapped by Mike Finley's phone call. Right now, all he wanted to do was grab his wife, jump into that bed, pull the covers up over their heads, and block out the rest of the world.

A pleasing thought, but that fantasy lasted less than two seconds.

Outside, a dog barked. Not any dog. Amber.

He'd locked her in the Tahoe, and from the persistent barking, Steve concluded she was getting antsy to greet Edie. He had debated about sneaking her into the hospital, but decided it wasn't worth the hassle since there was a good chance Edie would be coming home today.

When Steve arrived, he had pulled his Tahoe around to the far side of the lot, below the location of Edie's room. Shaking his head, he walked over to the window and looked out. Steve attempted to open it, so he could try to stop Amber's barking, but the locked window required a key. His hand raised to knock on the glass, when out of the corner of his eye he discerned movement off to the right side of the lot.

Near the service entrance to the trauma center, a man struggled with a woman, trying to get her into the passenger seat of a car. He shoved her against the seat while yanking the seat belt and shoulder harness across her squirming body. Steve could see her hands and feet were duct-taped together. A heavy bandage was wrapped around the woman's head and covered her eyes.

Steve's own eyes bulged.

"Oh fuck!"

Steve watched as Edie failed in her attempt to fight off the assailant. He took a wild guess at who the man forcing her into the car was.

He pounded his fists against the glass.

Trapped in the Tahoe, Amber's barking turned virulent.

Steve's eyes riveted on the locked window. He picked up the bedside chair, the forgotten gifts once again spilling to the floor. With as much force as his tired body could marshal, he swung the chair into the glass. An earsplitting ringing resonated in his ears, but only a slight crack appeared in one corner of the window. With the next blow, he hit the window harder. The glass pane exploded outward, sending shards down on the asphalt and nearby cars.

Farid Khan had just finished slamming the passenger door shut when the breaking glass caused him to look back at the building. He paused only a second before scooting around to the driver's seat and twisting the ignition switch. Tires squealed across the pavement as Steve jumped through the shattered window. A remaining sliver of glass in the corner of the frame caught his forearm, leaving a nasty gash. He ignored the cut on his arm and the sharp pain from the twisted ankle as he hit the pavement running to the Tahoe.

Amber moved from her usual position in the rear cargo area to the front passenger seat. Her barks escalated; front claws gripping for purchase on the dash. Khan's car skidded out of the lot, turning right onto Alexander Avenue.

Steve got the SUV started.

Pulling hard on the gear shift, he punched his foot to the floor and the Tahoe lurched forward. Amber, momentarily dazed by being flung back against the seat, resumed her barking and position clinging to the dash.

In pursuit, Steve caught sight of Khan on the straightaway, just passing the sewage treatment plant on the bay side of the road. Khan disappeared around the curve where the road turned away from the water. They headed inland near the southern tip of the Marin peninsula.

Steve fumbled for his phone, but his mind flashed on the items thrown to the floor when he'd picked up the chair in Edie's room. She always nagged him about hanging on to his phone. He'd recently taken her advice about fitting it into a sturdy case, so at least it probably didn't break—again.

Steve was sure Khan would take the 101 Freeway. He remembered the onramp, about a quarter mile away, just around the next bend. Probably head north, away from the city. Going south he'd be cornered into the FastTrak lanes on the San Francisco side of the Golden Gate Bridge.

Khan surprised him and bypassed both freeway entrances. He continued west. Steve punched the gas pedal, trying to keep up.

They entered the Golden Gate National Recreation Area. The lane narrowed, the aging asphalt rougher, intensifying the road noise of the Tahoe's tires. Khan's car disappeared behind the rocky cliffs after careening around a hairpin turn. Steve hit the brakes and skidded across the oncoming lane, losing traction in the gravel turnout. By the time he'd gotten back on track, Khan's car widened the gap by at least a third.

On the next few straightaways, Steve gained back precious yardage. When Khan reached the traffic circle, he cut to the right. The lane narrowed even more, the switchbacks grew tighter, and the guardrails disappeared. At the tee, Khan swung the car to the left and accelerated.

This road was wider, flatter, and better maintained. If Khan had taken a right, he'd be heading back toward the freeway and possible escape. This direction, Steve knew, was a dead end. It led to narrow and rugged hiking trails and the rocky coastline. Steve started to get a bad feeling about what Khan might be up to.

As the road narrowed again by the stables, Steve saw the turn-off for the historic balloon hanger.

"Been there, done that," he mumbled. He didn't think Edie would be up for another hot-air balloon ride. And Steve didn't have his shotgun with him.

Khan surged ahead, going way too fast. Just past the visitor center, Khan negotiated the viaduct over the marshy end of the lagoon and increased his speed as he passed the old beachside barracks of Fort Cronkite. Steve was now closing in on him. He gaped at the steel barrier gate ahead, but instead of hitting his brakes, Khan accelerated.

At the last moment Khan veered to the left, crashing through the wooden rail fencing. Sprays of greenish-red basalt, long ago scraped to the surface by shifting tectonic plates, riddled the hood and windshield of Steve's Tahoe as he bounced over the debris left in Khan's wake. The brined air slapped at his face.

"What the hell are you up to, you sick son of a bitch? Not a hell of a lot of real estate left," Steve said. Amber glanced over, but she never stopped barking.

* * * * * *

Edie could do nothing to loosen her bound hands and feet. She had worked non-stop since being forced into the car. Her head still hurt like hell from her prior encounter with Adolf Dinter at the Kessler Foundation. Seconds ago, she'd finally coaxed part of her blindfold out of the way but failed to get a clear look at her newest assailant.

But she did know who she was dealing with.

From the moment he had dragged her out of the hospital room, he'd barraged her with a sea of vile rhetoric and nasty promises. Much of what this lunatic spouted made little sense to Edie. She got the part about him needing to avenge the death of his father. He'd made that painfully clear.

His other rantings left her baffled.

She caught phrases of green monsters and gladiators and other bizarre threats. Khan's taunts turned into a sickening laughter as he screamed that she was all that mattered to him. The others could live to die another day.

He was either completely insane, or her head injury was more serious than she thought.

All that could wait.

So, the bastard she'd shot had a son. There seemed to be a never-ending supply of radical Muslims to fill the void, no matter what the good guys threw at them.

Edie remembered that day as clear as if it occurred yesterday.

Having discovered a terrorist cell embedded in the Idaho panhandle, and at the last minute thwarting a terrifying plot of destruction, Edie learned that two of the escaped leaders had been part of the same terrorist cell in Pakistan responsible for the embassy bombing that had taken her father's life.

Hunting them down on the San Francisco waterfront, Edie fired several slugs into the chest of Farid Khan's father, Abu Wajid Khan, as he dove to reach the detonator of a nuclear weapon hidden in a minivan.

Steve finished off the last remaining terrorist leader in a gun battle staged on a power boat motoring across the bay.

Having read about similar events in Steve's first novel, this current scene reminded Edie of a low-budget sequel. Today looked like a good start for his second manuscript.

"You got any kids, Khan?"

"Shut the fuck up you whore."

He took one hand off the wheel and reached into the center console. He kept checking the rearview mirror.

"Expecting company?"

Edie prayed they weren't alone, wherever the hell they were, but at the same time was torn at the thought of someone else, possibly Steve, getting involved with this maniac.

"Not to worry, this will be over in a flash. If this asshole behind us wants to join in on the fun, I will watch you all descend to Hell. I will be waving to you infidels while I ascend to Paradise."

A rush of air burst into the car and Khan waved his arm out the open window. Edie made out something in his hand, but the damn blindfold still blocked most of her vision.

Did she hear a dog barking? *Oh my God!*

With every ounce of strength she could rally, Edie leaned against the shoulder harness and twisted her shoulder to its limit. She thrust her bound hands as hard as she could at Khan. Futile, she thought. Not possible to do any real damage.

But Khan screamed out in response.

"The detonator. I dropped it. You fucking whore." Khan pounded the steering wheel, and the car began to accelerate again. The tiny black detonator bounced onto the rough terrain and tumbled down the incline.

"This is Allah's sign that my jihad is not to end today," Khan said and pointed the car toward the cliff. "It is always wise to have a back-up plan. And now more of you pathetic infidels will feel the brunt of my actions."

He jumped through the open window and landed on the spongy undergrowth just before the car reached the rocky downslope leading to the crashing surf below. Khan rolled his body away as the Tahoe roared by.

That last-ditch effort to strike Khan loosened her bound hands enough to grab hold of the blindfold. When she pulled it up, she wished she didn't. Although the car was decelerating from bouncing along the rocky surface, there was sufficient force to reach the point of no return.

Edie tried to undo her harness but couldn't make it happen. The scene transitioned in slow motion as the car began to slip sideways.

A horn beeped, followed by a jarring impact and metal-to-metal screeching.

Edie saw Steve's Tahoe grinding into the driver's side of the car. The effort decreased the forward and lateral motion, but the inertial force of the speeding vehicles persisted. Both cars bounced onto the steeper part of the cliff.

Finally, the force of the Tahoe did its job and slowed Khan's car. Its momentum had been reduced enough to snag onto the thick brush and the limbs of several lonely trees clinging to the coastal hillside.

That didn't work for the heavier Tahoe.

It careened down the remaining embankment. Edie looked on in horror as she saw Amber leap from the Tahoe's open window just before the vehicle disappeared over the edge.

The dog closed the distance and catapulted herself into Khan's car. Edie held out her bound hands and Amber's canines made quick work chewing away the duct tape. Edie finished the job of freeing her legs and releasing the harness.

Both doors were wedged closed by the heavy brush and limbs which Steve's Tahoe guided the car into. The only thing preventing it from plunging down to the surf.

At least for the moment.

She struggled to climb through the open window, trying to snake her way onto firmer ground. She felt the car shudder. It began to tilt, branches cracking against the strain of the vehicle.

Amber nudged her from behind, trying to push her to safety. The car started to break free from the weakened branches.

Chapter 51

Recovering, Farid Khan sprinted back toward the road barrier. Just beyond the end of the gravel path, in a copse of coyote brush and sage, he yanked off piles of branches, uncovering a hidden motorcycle. He'd scouted the area yesterday, leaving the motorcycle buried, and had then hiked back to the main road and public transportation.

Khan dug his hand into one of the saddlebags and grabbed the back-up detonator. After punching the button, the adjacent earthen bastion gave a violent shrug, and a huge fireball rose up from the edge of the terminal bluff.

Since the car had been below his line of sight, Khan started back toward the billowing plume of smoke to confirm his kill. From behind, he heard people shouting and the distant wails of sirens building in volume. A strong whiff of acrid fumes slapped his face as his eyes surveyed the contrasting black smoke against the azure sky.

Instead of continuing on, he turned, ran back to the motorcycle, and leaving a cloudy dust trail in his wake, drove off onto one of the many dirt trails in the park.

The whore's fate now rested in the hands of Allah.

The decision had been rendered, and one final mission remained for Farid Khan to complete. Everything needed to perform this task waited for assembly at the house back in Oakland. The tables had been turned, and now it was he who would live to die another day.

These infidel sayings were annoying, but sometimes appropriate. Perhaps his father would forgive today's failure at martyrdom in exchange for eradicating the lives of thousands of infidels.

* * * * * *

Edie was ten yards from the car when the blast hammered her to the ground. The concussive force sent her tumbling down the steep embankment. Her clothes ripped; exposed skin assaulted by the prickly fingers of coastal scrubs anchored to the precipice. She grasped at branches in an effort to slow her descent.

For several seconds, Edie couldn't see past the spreading clouds of black smoke, dirt, and debris draping around her. Through fits of coughing, she heard Amber barking. Catching onto a solid branch finally stopped Edie from rolling the rest of the way down to the ocean. The frantic dog nuzzled her one last time before scampering down the rocky coastline.

Amber barked louder at the surf crashing at her feet.

As her vision cleared, Edie's eyes focused straight down, watching the battered Tahoe bobbing in the breaking waves as it started to sink below the surface. Edie slid to the bottom, pulling herself to her knees next to Amber.

She reached the water's edge at the same time the sea swallowed up the Tahoe. The icy fingers of the Pacific masking its prey. Amber's barking accelerated as she bounded in and out of the waves. Edie scrambled into the frigid waters and fought the surf. She swam to where she had seen Steve's SUV go under.

Taking a deep breath, she dove below the surface. Fighting to see through the surf and reach the submerged

SUV cost her precious seconds of air as she spun around trying to regain sight of the vehicle. Chest bursting, she resurfaced long enough to fill her lungs once more, knowing Steve had no such luxury.

In a more controlled dive, she zeroed in on the SUV. Through the open window of the Tahoe, Steve's image materialized. He wasn't moving. Edie watched the water gushing through the open windows, expelling the remaining air pockets and engulfing Steve's inert body.

The SUV lay stuck at an odd angle on the rocky bottom, but it had landed on its wheels, so she could pull open the door once the water level rose high enough. She got the seat belt off and tugged at his body, yanking him out of the Tahoe. Her lungs again crying for air, but this time she was determined to bring Steve with her.

With all her might, she pumped her legs and pushed toward the surface.

Barely keeping her own head above the incessant waves pounding around her, no matter what she did, Steve was too heavy to keep his head above water. Edie, her strength already compromised from her head injury, fought a desperate, losing battle.

With every second, her own lungs swallowed more and more of the salty sea and less life-giving oxygen. Her arms all but tore from her shoulders as she wrestled to hold onto Steve while spitting brine from her throat. They were both going under, but she refused to let go of Steve's motionless body.

Something bumped into her arm and grabbed Steve's collar. Amber had a tight grip on her master, and with Edie's help they maneuvered Steve back to shore, dragging him through the surf to safety.

On the edge of exhaustion and the verge of panic, Edie knelt at the side of Steve's body. She pushed against his shoulder and hips, turning him onto his stomach. Everything she remembered about first aid training started to evaporate.

In a rush, she scooted around Steve and grabbed his arms and pulled them over his head, making sure his face was turned to the side. A small amount of water expelled from his mouth. Next, she flipped him over again and placed her ear against his chest. She heard his heart pounding but didn't see his chest moving.

Still not breathing.

She placed a palm and fisted hand on his sternum.

"Not strong enough to—" she muttered and changed her mind.

She pulled his head back and started to pinch his nose. As she bent down, taking in a deep breath, Steve's body spasmed and his chest heaved. Edie yanked his shoulders over and Steve spit, coughed, and vomited. His chest heaved several more times and then resumed a more rhythmed action.

Edie collapsed next to him. Through tear- and salt-stung eyes, she looked to the heavens above the California coastline and realized that somehow they were all still alive.

Amber licked both their faces. Satisfied with the situation, she scooted over to a pile of driftwood and selected a prime specimen. Proudly, she returned and dropped it onto Steve's stomach.

* * * * * *

After Farid Khan had driven his motorcycle back toward the freeway onramp, he pulled to the side of the road at the highest lookout point at the entry to the recreational area. Placing the binoculars to his face, he focused on the ebbing smoke and flames, and the influx of emergency vehicles. The authorities had set up a perimeter, keeping the gaping onlookers back from the action.

Khan bellowed out an anguished scream when he witnessed paramedics hoisting two baskets up and over the rocky cliff. Edie Pauling was securely anchored in one, and she was breathing. A white dog sprinted around the site barking as if issuing orders to the first responders.

Khan threw the binoculars over the railing, jumped back on the motorcycle, and skidded out of the parking area, scattering several tourists in his wake.

CHAPTER 52

SOON AFTER DOWNING HIS ONE and only martini yesterday afternoon, Arthur Constantine had been chauffeured from his beach house on the outer banks of the North Carolina coast to a nearby private airport. He was the only passenger on a customized Gulfstream G650ER. As the elegant jet traveled in a southerly direction, Constantine felt the sleek aircraft bank. His ears popped as they next began losing altitude, in a slow downward spiral. Reflexively, he stared out the starboard window.

Intent on the landscape below, Constantine hadn't seen the door to the cockpit open. A bony hand grasped his shoulder.

"I never tire of seeing those monuments, Arthur. They serve as a constant reminder of who we are, and why I'm here. Without their guidance, all would be lost."

Constantine recoiled at the electric jolt from the light touch of the old man's fingers. His skin crawled, but when he turned to face Mr. Clean, he plastered a half-convincing smile on his face. He glanced toward the open door to the cockpit and the one empty chair. His eyes widened, but before his lips formed the question, Mr. Clean shrugged shoulders bonier than his fingers.

"My grandson, Bartholomew, has taken over the controls. He's coming along quite nicely. There are very few people I trust up there."

Mr. Clean's eyes stung into Constantine. "And I trust even fewer people on such an important mission as this. We are about to see if this trust is justified, Arthur."

Constantine swallowed hard, looking at his empty hand that should've been holding a filled martini glass. His finger pointed out the window. He spoke a few halting words. "Is this our destination? The same as the last time we met? The Georgia Guidestones?"

"No, Arthur, not this time." Mr. Clean released Constantine's shoulder after one final squeeze. "After picking you up, we were so close, and it never hurts to remind ourselves of the ultimate goal. From here we are heading west. Current events have dictated another change."

Mr. Clean got a faraway look in his eyes. "I'm sure you are old enough to remember a prophetic song from the fabled Sixties. An old Bob Dylan tune. When Bartholomew was a child, I often recited him the words to 'The Times They Are A Changing'. Similar to the talented Mr. Dylan, I can't carry a tune, but the words… the words are more than sufficient. Don't you think, Arthur?"

Patting Constantine's arm, Mr. Clean smiled. "It is time to introduce you to the next phase of our plan, and to make you an offer. One I'm sure you will agree to. I am absolutely certain of this."

The only thought crossing Constantine's mind at the moment was that as he understood things, Mr. Clean had been bankrolling the beltway political consortium to further the aspirations of the greedy politicians in D.C. because of Constantine's power of persuasion.

Where in the hell did this new idea come from?

And who the hell was in charge?

And in charge of what?

Mr. Clean took the seat opposite Constantine. "Since Bartholomew seems to have things under control up front, why don't we discuss those unpleasant events you've been pouting over. I know right now you're annoyed with that young rascal in the White House. Perhaps when you become aware of the bigger picture, you can move on. Soon, he will no longer be a concern."

Constantine stared back at the old man.

"But I must admit, I'm having a few problems of my own, Arthur. I'm hoping things will be sorted out before we land. But if not, it doesn't hurt to take care of affairs myself. Seems all this nasty business is related."

Mr. Clean sighed. "My, my. What to do… what to do."

CHAPTER 53

ALTHOUGH THE GRANITE IMAGES HAD long since disappeared below the evaporating contrails of the Gulfstream, and the cloud layers cushioned his views of any earthly anchors, Arthur Constantine preferred the muted blankness of the cold exterior to the stark reality of his insane host.

"Don't you see, Arthur," Mr. Clean said, "when you look at the bigger picture, it matters little what your good friend President Griffin does. We are patient and have been at this for quite some time and have had to readjust our strategies on numerous occasions. And these latest ripples might be put to good use. Right now, everybody's itching for a fight. We need only one more—shall we say, major conflict—before it all comes together. As long as all the players are in position."

Arthur Constantine had just finished pouring out everything he had learned of what transpired in the Situation Room. It had started with the frantic phone call from Senator Whitcome, who had a front row seat to the unfolding drama of the U.S. Special Forces raids on key terrorist camps. At the last minute, the president had pulled everything out of the fire. For the moment, any attempt to derail his administration had been shut down.

Hearing the last words of his host, Constantine stared back disbelievingly.

"I don't understand how you can be so calm when this whole plan is crumbling right in front of us." Constantine paused, looking away from Mr. Clean, not sure of his next words. "I've heard rumors regarding potential problems in California. There have been several incidents. My sources tell me the Uteroprost trials have come under suspicion. Surely this must trouble you. The company you've invested in stands to lose billions, not to mention the potential legal issues that are sure to follow."

Mr. Clean smiled but shook his head. "Your sources are once again correct, Arthur. In fact, we are right now heading to California. Yes, it is time to make a few important decisions."

He leaned forward and said in a lower voice, "This current dilemma may represent a great opportunity for us all. *My* sources are telling me much bigger things are about to happen. You, Arthur, will need to decide if you are to be a part of it. If you think this is all about ConnorCare and the impeachment of President Griffin, you've got a lot to learn."

Leaning closer to Constantine, Mr. Clean smiled, but the darkness behind it made Constantine's blood thicken and his heart struggled to keep pumping. "Arthur, I've spent good money over the last few decades, as did many others, to assure the correct individuals got elected to key offices. The debacle involving President Connor did not serve the organization well. You fools in Washington got a little too greedy and took it upon yourselves to improvise."

"But the people I worked with had—" Constantine attempted to explain.

Mr. Clean waved an arm, cutting off any further words. "Please, Arthur, I am familiar with the details, the excuses, and the fallout from this dubious excursion. That is why Tyler Griffin is sitting in the White House. What's done is done, and now we will use his little victories to move forward with our agenda. At some point, a dramatic increase in violence would be inevitable. Let's just say the time has come sooner than we expected but, nonetheless, it is here."

Mr. Clean stood and looked toward the cockpit. Before walking away, he said, "I hope you are ready for it, Arthur."

CHAPTER 54

"WELL, ISN'T THAT SWEET." Catori said. "Matching head bands. You guys wouldn't be trying to mock my tribal heritage, would you?"

Steve and Edie pulled chairs up to Catori's hospital bed in Saint Francis Memorial Hospital. Following today's ordeal, they'd been treated and released from Marin General after sustaining only minor cuts and bruises. In addition to the slash on his arm from leaping out of the hospital window, Steve had a cut on his head, similar to the one Edie received from the security guard's pistol.

The obliging E.R. nurse had made sure the couple's bandages were the same color and had also added identical inked-on designs to them both.

After rushing to Saint Francis Memorial, Steve and Edie were relieved to see Catori now undergoing appropriate medical treatment and recovering from the tribulations she endured at the Kessler Foundation. Once off the Uteroprost treatment regimen, Catori's skin began healing. Her exotic bronze complexion on a path returning to its alluring charm and beauty.

Catori hit the button, tilting her bed higher to make better eye contact with her guests. "So, Steve, my mind's a little fuzzy about what happened during our hot-air balloon ride. But from what I've been told, they later found Edie's purse in my hospital room at the Kessler Foundation. Is that right?"

Edie nodded. Steve just stared and edged back a little in his seat.

"And you never talked Edie into that *really sexy* Flash-Bang holster, did you?"

Steve looked over at Edie, then back to Catori, shaking his head.

"That would mean Edie was not in possession of her lawfully licensed firearm."

Steve shrugged; then nodded.

Catori clicked the remote button again, moving her closer to Steve. "You in the habit of shooting at unarmed African American women?"

"She didn't have her hands up. How'd I know they were shackled to the basket?"

Edie whacked him with a solid punch to his shoulder. He assumed that answer was still a safer bet than stipulating he only shot at the unarmed African American woman he was married to.

Catori turned to Edie. "What's the word about Farid Khan? Any updates from Agent Finley?"

Edie shook her head. "The interrogations have stopped. Before getting any useful information, the courts forced the military to complete the prisoner transfers. The latest efforts from the legal groups have apparently won out for now. Until the higher courts rule, we're being forced to process these enemy combatants through the American legal system. If they're not killed in the battlefield, once detained, the current orders require Miranda rights, legal representation—you know, the whole nine yards. Mike Finley told Steve he's working a few angles, but he's not sure where it's all going to lead."

"If I ever set eyes on this Farid Khan," Steve said, eyes flashing, "I think I know how to limit his legal options."

Edie's mouth dropped at his vehemence but nodded in agreement.

"Local law enforcement have any luck finding Khan?" Catori asked.

"Nope." Edie frowned. "They found what they think is the abandoned motorcycle he used to escape. That was near the lagoon in Tiburon. From there, it looks like he vanished."

Steve turned to Edie. They'd rushed over to see Catori as soon as they were released and had given statements to the authorities, so they hadn't had any opportunity to talk about what happened. "You remember anything Khan said to you that could give us any clues?"

"Oh, he talked a lot," Edie said, her face clouding over. "Most of it about me." She sighed. "He uttered a lot of things in those last seconds, but I still can't separate fact from fantasy."

Steve placed an arm around her shoulder, pulling her closer.

"He grabbed me from behind and blindfolded me. Never stopped screaming about his holy jihad to avenge for me killing his father. I only got slight glimpses of his features through the edges of that damn blindfold. No chance I'd recognize him, even if he walked into this room right now. But there was also some—"

Everyone jumped when the door sprang open, banging against the tray table Steve had wheeled away from the bed. Everything on top spilled to the floor.

"Oh my god," the candy striper squealed. "I'm so sorry." She cleaned up the mess and exchanged the water pitcher on the bedside table with a fresh one.

After she left, no one said a word.

"Probably not him," Steve said eventually.

Edie, relaxing a bit, said, "Don't think she'd be hiding much under those red and white stripes?"

"Anything's possible, that's why I needed to take a closer look. In my professional opinion, I'd have to say everything fitting beneath that jumper belonged to her."

Edie exhaled and smiled. She patted his hand. "I'll attribute any indiscretions to your head injury."

Steve pointed to the bandage on his arm. "My arm hurts too."

Edie's short-lived light behavior suddenly turned serious.

"What is it?" Steve and Catori blurted together.

"I—I'm not sure. Probably nothing. I can still hear Khan babbling. The whole time: he never stopped. Clearly, I was his primary target, but there were other things as well. None of it made sense. He talked about striking a greater blow against the infidels. I heard a bunch of nonsense words about gladiators, I think… and green monsters. He sounded almost delusional, but…."

Edie pulled away from Steve's arm, her hands rubbing her face. "I don't think we've seen the last of this asshole. And I don't think I'm his only target."

Before leaving, they both gave Catori hugs and wished her a speedy recovery.

Neither noticed the haunted expression on Catori's face.

CHAPTER 55

FOR A CHANGE OF PACE President Tyler Griffin faced the nation from the James S. Brady briefing room. With the success of our Special Forces raids on key terrorist training camps across the Middle East, he expected a more welcoming reception from the White House press corps.

He was mistaken.

Standing at the podium, the president prepared to outline the details of the daring plan. His political advisors had urged him to parade the released Navy SEALs in front of the nation, but Tyler Griffin refused to turn this into a bigger media circus than it already was.

"My fellow Americans," the president said. "Over the course of the last several months, you have been bombarded with numerous reports and accusations against my administration. In the interest of national security and the safety of the three Navy SEALs involved in a dangerous and classified operation, I was forced to remain silent as to my knowledge and motives regarding the mission."

The president paused and looked around the room. He didn't see a whole lot of friendly faces. Members of the press never appreciated being used as pawns, even in the light of national security issues.

"About a year ago, a person came to me and presented a plan conceived by the three Navy SEALs who were recently released from captivity." At this point, Griffin wasn't about to reveal Edie Pauling's name to the nation, due to the disturbing facts discovered in one of the terrorist training camps and the unresolved search for Farid Khan. There appeared to be more than enough fatwas placed on Edie's head by any number of terrorist organizations. And Griffin concluded that if a few unnamed federal agencies were permitted to issue similar religious decrees, Edie would be on top of their list as a result of her past probing stories pointing out incompetence and corruption among the ranks.

"These brave Navy SEALs volunteered to march into the hands of our enemy under the guise of deserters to their country. Let me make this crystal clear. These three individuals are not traitors. They are heroes. For months, they systematically fed misinformation to the terrorist groups. And while in captivity, they were forced to undergo unbelievably cruel sessions of torture in an effort to beat the truth from them. They endured the most dehumanizing interrogation methods known to man. And let me make this clear as well. I am not talking about what our media decries as torture or what our interrogators define as enhanced interrogation techniques. The images of what these brave soldiers suffered will haunt me to the grave."

Tyler Griffin turned his head away from the podium, took a deep breath, and swallowed hard before continuing. His eyes still glistened from the impact of his own words. "The detainees we traded for the so-called defectors were specifically chosen for their known importance and ties to key terrorist groups. Due to our limitations and restrictions in regard to our own interrogation techniques, we had been unable to extract the kind of information needed from these individuals. Before releasing the four terrorist leaders, we implanted sophisticated tracking devices that enabled our intelligence forces to follow them back to several major terrorist training facilities across the Middle East. Somehow these centers of terrorist activities had gone unnoticed by all other intelligence gathering operations or our state-of-the-art spy satellites."

The president picked up a glass of water. While drinking, his eyes scanned the faces of the assembled press corps. "A few key leaks from my administration were done deliberately. They were calculated to strengthen the deception in order for us to appear desperate and weak to our enemies."

These leaks, the president left unsaid, were made to his political opponents, not the media. The implications from the leaks were too good to be true. Griffin's enemies were ready to nail him to the wall. Not many bothered to do any fact checking. The vast media machine did the rest.

"During the course of the clandestine portions of this operation, my administration acted in full compliance with our laws. When the military operations involving the movement of U.S. Special Forces troops into Syria, Afghanistan, and Pakistan to seize these specific terrorist training sites took place, I signed the necessary national security disclosures, and the congressional notifications were carried out in accordance with those same laws. And—in an effort to prevent any *accidental leaks*," the president deliberately emphasized those last words, "from jeopardizing the mission, we waited until the last possible minute to distribute the notifications to the appropriate committee members, as well as the house and senate majority and minority leaders."

Placing both hands firmly on the podium, the president said, "I'm pleased to report that the raids on those key training camps were a complete success. Our Special Forces troops sustained only a few non-life-threatening injuries, and no casualties. They accomplished the safe rescue of the remaining hostages within those particular camps as well. Our intelligence agencies are right now combing through the uncovered data."

He tempered his next remarks with words of caution. "This fight is far from over. We must prepare for a long and vicious battle."

He appeared to address the following words directly to the terrorists. "If the battle is brought to our shores, we will not waver in our resolve to defend our freedom and stamp out those who threaten our existence. And so there are no mistakes in regard to our commitment to the fight, under advice from my military commanders, I am sending proposals to congress outlining a long-term program to strengthen our military forces, including the modernization and the bolstering of our nuclear arsenal."

The president signaled he was ready to take questions.

The CNN correspondent raised his hand and was selected by the president. "Mr. President, we have heard from an unconfirmed source that the Department of Homeland Security conducted a raid on an Islamic retreat in northern California and has taken control of their mosque. Does this have anything to do with what just took place in the Middle East?"

Before the president responded, the reporter added, "Muslim leaders across the country are claiming you've violated privacy rights. And this represents an escalation of your administration's attempt to profile Muslim communities. Could you comment on those charges?"

"I am not aware of any such activities," the president said choosing his words carefully, "or any federal agencies targeting innocent people or any legitimate religious organizations. And let me emphasize this. Law-abiding, peaceful American Muslims have nothing to fear from the government. In case there's any confusion, I'm talking about U.S. Constitutional law, not Sharia."

The president took several more questions before spinning around and departing the press room. The shouts of additional questions echoed behind him as he sped off with a phalanx of secret service personnel running interference.

Instead of heading to the Oval Office, Tyler Griffin descended to the security of the Situation Room. After the door to the inner conference room swung shut, he faced the occupants seated around the table.

"Finley. Glad to see you're back from Kandahar. Now—what the hell is going on in California?"

"Mr. President," Agent Mike Finley said. "Last night we deciphered several more records from the Syrian terrorist camp. The one where we found the troubling information about Edie Pauling. Right before Justice removed the last detainee from our military base, we coaxed additional information from one of the men—data we couldn't quite understand. At least until our intel guys brought us these new documents."

The president interrupted. "According to what happened in San Francisco, we've substantiated the earlier fears about this Farid Khan having a hard-on for Edie. But as I understand it, we were almost too late… again."

"Ah, yes sir, I'm afraid if it wasn't for Casella's damn dog, things might've turned out a lot worse."

Tyler Griffin twisted his head. "You and I owe that dog a lot ourselves, wouldn't you say?"

"Yes, sir, and probably her owners as well," Finley mumbled.

"I spoke to Steve and Edie this morning, as did you from what I hear."

"Yes, Mr. President. And as we discussed, Farid Khan has disappeared again. But we just got intel back from our guys in California. This so-called Islamic community the press just questioned you about turned out to be a terrorist training camp."

"I hope we were not surprised by this. Apparently, our media friends are on top of this as well, but from a completely different angle. The media appears to be bent out of shape because of your unfair profiling practices."

"No, sir. Very little surprises me anymore. But until we had solid data from our interrogations in Kandahar, the Department of Justice refused to issue any warrants for—"

The president leaned forward holding up his hand. "You obtained warrants to enter the mosque?"

Finley shrugged. "Well, we're counting on your power of persuasion to remedy that little detail."

"Glad to see we're making it easy for our congressional opponents to regroup and pick up the fight, but right now, please tell me you got something worthwhile to report."

Finley smiled, waving a piece of paper. "Guess where this leads us?"

Chapter 56

Catori Torrence remained motionless IN her raised hospital bed after Steve and Edie departed. Located on one of the upper floors, her room faced east. She continued to gaze out the window at the San Francisco skyline. The epic storm had long since dissipated, leaving the sky a brilliant California blue. For the time being the typical coastal fog remained absent, allowing the normally dreary neighborhoods in the city a chance to bask in the warming rays of the sun. The clean-up from the storm was underway and soon the resilience of the Bay Area would wipe away any evidence until the next disaster struck.

The ordeal Catori had faced at the clinic left her drained, and her eyes grew heavy. Inside her heart, something tore at her soul. The fear she had felt for Edie upon awaking the other day at the clinic persisted. In fact, if anything, the terror was greater and more threatening than ever. She sensed that not only her friend might be in trouble, but that larger evil still brewed and festered behind the bright sunshine.

Like the lid of a coffin slamming shut, Catori's mind plunged into darkness, her sapped strength no longer fought off the sleepiness or fended off the visions. As the light disappeared, Catori's body became entombed in a damp and murky grave. This did not disturb her. Instead, it energized her resolve.

When Catori was growing up, her grandmother, Lomasi, had taught her many things about the underworld and the need to face the demons. Her father, a hard rock miner, had given her the skills to navigate the many abandoned tunnels hidden deep below the reservation.

Catori's viewpoint shifted, and she now gazed at skeletal remains uncovered from beneath the surface. They lay, not scattered in the abandoned mines of the Idaho panhandle, but nearby, below the unstable earth of the city by the bay. Men stood around the ancient bones, pointing and whispering. Heavy machinery, now dormant.

She visualized miles and miles of tunnels at different depths, crisscrossing above and below the bony relics. Above, crowds of people scurried about. A number of them descended, while others returned to the surface. Many remained perched high above the earth, enclosed in gleaming towers of glass and steel. A heavenly garden floated somewhere in between.

She heard the waxing and waning of shifting frequencies rattling in her head. Numerous large and terrifying objects rumbled by at frightening speeds. For an instant everything stood still. The last thing she witnessed was the violent convergence of every layered image that had come before. The past, present, and future smashed together, and in a flash, Catori's vision disappeared.

The scream escaping from her mouth was real, and two nurses reacted by trying to hold Catori's contorting body to the bed. Her hospital gown had soaked through, and the sheets clung to the cold dampness punctuating her sobs.

As her beating heart returned to normal, Catori's body relaxed, and the nurses loosened their grip. With a rapid fluttering, her eyes opened. A glaring light assaulted her, causing her hands to fly to her face. As her eyes adjusted, Catori's fingers slowly splayed. Out the window, the sharp sunlight danced and reflected from a distant glass and steel structure.

In a moment of clarity, Catori turned to one of the nurses. Her finger still shaking, she pointed and asked, "What is that building... the tallest one you can see... with the sunlight shimmering on its surface?"

They answered her question. Puzzled, they also responded to her next request before an absolute fatigue hit Catori, and her eyes once again slammed shut. This time she fell into a deep and dreamless sleep. No more visions.

CHAPTER 57

YESTERDAY, FARID KHAN HAD WASTED no time after dumping his motorcycle and turning to public transportation to work his way back to the hideaway across the bay in Oakland. His backpack held a change of clothing, so he showed no outward signs of the dramatic attempt to kill the infidel whore. The torn and soiled garments were shed and discarded in a public restroom.

Inside, Khan's mind contorted in rage. He had been so close. His finger had been set on the detonator when the whore had struck back. He could still hear the relentless barks assaulting him through the open window as his suicide vehicle skirted the edge of annihilation. When he had glanced in the rearview mirror, the ghostly image of a large white creature with devilish eyes stared back at him.

The ancient prophet had despised dogs. Proclaimed they were dirty and defiled all humanity. Khan had witnessed pure hatred in the eyes of this creature. Almost as if it had been waiting for eons to return the favor from Mohammed's curse. Had the prophet been wrong? His decision to exterminate only the black dogs may have come back to bite Farid Khan in the ass. The devil can be disguised in many ways.

Why had the white creature shown up at the instant he had dreamed of since his father's death? Had it been mocking his failure to kill the woman? Or had it played a role in blocking his success? Perhaps a sign from Allah that he had other work to do.

For now, he would forget his personal failure and submerge himself in this last holy jihad. He appreciated that although he would act alone on this mission, there were many others already embedded in this land of infidels, and droves of other dedicated jihadists at this moment journeying to this same land to exact revenge on the Great Satan for interfering in the only true religion.

The time had come for Islam to once again reign supreme. This next step, although small in the larger scheme of things, would serve to awaken the infidels to their coming demise. Khan stared down at his hands. They no longer trembled from the inner rage.

His fellow passengers paid him no attention as they sat in ignorance, senses dulled by a relentless obsession with their precious electronic devices. Machines had taken over their souls, and no one sensed the presence of extreme power. Someone who had the ability to end their useless existence in a flash.

As the train stopped at Khan's exit, he took a last look around at the pathetic infidels and stepped onto the platform at the Oakland Coliseum BART station. Once outside, he hastened to complete the short walk to his temporary home.

Now that Farid Khan committed himself to this last task, he needed to finish up his duty to Allah. Once again, he'd be ready to martyr his soul. This time he would not fail. He rejoiced in the coming opportunity to join his father in Paradise.

Chapter 58

Catori didn't know how long she had slept but awoke invigorated and determined. While she rested, the nurses left the requested laptop on her bedside table. Catori pushed the button to raise her bed back up into a sitting position. She placed the untouched tray of food at the foot of the bed and set the laptop on the wheeled bed stand and got to work, sensing she had little time left.

From what though, she could not fathom.

As she booted up the computer and accessed the hospital's wireless internet service, an image of Amber materialized in her psyche and licked at her memories.

She once again thought of her grandmother, Lomasi, and her visions of Coyott, the legendary ghost of the ancient god of light. When Lomasi had first seen Amber padding alongside Steve and Edie, she was certain the creature of her ancestors had returned. It would either save the world or lead it down a path to complete destruction.

On Lomasi's deathbed, Amber's presence had helped ease the matriarch into her final resting place, guarding her final moments on earth and guiding her on the long-awaited path to meet up with her ancestors.

A chill pulsated through Catori's body. Perhaps the complete legend of Coyott had not yet been written. Only months ago, Catori's hands had helped with the birth of Amber's puppies. Just as Catori represented the next generation in the Torrences' ancestral role in the Kootenecti tribal traditions, the progeny of the ancient god of light could be preparing, as well, for the next great fight.

For now, Catori Torrence put aside her mystic ruminations and clicked on Google to begin her search for answers. Her fingers flew across the keyboard, entering in key words and questions from her disturbing vision.

As she did this, her mind ricocheted between the images in her head and the discordant phrases Farid Khan had shouted at Edie.

With the help of a high-powered search engine and a modern web browser, Edie's images of gladiators and green monsters started to take on a concrete meaning, and the ancient buried bones from her last vision steered Catori down the path.

CHAPTER 59

THOUGH ONLY A FEW DAYS had lapsed, it seemed like another lifetime since Edie had stood on the deck to what she now considered her home, gazing across the vibrant Sonoma Valley and the bordering coastal mountains. The same home where several years ago she charged headfirst into an adventure taking Steve and her on a journey yet to be completed.

Before that day, they had never met, but a troubling past pulled them together, leading them on a path to discover a far-reaching cover-up that sent a devastating chill across the nation. As they got closer to the truth, the desperate actions of the conspirators served only to bind the motivation and emotions of this once unlikely pair.

Edie now gazed at the sun setting behind the western ridges flanking the Sonoma Valley. The kaleidoscope of colors wheeled one last turn as the darkness grabbed the baton and once again ruled the night.

Steve stepped up behind her, his strong arms encircling her waist. She leaned back into his embrace, her head resting in the nook of his shoulder. She felt Amber's muscled flank gliding across her knees. While less anxious about Catori's condition and her chances to make a full recovery, she realized they faced unanswered questions and other imminent dangers. For the moment, she relaxed and absorbed the love and support flowing into her body.

Steve kissed the side of her neck and whispered in her ear. "What's going on in that beautiful head of yours, Edie?"

"I'm remembering the first time I ever set foot on this deck."

Steve didn't respond but held her a little tighter.

"I remember being scared, mad, frustrated… and lost."

Steve shut his eyes and nodded. "I know. Been to that same place. And without you showing up that day, I'd have gone to my deathbed fighting and screaming, trying to fix what my father had done. Instead of understanding how wrong I was."

"Steve," Edie said. "I also remember it took more than a year before I got to see the inside of this house."

Edie turned with a sudden hunger and grasped Steve's cheeks and kissed him hard. He responded by scooping her up in his arms and carrying her into the bedroom. They tore at their clothes until the discarded obstacles lay heaped at the side of the bed.

Holding hands, they stretched out their arms and stared into each other's eyes. They pulled themselves onto the bed and drowned in a healing passion, ignoring their physical wounds and cementing their bonds to a strength that could never be broken. As the night marched on, they rekindled their heated embrace and fed a fire that could not be quenched.

Amber, the ghost of the ancient god of light, checked on her three puppies, Max, Greta, and Sophie, leaving Steve and Edie to tend to their wounds.

The night inevitably slipped away, and the sky gradually grayed. The slow unveiling of the new day came, but Steve and Edie slept in, lost in each other's arms.

Much later, the familiar harsh bleeps from Edie's phone penetrated their temporary respite. This particular ringtone meant the lingering embraces of post-coital dreams would be instantly severed.

Chapter 60

Farid Khan had worked long into the previous night. He caught a few hours rest and then vacated his hideaway in Oakland before dawn shattered the darkness. As he slipped from the house for the last time, he took one final look around and nodded. Satisfied that none of the remaining items, even if found in time, would alert the authorities to his next actions.

If they somehow managed to enter the premises unscathed, they'd be concerned that something bad was on the horizon, but he'd left no telltale evidence of his intended target or when he would strike.

Since returning to the house following his failed efforts to send Edie Pauling to Hell, he'd half-expected government agents to break down his door before allowing him to finish his preparations.

Now, as he closed the front door and walked down the sidewalk, he laughed at this unwarranted anxiety. His leaders had overestimated the ability of this weak nation and their resolve to fight back. They were too shackled by their laws and afraid to appear insensitive to those who planned to annihilate them. In the end, their own system of justice would lead to America's ultimate demise.

Although the backpack felt heavy, his stride remained light. Khan checked his watch and, in his head, ticked off the timing of the subsequent steps once again. He spent the next several hours sitting in a local café, and then wandered about the neighborhood, double-checking for any signs of heightened security concerns. With all the official credentials in place, he headed for his final destination.

Behind him, the deafening roars of the monstrous beasts and the cheers of the clueless spectators echoed in his ears. A reminder of the ancient Roman gladiators.

From the last days of the Roman Empire, to the final days of the Great Satan. Things hadn't changed all that much. It was now time to finish his work.

CHAPTER 61

STEVE AND EDIE CLIMBED INTO her red Mustang convertible. Steve's Tahoe had suffered a fate similar to his previous SUV. Only this time it got totaled by water damage instead of being charbroiled in the middle of an Idaho panhandle forest fire.

Soon after Edie's wake-up call from Agent Mike Finley, they were driving through the town of Sonoma, heading for Oakland. With the top down, Amber's coat fluttered in the early morning breeze. Tufts of shedding fur flew through the sky and came to rest on the dewy vines lining the road.

"What time did Mike say he'd get there?" Steve asked above the roaring engine and the cool air rushing over the windshield. He needed something to occupy his mind.

Why the hell did I agree to let her drive?

Edie's excuse about her concussion being older than his didn't help soothe his anxiety. His defense of being conscious as a justification for him getting behind the wheel didn't sit well with Edie either. But being a thoughtful husband, he relinquished his power of control and settled into the passenger seat.

He could've wrestled the keys from Edie but opted to avoid the scene. Looking back at Amber, he didn't notice any signs of fear on the dog. In fact, the wind gusting through her open mouth only served to exaggerate the smile on Amber's face.

"Not sure. His first stop was in Mendocino County. The site of a terrorist training camp discovered by DHS. The media got wind of the raid, and the president wants to put a lid on this before things spiral out of control."

"Is that possible?"

Edie shrugged as she downshifted into the next curve. "Both sides of the aisle have united on this one. All Tyler's old enemies have joined forces and circled the wagons. They smell blood in the water. They'd like nothing more than to sideswipe the outcome of those successful raids on the terrorist camps overseas. Already we're hearing accusations of an administration gone rogue. Abusing its powers and thumbing its nose at the legal system."

"Didn't somebody tell me Tyler Griffin was born with a copy of the constitution in one hand?"

Edie ignored Steve's comment. "For now, it's in everybody's best interest to determine what the hell Farid Khan is up to. Tyler told Mike—it's his top priority."

"So, when you said Mike's headed to Mendocino to smooth things out?"

"I'm guessing he's about to promote a more open line of communications with the local Islamic leaders."

Steve didn't think her explanation rang true. "And if the media gets in the way?"

Again, Edie ignored Steve's comment.

She navigated the MacArthur maze at a speed well above the safety limits designed by the engineers. A rare opportunity to do so, since traffic usually ground to a halt at this crowded Bay Area freeway exchange.

As they exited the freeway, Edie glanced at the Oakland Coliseum and its packed parking lot. Approaching the entrance, her foot tapped the brake pedal for an instant; then she popped the gearshift into second and accelerated.

Steve caught her hesitation and looked over his shoulder. He gazed at the crowded stadium but could only imagine the thunderous reverberations of the awesome vehicles taking part in the Monster Jam event, over the revving engine sounds screaming from Edie's Mustang. His gut twisted, and he wondered if it was only in response to Edie's driving. He turned to Edie and noticed the troubled look on her face.

Before he had the chance to digest this, Edie slalomed the mustang through several side streets and hit the brakes as they closed in on the perimeter of flashing lights and barriers swung across the road. They stopped several blocks east of the stadium.

Armed officers cordoned off the area surrounding the house where Farid Khan had been held up. The booby traps all disabled, and the entire scene examined. They found enough explosives in the house to flatten a good part of the neighborhood, but the bomb squad had done its job.

What remained inside gave little clues as to where Farid Khan had gone, or what he was up to.

Steve and Edie worked through the various checkpoints. They entered the house while watching the crime scene techs packing up equipment and backing out. Steve kept Amber tethered tight to his side, feeling the tension in the lead build.

They stood in the dining room, staring at a crumpled eight by ten photo of Edie. It was propped up against an empty soda can in the middle of the table. Steve dropped Amber's lead and put his arms around Edie. Amber darted about the house, alternately sniffing the air and grinding her nose into the filthy carpet. Throaty growls filled the quiet dwelling with ghostlike sounds.

Steve took note of the telling signs of early corrosive changes on the metallic surfaces in the house. The strongest damage appeared centered in the dining room, where the metal cover plates on the wall switches and the intricate wrought iron chandelier hanging over the sturdy oak table were surfaced with an encrusted flaky reminder of an underlying chemical reaction.

This stuff must've been sitting here a while. The hairs on the back of his neck bristled with the thought of how many other places similar to this lay hidden in unsuspecting neighborhoods in different parts of the country.

"I guess him coming after me is old news," Edie said, breaking his reverie. "We need to find out what the hell the son of a bitch is going to do now."

With no small effort, Steve reeled in Amber, and they headed back outside.

His phone chirped, and he checked the screen. "A text from Mike Finley. He just left the mosque in Mendocino County. He's on a chopper right now heading here. So far they've got no other leads on Khan. Besides the obvious. Whatever the target is—it must be somewhere close to here. He attached a photo," Steve said as he opened the message. "Shit. They found detailed schematics for a specialized detonator." Steve enlarged and scrolled around the image and shook his head.

"What kind of a detonator are you talking about?"

"It looks like a type of impact detonator. But with a few modifications."

Edie shivered. "Good thing he didn't use one of those in his car when we went joy riding. Otherwise neither of us would be standing here. What now?"

"Mike said we're to meet up with him. They're going to land the chopper in the rear parking lot of the Oakland Coliseum in about forty minutes."

"We just passed there, and the stadium's packed because of that Monster Jam event going on. Where the hell is he going to put that thing down?"

"I don't think that's much of a deterrent, at least for any helicopter pilots I've ever flown with." Steve stopped and pointed over Edie's shoulder. "Besides, look at the traffic on the freeway. I think the show's over and everybody's hitting the road."

Steve got behind the wheel, getting no arguments from Edie. He found a service entrance to the coliseum, and after flashing his credentials, he pulled inside and parked.

This time Edie's phone rang.

After checking the caller ID and reacting to the caller's frantic words, she punched the speakerphone button so Steve could hear the urgent message. They listened to the panicked voice of Catori Torrence. Edie tried to slow her down but that only made Catori's voice sound more desperate.

"Edie, listen to this." Catori's rattled words spilled from Edie's cell phone.

CHAPTER 62

EDIE PLACED HER PHONE ON the Mustang's center console and grabbed the front of the seat cushion, her knuckles turning white and her hands visibly shaking. Steve placed a hand on Edie's shoulder and stared at the phone. From the back seat, Amber plopped her front paws on the console and nudged the phone with her snout.

"We're listening, Catori. You're on speakerphone," Steve said in a slow and calming voice.

"I got a real bad feeling right now. Where are you guys?"

"We're parked behind the Oakland Coliseum," Steve said. "The feds got a lead on Farid Khan and we're checking it out."

"So, you know where he is?" Her voice rose in a hopeful tone.

"No. They found his hideout, but he's gone. And no signs of where he's headed."

Catori let out a long breath. "Oh crap. I think I know what he might be up to. I don't know how he'll do it, but I've seen the end results." The words began tumbling out of Catori's mouth, sounding all the more eerie coming from the tiny speaker on Edie's phone.

Steve prided himself on being a simple man. Edie reminded him of that fact on a daily basis. He was pretty sure she didn't mean it as a compliment. As he listened to Catori's tale unfold, he figured Edie didn't need to discuss those limitations today. He knew Catori well enough to take whatever she said seriously. Amber rested her head on the console, her eyes darting between Steve and Edie, low whimpering sounds emanating from within.

"You got all that from what Edie remembered Khan screaming at her?" Steve asked.

"I had a little help from Google too. And I think the images of the skeleton found during the initial excavations at that same site sealed the deal. Did you know they had dug up the ancient remains of a Native American?"

Even being a simple man, he presumed Google didn't have the correct algorisms to come up with the bizarre conclusions he'd just heard from Catori. He glanced at his watch and cursed. He remembered that the blaring engine noises and earsplitting rock music coming from inside the coliseum had stopped some time ago. Over his shoulder, he watched the last of the departing spectators scurrying down the exit ramps.

They had little other information to act on, but Catori Torrence had long ago proven that she was no ordinary young lady. Steve had listened to her on previous occasions and didn't doubt for a second—the reliability of her warning.

"Let's go," Steve said. "I don't think we can wait for Finley." He pointed across the tracks and beyond the warehouses to the distant transit platform. "That's gotta be the train. Hard to tell from here, but it certainly doesn't look like a normal BART train."

Jumping out of the car, Steve reconnected Amber's lead to her service harness and they sprinted up the stairs to the pedestrian bridge. A few stragglers were still exiting the stadium, but most of the lucky patrons who'd won the tickets were already seated or were just boarding the brand-new prototype BART train for its inaugural trip to the opening ceremonies at the Transbay Transit Center in the heart of downtown San Francisco. This train would be the first to transit the recently completed second Transbay tube via the new Green Line transfer point on the western outskirts of Oakland.

* * * * * *

Earlier today, Farid Khan had walked along the Coliseum BART platform. He was there when the newest generation BART train halted on the tracks. It was Sunday, and the Green Line normally did not run today. While the workers fitted the exterior of the lead car with the inaugural banners, Khan, in proper attire, and with the appropriate credentials, stepped inside the train. Starting from the rear car, he walked the entire length of the ten-car train, taking his time, inspecting the interior.

He had just taken care of the legitimate operator for this trip and had hidden the body in one of the dumpsters along the alleyway below the raised station. As per the instructions given to him by the leaders in the Mendocino training camp, he entered the codes for the operator cab in the lead car and got to work inside modifying key elements of the train's automated control system.

When the time came, Farid Khan would be in charge of this particular train's speed, track selection, and communications. After tucking his heavy backpack under the cab's seat, he sat down and awaited the designated start time for this historic trip to the new Transbay Transit Center in downtown San Francisco.

On schedule, the Monster Jam's final event ended, and the winners of the tickets to attend the opening ceremonies in San Francisco filed onto the prototype BART train for the first trip on the new Green Line run through the long awaited second Transbay tube. At the moment, the modified line, which routed through the new Transbay Transit Center, ended a few yards west of the terminal in San Francisco.

This train's first and only stop for today would deliver the lucky ticket winners from the Monster Jam attendees in time to participate in the grand opening ceremonies.

In anticipation of this monumental event, the newly constructed neighborhood that surrounded the terminal structure bustled with activities and entertainment. San Francisco was proud of this stunning concept and the ushering of the Bay Area into the twenty-first century of state-of-the-art public transportation. Part of the far-reaching vision was the incorporation of business, residential, and recreational facilities into this transformed part of the city.

Today the entire downtown area overflowed with tourists and dignitaries from around the world to take part in the unveiling of the future of public transportation in America. While today represented only the first phase in this futuristic project, it signified an important milestone in painting the new canvass of urban revitalization and the nation's commitment to the inner city.

Sitting alone in the locked operator's cab, Farid Khan listened to the news reports hyping the day's ceremonies and savored the opportunity to deliver a defining moment of his own. This newest rendition to the fleet of cars in the BART system was indeed an impressive sight.

Khan had prepared for today using mock-up representations of this high-tech cockpit before leaving his compatriots in Mendocino, but sitting here now and gaping at the actual prototype gave him a sense of almost unlimited power. He had watched the men cast gallons of gasoline on the model used in Mendocino and ignite the structure, destroying all evidence of the proposed target.

Under his seat was enough explosives to decimate at least several city blocks and crush the entire Transbay Transit Center. Based on calculations he'd seen, there was a strong possibility that the foundation of the tallest skyscraper in the city would also be undermined by the underground blast, which would be centered a few short yards to the east of the city's newest high-rise.

Instead of the automated control systems from the BART's transportation center throttling the train down to a gentle stop at the new platform in the Transbay Transit Center, Khan's modifications would assure that the ten-car train would hit the barriers at the end of the platform at the train's top speed. The impact detonator in his backpack would do the rest. Khan was confident that this device fit in well with the sophisticated instrumentation surrounding it.

Khan's leaders provided him with a different version of the original Lawrence Livermore National Laboratory design. In this modified iteration, when the forward motion of the train was interrupted by the massive concrete barrier at the literal end of the track location, the vaporization, and sudden release of several thousand amps of current from the charged capacitive component would drive the pellet through the insulating disk and trigger the main charge. Khan had seen the original test models work on several occasions at the facilities in Mendocino.

Farid Khan had no problem being a martyr for the jihad. It was the least he could do after failing in his effort to kill the infidel whore who'd shot his father. Watching the last of the passengers board the train, Khan smiled and listened to the final preparation orders to depart coming through the communications system at BART Operations Control Center.

Over the subsiding din of the crowd, Khan's trance broke, and his gut froze at the sudden emergence of escalating barks blasting through the cab's speaker system. Checking the video monitors on the control panel in front of him, Khan's eyes opened wide in disbelief at the sight of a familiar large white dog charging along the platform in front of a man who he had also seen before.

For an instant, he thought that he had caught the image of the infidel whore who had escaped his reach. When he looked again, those views were obscured by the remaining people who rushed to get on board the train. Only the terrifying shrieks of the beast still echoed about the tiny enclosure surrounding him.

He uttered a number of prayers and curses in Farsi. He closed his eyes, willing the doors to shut and the train to move out.

"This will not happen again. If the creature jumps onto the train, it too will die. Of that I am certain." He prayed that the fleeting vision of the infidel whore had been real, and that she too had boarded the train.

CHAPTER 63

ARTHUR CONSTANTINE CLOSED HIS EYES as the Gulfstream lifted gracefully off the tarmac at the Charles M. Schulz Sonoma County Airport in Santa Rosa, California. Mr. Clean and his grandson, Bartholomew, were seated in the cockpit. The last several days had twisted Constantine's world apart.

A stark black and white cartoon image of Charlie Brown came into his head, and he envisioned the cartoonist's words:

And when I'm lying in my bed, I think about life and I think about death, and neither one particularly appeals to me.

Apparently, Bartholomew was more than a pilot. Much earlier, after the cross-country flight from the East Coast, the Gulfstream had landed at this same airport. They were met by four men in a Suburban who drove them to an isolated property west of Santa Rosa. Constantine tried to blot out the horrifying events that followed in what he now knew to be the headquarters of an organization known as the Nordic Brotherhood.

After leaving the Nordic Brotherhood compound on the outskirts of Sebastopol, they drove further up the coast to an opulent cabin perched high on a cliff with stunning views of the Pacific Ocean.

During the entire stay, Constantine had been left to his own imagination, seeing Mr. Clean and his grandson, only at dinnertime. Their conversations never referred to what had transpired on the Nordic Brotherhood compound. Mr. Clean talked vaguely of the future in a way that left Constantine begging for the good old days.

While at the cabin, Constantine spent most of the time in his own room, with its private balcony cantilevered over a precipitous cliff. He gazed for hours at the surf's unremitting crashing against the jagged rocks. At times, he half-expected to feel steely hands grasping his shoulders and heaving him up and over the railing. At other times, he contemplated climbing over the railing himself and leaping to his death.

Today, with Bartholomew driving the Suburban, no words were spoken on the return trip to the airport in Santa Rosa. The corporate jet climbed to its cruising altitude after a sweeping bank away from the coast and began its eastward journey high above fluffy layers of clouds, surrounded by an emerging infinite ceiling of distant stars and planets blotted out by a blazing sun.

This time when the door to the cockpit opened, Bartholomew's image filled the space. He took a step forward and closed the door behind him. Constantine had wanted desperately to keep his eyes shut, but they had reflexively fluttered open at the sound. Towering over him, Bartholomew's face was fixed with an unearthly smile.

"Do you mind if I sit here, Mr. Constantine?"

He had already seated himself across from Constantine before completing the sentence.

Bartholomew leaned forward with his arm outstretched toward Constantine. "Welcome aboard, sir."

Constantine automatically reciprocated the gesture, and he met the crushing handshake with a clammy, trembling grip.

"We haven't had much time to talk, but I assume you will be staying with us and continuing to work with the usual suspects in D.C.?"

Constantine could barely swallow, let alone breathe. His throat a microclimate as dry as a desert landscape. No words could be formed. Although a considerable time had passed since witnessing the carnage, the lingering scents of cordite against an overwhelming backdrop of bodily fluids on the Nordic Brotherhood compound still engulfed his senses.

Constantine finally nodded.

Bartholomew stood and patted Constantine's shoulder. As he walked back to the cockpit, he paused and looked over his shoulder. "Help yourself to a drink, Mr. Constantine. Grandpa will join you in a few minutes."

The same image of Charlie Brown reappeared in Constantine's head as he frantically fought with how in the hell he could escape from these insane people. Luckily, he had planned for the day when the need might arise to make a hasty exit.

A good deal of the funding for his upcoming escape strategy had come from a portion of Mr. Clean's donations to the political strategies he'd orchestrated in D.C.

CHAPTER 64

FROM THE SECOND STEVE CHARGED up the stairs, Amber pulled, lunged, and barked her way across the pedestrian bridge linking the Oakland Coliseum to the BART platform. Edie followed a few steps behind. As the last of the passengers boarded the train, the flashing warning lights blinked their countdown for an imminent departure.

They stood near the last car of the ten-car train, with Amber's efforts in pulling Steve getting beyond his control.

"I don't think there's any doubt that son of a bitch is on this train. We can't identify him, but Amber sure as hell can."

"Okay, Steve," Edie said. "Let's go find the bastard."

Steve jumped across the car's threshold with Amber leading the way. At the last second he pushed Edie back onto the platform. "Sorry, Edie, you need to stay here. See if you can find somebody to shut this damn thing down before it gets into the city. My guess is we have less than fifteen or twenty minutes. This is supposed to be an express. No stops on the way."

Before Edie reacted, the doors slid shut and the train started inching forward.

To the closed door, Steve mumbled, "I think we both know what's going to happen when this train makes the next stop."

* * * * * *

Edie shut her eyes, cursed, and reached for her phone. She sprinted back across the pedestrian bridge.

"Where in the hell are you, Mike?"

By the time Edie finished giving the short version of the situation to Finley, she had reached her Mustang and was rocketing toward the exit. She had a good idea where to go, but not a clue of what would happen once she got there.

"Edie," Finley said, his voice crackling through the Bluetooth. "We're still at least fifteen minutes out. Can't get through to the BART Operations Control Center. Something's blocking all outside communications with them. I'm diverting to that location, but you might get there first."

Finley relayed the exact address to Edie as the Mustang fishtailed onto Seventy-Third Street, heading for the 880 Freeway. Hitting the onramp, Edie punched down on the gas and used as much of the narrow breakdown lane as possible to skirt around the slower moving traffic. She cut the wheel hard and slid into the left-most lane. The Mustang sprang ahead as Edie shifted smoothly into high gear and narrowed the distance to her destination.

Her Mustang lacked flashing lights and sirens, but it was a bright fire engine red. She was thankful Steve was not a passenger. Several minutes later, her foot hit the brake pedal and she skidded back across multiple lanes onto the exit ramp. She had a brief image of her dad teaching her to drive on those lonely country roads in the Garden State. She could understand why he kept his eyes closed for most of the lessons.

* * * * * *

The train jolted and then slowly accelerated away from the station. Steve got his bearings, sweeping his eyes over the interior of the car. The space, although filled, was not as overcrowded as an ordinary commuter train. The issued prize tickets had set the capacity at a more reasonable level. This would hopefully make Steve's task less daunting.

The passengers gawked at the sight of Amber working her way up the center aisle with her head darting in all directions, checking things out as she charged forward. Steve hung his credentials over his neck, the laminated badges swinging across his chest. This did little to calm the anxieties of the supposed lucky ticket winners. From the expressions splotched across most of their faces, it did more to heighten concerns for their safety.

After clearing the back seven cars, with three more to go, Steve realized he hadn't seen any BART security forces at all. He didn't know if that was good or bad, since more than likely he'd have a lot of explaining to do and may not have been believed before time ran out.

How in the hell did Khan arrange for this lack of security?

As he cleared each car, with no sign of Khan, Steve felt Amber pulling harder toward the front of the train. Reaching the lead car, Amber lunged forward and barked. She ignored the frightened passengers and headed directly toward the operator's cab in the front.

Using all his strength, Steve stopped Amber about midway. He waved his credentials above his head and ordered the passengers to get out of the lead car and move rearward through the passageway. Even recognizing the futility of it, he advised them to tell the rest of the passengers in the adjacent cars to get back as far as they could. One look at the enraged dog pulling at her lead was more than enough incentive for the passengers to comply with Steve's commands.

For the last several minutes the train had been traveling underground, but it now resurfaced and slowed. Steve felt the rumbling scrapes below the wheels as the train switched to a different set of tracks. He knew they had just transferred to the line connecting them to the new Transbay tube. A second later, this was confirmed as the train once again accelerated and dipped beneath the surface on the final run under the waters of the San Francisco Bay.

As darkness surrounded the speeding train, the glaring lights inside the car blinked, creating a harsh, but illuminated path to the front of the car. With the increasing vibrations and rocking of the train, Steve understood they were accelerating to maximum speed— approaching close to eighty miles per hour. In several minutes they'd be clear of the submerged tube and making their final stop at the concrete barrier just west of the Transbay Transit Center.

Steve released Amber and she charged to the front of the car, crashing wildly against the locked door to the operator's cab.

A loud crackling noise burst down from above Steve's head.

"If you would kindly secure the creature, we could spend the last few minutes discussing our options." The disembodied voice from the recessed speakers bounced around the empty car.

Steve regained control of Amber.

"Now back up to the center of the car, so we can begin our little chat."

Steve did as he was told.

He got a good look at Farid Khan as he exited the operator's cab. The door slammed shut with a solid click behind the lone jihadist.

Steve had withdrawn the semi-automatic pistol from his holster. Due to his department's new firearms regulations, he was no longer limited to the tiny concealed pistol he used to carry in his pocket holster. He aimed the weapon at Khan. This act appeared to have a calming effect on Amber. When Steve did this, Amber, for the first time since entering the lead car, took her eyes off her prey and glanced up at Steve.

"What exactly are the options you wish to discuss? You've got about five seconds before I exercise my option of emptying this magazine into your sick brain."

Farid Khan shrugged. "There are no options."

He looked over Steve's shoulder. "I was hoping to say goodbye to the infidel whore who killed my father. It's a pity she didn't join you for this final ride. But, at this point, I guess your death shall suffice. At least she will have to live with the fact that I killed her lover, and it was all because of her actions. By my calculations, we have less than a minute before the train impacts the construction barriers. You might as well put down your weapon, as we both know your rules of engagement do not allow you to shoot an unarmed man."

Khan lifted his arms and rotated his body a full 360 degrees. A sickening smile spread across his twisted face. "We shall both die at the same instant. You going straight to Hell with thousands of other infidels, and me ascending to Paradise."

Steve stole a quick glance at his watch and returned his stare to Khan. He shrugged and allowed a small smile to counter Khan's expression. "Since I got married, my rules of engagement have changed. You first, asshole."

Steve squeezed the trigger five times. The impact slammed Khan back against the door to the operator's cab. The spent cartridges bounced around Steve's boots. Blood smeared down the door of the cab as Khan's body slipped to the floor.

Sprinting forward, Steve shoved Khan aside and grasped the door handle.

Locked.

He emptied the remaining rounds into the locking mechanism, but it held tight. He made the effort of pulling on the emergency braking levers.

But, of course, they'd been deactivated.

Ahead, through the locked enclosure, the faint glow of the station lights came into view. At first it looked only as bright as the dimmest flickering of a single candle. But the light grew more brilliant with each passing second. Steve knelt down, leaning against the side wall. Amber padded forward, and he hugged her neck as she licked his face.

* * * * * *

Edie jumped from the Mustang and ran toward the entrance to the BART Operations Control Center. At this point in the BART system, the Green Line ran underground close to where she now stood. She had a hunch that the train Steve was on had already passed by. Edie sensed the sounds and vibrations below her feet. Her eyes shut for the briefest of seconds. Blinking them open, she plunged ahead.

Entering the building, Edie flashed her White House credentials amidst a slurry of executive rhetoric and threats. This got her into the inner sanctum of the command control center and in front of the person in charge.

A true bureaucrat, the bored administrator listened to Edie's story. After asking several questions for clarification, he showed no sign of urgency, but admitted they were experiencing a temporary loss of communications with the very train Edie had just mentioned.

"Not to worry, Ms. Pauling, I can assure you that we are in complete control of this particular train and there is nothing to be concerned about."

At that moment, a technician approached and whispered something in the manager's ear.

In response, the manager said, "Oh my, perhaps we should throttle back on the speed."

"What's going on?" Edie said.

"Just a minor glitch in the system, we'll have it fixed in a second." He walked over to the console where the technician worked at the keyboard. Edie looked over his shoulder.

The technician flashed a worried glance at his boss. "No response. The train's not slowing down. In fact, the speed is increasing. Almost at maximum for the new engine design. Way above normal safe operating speed."

For the first time, the manager showed a little emotion and took action. "Override immediately and activate the seismic safety braking system for the train."

Several seconds later, the frantic technician shook his head. "Still no response. Somehow whoever's in the cab has completely taken over control of the train. In thirty seconds it's going to smash into the concrete barriers on the other side of the terminal."

Edie grabbed the manager's arm. "What the hell can you do to stop that train?"

He shrugged off her hand and said, "Nothing. Only cutting power to the entire BART system can stop it now."

"What the hell are you waiting for? Do it!"

"I don't have the authority… and there's no time." He turned away and stared at the panoramic display of the massive transportation grid plastered on the front wall of the control room.

"I'm giving you the authorization," Edie shouted. "Shut the fucking power off. NOW!"

When the manager turned to face Edie, he saw the pistol aimed right at his chest.

* * * * * *

Steve chanced a glance through the windows of the operator's cab. The lights grew brighter by the second. And then they became the only lights remaining.

The interior train lights flickered and went black.

Then the lights on the control console in the cab extinguished. At first he didn't recognize what was happening, and then he sensed the train's speed decreasing. Gradual, but the forward momentum waned.

He stared at the lights ahead.

They were becoming larger than life. The train continued to slow down. But still barreled forward. The lights of the station now surrounded the train in a surreal glow. He watched throngs of people pointing and backing away from the platform.

And then the lights on the platform faded, and the interior of the car dimmed. Steve looked again through the front window of the cab. The tunnel surrounding him grew dark. He experienced the sudden sensation of entering a tomb.

Ahead he saw a series of blinking red lights.

They got larger.

And closer.

He couldn't turn away from the lights as they filled more and more of the window. He wanted to shut his eyes, but they remained wide open. Amber whimpered as Steve realized he had tightened his grip on her.

Steve's eyes blinked in rhythm to the flashing red lights ahead. It took several seconds before he realized they were no longer getting closer.

The train had stopped about two or three feet from the barrier.

Steve turned to Amber and scruffed her neck. "Well, girl. I'd say Edie finally remembered to shut off the lights."

Amber licked his face, smiled, and chuffed in reply.

CHAPTER 65

STEVE REMAINED LEANED UP AGAINST the wall near the front of the car, still holding onto Amber when the doors popped open. A team of bomb squad technicians entered the BART train. Before he comprehended their actions, several men whisked him out of the train and guided him to the outside of the new Transbay Transit Center.

As he looked around, Steve saw crowds of people being escorted away from the vicinity. He peered at the skyscraper towering high above the new terminal and rooftop gardens, also in the process of being evacuated.

There was a mobile command center on scene and several first responders pointed him in that direction. The door to the mobile unit opened before Steve reached the steps. Two agents filled the doorway. One of them bounded over to Steve and grabbed his shoulder.

"Steve Casella, I presume," the agent said. "Just got the word. The explosives are secured. Nice work down there."

Catching his breath, Steve said, "I was just along for the ride. The one who pulled the plug is who deserves the credit."

All eyes turned skyward at the thumping sound of two approaching helicopters. They came in fast and landed on the nearby rooftop garden. As the blades spun down, the stairs of the first helicopter dropped open and two familiar figures jumped out. Crouching, Edie and Agent Finley ran under the slowing blades. Steve released Amber's lead and gave her a head-start up the escalator. He did a credible job of keeping pace.

Mike Finley stood back as Steve embraced Edie amidst a jumping Amber, who appeared as hell-bent as Steve in greeting her.

Steve whispered in her ear. "I forgot to tell you, but last night you left your hair curler plugged in. Under the circumstances, I think I'll forgive you."

"Bet you never thought a cute little black girl like me would have to add curls to her naturally straight hair."

"I might've said that at one time, but I've since learned my lesson. I'm keeping my mouth shut."

Steve turned to Mike Finley and shrugged.

"You worried because she's one of the president's most trusted advisors?" Finley said.

"Guess you've never been married, Mike."

CHAPTER 66

PRESIDENT TYLER GRIFFIN STOOD IN the sunroom at his family's retreat in the northwest hills of New Jersey. Dressed in an old corduroy work shirt, faded blue jeans, and scuffed, but immeasurably comfortable cowboy boots, he wiped his hands on his shirttails. He had spent the morning cutting logs and splitting, by hand, enough firewood to get him through the remainder of his first term. He had a newer and more powerful chainsaw but insisted on using his father's old relic.

Years ago, his dad showed him how to safely operate, maintain, and repair that particular power tool. Over the years Tyler had rebuilt it so many times, he doubted any of the original parts remained, except for the memories of the time spent with his father.

His dad had dared to dream, just as his ancestors had desired to make America their new home. He had been taught that this country, unique in history, had given them the chance to succeed. He also instilled him with the responsibility to pay it back and leave the coming generations something to build upon. Tyler hoped he would not let his father down.

He turned back to the woodstove set against the beautifully crafted stone wall at the rear of the sunroom. The fire crackled, sending sparks fluttering to the tiled floor. He breathed in the reassuring scents of the aged oak pieces as they burned. He knelt down, closed the airtight doors on the stove and adjusted the damper.

Since his inauguration, Griffin had spent little time back in his home state. His presidency had been an uphill battle from the start. He looked forward to some needed relaxation.

The guests would be arriving in a few minutes and there was no time to clean up and change his clothing. He wanted to thank them for exposing the corruption and helping to put together the final pieces of the events surrounding the failed clinical trials held at the Kessler Foundation and the potential role of ConnorCare in allowing for such a travesty to take place.

Just last week, congress passed a bill to repeal the complicated and poorly understood healthcare law dumped on the nation by President John Connor. Tyler Griffin had vowed to not only repeal this draconian legislation but would work with congress to implement a bipartisan plan to change our healthcare system and make it an example for the rest of the world to follow. Never again would the United States try to mimic mediocre systems used in other countries.

ConnorCare was no longer the law of the land.

Informed by his security detail that the limousine had just passed through the outer two checkpoints, Griffin turned from the woodstove and looked through the expansive sunroom windows.

His two guests were surprised when the door to the two-story stone colonial house opened and the president himself greeted them.

"Ms. Mendelschein, Dr. Johnson. Please come in." The president ushered his guests into the family room and invited them to sit. "I wanted to personally thank you for all you've done to shed light on the unconscionable acts taking place at BioCoGen and the Kessler Foundation. And thank you for taking the time to meet with me here. Since you requested to keep a low profile, this location should provide us with enough privacy."

Following the close call in the steam cleaning unit at BioCoGen's animal facility, Clarissa Mendelschein and Dequain Johnson were detained at the company's guard house at the main gate. Once the weather cleared sufficiently, Adolf Dinter and Joseph Stock picked them up and deposited them both in a locked outbuilding on the Nordic Brotherhood's compound.

The plan was to have a little fun with the Jew and the nigger before taking care of them for good. Two hot-blooded subjects might provide an added incentive for hands-on training activities for the new recruits. And a much-needed diversion for the old-timers as well.

Unfortunately, they were interrupted by the sudden appearance of a Suburban. At the time, Dinter and Stock were downing brews with Karl Luntz, the leader of the Nordic Brotherhood, and Dr. Kessler, head of the Kessler Foundation. Aside from Clarissa Mendelschein and Dequain Johnson, locked away in one of the buildings at the far side of the compound, no other members of the organization had been present.

Although surprised, Karl Luntz enthusiastically greeted his visitors. Dinter paid special attention to the odd-looking old man. After several minutes of small talk, the old man turned to one of the younger men with him and simply said, "Bartholomew?"

Events occurred fast, and before any of the Nordic Brotherhood members understood what was happening, their bodies lay dead inside the house. Mrs. Luntz had been in Santa Rosa shopping at Costco in preparation for next week's training event.

Mr. Clean knew nothing of the presence of the two prisoners locked away at the other end of the compound.

When they had arrived, Karl Luntz told Mr. Clean there were no other members currently on site.

Luckily for Clarissa Mendelschein and Dequain Johnson, information regarding their disappearance had been given to Agent Mike Finley by Edie Pauling after she survived the harrowing hot-air balloon ride. Steve added his description of the telltale tattoos he'd recalled on a couple of the security guards at the Kessler Foundation. When DHS agents finally arrived on scene, they found the stranded prisoners and began to put more pieces of the puzzle together.

"I am also indebted to you for passing on those papers to Edie Pauling," the president said.

Clarissa and Dequain exchanged glances and Clarissa shrugged. "I hardly knew Ms. Liebermann. I thought it might be a joke, but I understand she knew Dr. Kessler quite well. The note she attached to it was so cryptic. Then... that awful accident... stepping off the curb. I heard Tiffany died instantly, and they never found the driver. A hit and run. Oh God, how awful."

The president didn't comment. He just nodded his head.

"Then I remembered way back when she did those interviews with Edie Pauling. I hoped she might make some sense out of it. What does it all mean, Mr. President?"

Clarissa never got an answer.

After Clarissa Mendelschein and Dequain Johnson left the president's retreat, Tyler Griffin walked over to the bar in the family room and mixed himself a drink.

He mumbled, "What *does* it all mean?"

He sat down in the leather armchair facing the panoramic views to the south. This next plan hadn't been given much thought, and he hadn't confided in anyone except Agent Mike Finley. Rather than speaking to Steve alone on this matter, he decided to approach the subject with both husband and wife together. He wasn't playing fair, but so be it.

CHAPTER 67

ALMOST EIGHT MONTHS AGO, ARTHUR Constantine had returned home from his trip to California on Mr. Clean's Gulfstream. Now, a drained martini glass in hand, he gazed out the window at the sea. A far different picture than the view he remembered from his old beach house on the outer banks in North Carolina.

Below him, the shimmering waters of the South Pacific appeared bluer than the cloudless skies stretching to an endless horizon. Besides the other tiny islands in relative proximity to Constantine's new home, the nearest tangible land mass lay at least a three-day boat ride away. There were no airports on any of the islands, and larger ships could not even make port in the treacherous waters of Bounty Bay, entrance to the previously only populated island in one of the most remote human outposts in the world.

With an infamous past, first settled by Fletcher Christian and a small band of mutineers and an unwilling group of Polynesian natives, the Pitcairn Islands were now the home of Arthur Constantine.

After returning from his harrowing trip to California, armed with the knowledge that his eccentric benefactor was indeed insane, Arthur Constantine pretended to go along with the program until he'd put together his escape plan. He even went so far as to fake his own death before beginning the circuitous route to his current destination. A three-month journey, not following any specific path. He simply melted into the night and crisscrossed around the globe until he reached the end of the world.

Constantine had plenty of time to think since first arriving here. From the battered old freighter moored in the tiny harbor, he'd watched the native crew hired from distant ports. When the time was right, standing on the deck of his new home, he'd gazed at the freighter as it erupted in a ball of flames and sank to its final resting place atop the once pristine coral reef.

Except for one young Polynesian girl he'd kidnapped for his own pleasures, the workers who'd slaved over building his home, along with the crew of the leased freighter, perished in the deliberate destruction of the old ship.

He had assembled the crews and purchased the building materials from a variety of pacific ports spaced hundreds of miles apart. With the promise of great sums of money for their labor, no one asked too many questions as to their destination. Whatever remained of their bodies now contaminated the reef and fed the sharks.

Constantine had already grown tired of his sex slave and questioned why he'd not just left her on the old freighter with the rest of the ill-fated crew. Looking out over the endless sea, he often envisioned his former life and the power he yielded in the world's most powerful nation.

At one time, he had it all.

A puppet master, pulling the strings on the most influential people in the most politically driven city in the world. He had been in the driver's seat orchestrating deals that changed the course of history. It had shocked him to the core to learn that he had been used by someone more sinister than himself and his own unsavory band of conspirators.

Events and signs that he had ignored for many years, now began to make sense. He had thought he was in control of the most important aspects of political maneuvering in the nation's capital.

Too late, he learned the truth.

He had at least recognized Mr. Clean's latest offer for exactly what it was: a threat to go along with the program and push the politicians in D.C. in the appropriate direction to assure the inevitable outcome of Mr. Clean's specific dream. Constantine had used many of Mr. Clean's techniques for persuasion, as he did to make certain individuals disappear when their usefulness had expired.

What haunted Constantine the most was the possibility that Mr. Clean was not actually insane. He knew little of the man himself. Years ago, Mr. Clean had come to him. He had appeared like a ghost in the night. And just like a ghost, there was nothing concrete to paste to his image. He had no past, and no apparent ties to anything in the present. The only tangible element was the unlimited funding he provided for Constantine's colleagues to use for their nefarious activities in the high-stake games being played in Washington, D.C.

Constantine realized he had to tread lightly when tracking down any information about Mr. Clean. During that last trip to California, he became acutely aware of the man's reach and power, not to mention his brutal methods in problem solving. Also, Constantine trusted very few people. So, he began and ended with his only clue to the man's identity.

The Georgia Guidestones.

Constantine didn't fancy himself a conspiracy theorist. His conspiracies had always been real and carefully choreographed. To him, all these crazies spouting out propaganda on secret organizations, world domination, apocalyptic disasters, and the massive culling of the world's population had always been nothing more than sheer fantasy.

The podium for lunatics.

But what if a wealthy lunatic, one with unlimited funds and worldwide connections dabbled in such nonsense?

Constantine found intricate webs of intrigue in his research, but every trail led to a dead end. Mr. Clean was still as ephemeral as the late-night breeze tingling the clustered leaves in a grove of white ash. Constantine had gathered up what little information he'd assembled and placed it in a FedEx overnight envelope. The next day he dropped it into a shipping kiosk and conspired to fake his own death in a fiery boating accident a mile offshore, due east from the Cape Hatteras lighthouse.

* * * * * *

As usual, on that fateful day, Derrick Pranchard had been in a hurry and was just locking his door when FedEx delivered the sealed package from Arthur Constantine. He shoved it into his briefcase and dashed down to the waiting taxi. He'd spent the remaining part of the day and a passionate overnight rendezvous at the Georgetown apartment of Tiffany Liebermann.

On his way to a committee meeting at the capitol building the next morning, Pranchard came across the forgotten envelope when he opened his briefcase looking for a cigarette. He scanned over the documents and laughed. Perhaps Arthur was becoming as fruity as this mysterious character he always alluded to. He shook his head and dropped the entire contents into the wastebasket next to Tiffany's desk.

He headed out the door to another waiting taxi, but never appeared for his committee meeting, and was never seen or heard from again.

It would be several days before Tiffany Liebermann discovered the package from Arthur Constantine. After Pranchard had left her lounging peacefully in bed, she eventually got herself showered and dressed and left him a voicemail to be prepared for another night of unbridled sex. With no response by the next day, she became pissed. Then worried. She had barely processed the violent deaths of her associates in California, and the just learned boating accident of Arthur Constantine.

And now Derrick Pranchard had vanished.

When she came upon the discarded envelope, she at first ignored it. But eventually it began to nag at her sanity. She considered it a bad omen. But what to do with it? Burn it? Or pass it on. But to who?

She recognized the veiled references to Dr. Kessler's clinic, but he was dead. Maybe someone else at the clinic would know what it all meant. At this point, she just wanted to get rid of it. Let someone else deal with whatever the hell was going on. Then she remembered the name of the person at the Kessler Foundation who had arranged for her rally and introduced her on stage: Clarissa Mendelschein.

* * * * * *

Sighing, Constantine glanced toward the bed, listening to the quiet breaths coming from the naked, bronzed body of the young girl on top of the scattered covers.

Perhaps he wasn't quite done with her yet. He'd been careful not to bruise her shimmering skin too severely so far, but his lust for power had been getting the best of him, and lately, he found it more difficult to restrain his actions.

Constantine chose to ignore any involvement with the small indigenous population on the nearby island. That was why he'd selected one of the uninhabited islands as his destination. The thought of wielding his clout on the unsuspecting people had been tempting, but he decided to leave the local politicians alone to their own devices. When the time came, he'd delve into one of the younger local girls on the island, but for now he'd make do with what he had.

He paused, thinking he heard something unusual, out of sync with the tranquil island sounds. He turned back to the window, his eyes once again scanning the horizon, but he saw nothing.

Then the buzzing became steadier, no longer wavering in the sea breezes rattling the leaves of the nearby trees. In the distance, a glint of sunlight momentarily reflected back at him off a non-descript object in the sky. He could make out the image of what looked like a large bird. The droning noise grew more persistent as the image in the sky loomed larger.

It was no bird.

Constantine froze in place.

He recognized the object, and instantly knew who had sent it. No need to turn and run. No place to go. He was already at the end of the world.

Arthur Constantine closed his eyes, accepting his fate.

From the east, beyond the horizon, a large yacht bobbed in the slight swells of the tranquil seas. On the ship's stern deck, under a large umbrella, Bartholomew sat in one of the cushioned lounge chairs. He ignored the tall frosty gin and tonic sitting in the built-in glass holder in the chair's armrest. The picture-perfect Pacific played with the brilliant rays of sunlight and spread its warmth and light for the thousands of miles of deserted seas around him.

His eyes focused on the laptop screen resting on his lap. His nimble fingers worked the keyboard, relaying commands and watching the precise changes in the flight path respond to his touch. The compact suicide drone known as a Switchblade maintained a westward trajectory at an altitude of approximately one hundred feet. The modified drone had been launched from a tripod-mounted tube launcher fastened several feet in front of Bartholomew's deck chair approximately ten minutes earlier.

After receiving the last transmitted commands from Bartholomew, the Switchblade headed directly at Arthur Constantine's new house built on one of the highest bluffs on Henderson Island. Satisfied with the final course adjustment, Bartholomew reached for his gin and tonic, taking a long draw on the ice-cold cocktail.

Once the Switchblade reached its destination, it would explode on impact. The warhead carried enough explosives to demolish the house and kill any living thing inside. There was no question of Constantine being in the house. Several days ago, two of Bartholomew's men had snuck ashore late at night and planted surveillance devices. They could have taken care of Constantine and his servant at the time, but Bartholomew hadn't traveled all this distance for something as mundane as that.

Ever since he'd heard about these Switchblade drones, he'd wanted an excuse to play with one. In fact, it was Arthur Constantine who had mentioned their use several years ago in a failed assassination attempt on Tyler Griffin, who at the time was the vice president. Bartholomew had no intentions of botching this particular mission.

As he placed his empty glass back in its holder, he watched the images on his laptop go black. Looking up, he saw plumes of thick black smoke rising above the horizon. Several seconds , the rumbling of the explosion reached his position and disturbed the calming sounds of the lapping waters caressing the huge yacht. He debated the wisdom of remaining in the vicinity for several more days to examine his handiwork. He had this picture in his head of the remains of Constantine's burnt body being ravaged by the hordes of rats who occupied this tiny island in the middle of the Pacific Ocean.

On his long journey to this destination, Bartholomew devoured every piece of information he discovered on the history of the Pitcairn Islands. For some reason he became fascinated by the fact that no matter what well-meaning authorities had tried, they never rid this little piece of paradise of the growing rat population brought here years ago by unwitting sailors.

Bartholomew felt certain that his grandfather would appreciate this historic tidbit as well.

CHAPTER 68

STEVE WAS SITTING AT HIS favorite place to write. The modest desk in the corner of the large cathedral-ceilinged room faced the expansive windows overlooking the Sonoma Valley. In the distance, to the south, he could see the city of San Francisco rising above the bay waters. Today the skies were clear. No blankets of fog to shroud the lower buildings of the city.

His mind mimicked the open views, and his fingers tapped the keyboard. He anticipated the light at the end of the tunnel, as the first draft of his second novel neared completion. His editor had the good graces to ignore the previous deadline and give him needed space to regroup and recuperate from the harrowing series of events. But now his agent had begun chiding him to finish up.

Edie had been spending a lot of time in Washington, D.C. She was due home today, and Steve looked forward to a break from his writing.

From across the road, Steve heard Amber barking. He got up from the desk and walked over to the front window, pulling aside the lacy curtains. The door to the dog training facility swung open and he saw Catori Torrence standing in the doorway, the brilliant sunlight reflecting off her bronzed image.

She had taken on a large portion of running the classes herself. Today's class in basic obedience had finished about a half hour ago and Steve had heard the handlers' cars pulling away. He watched Amber dashing back and forth across the front yard, and then he heard the sound of a car approaching.

Edie pulled her Mustang next to Steve's new SUV. Checking his watch, Steve confirmed it was not too early to fix up a pitcher of martinis. He got to work in the corner bar. He placed three glasses on the counter and grabbed the stainless steel shaker.

Steve had already turned away from the window by the time Edie's car door opened. Amidst Amber's enthusiastic greeting, Edie retrieved her small carry-on bag from the rear seat. She reached back in to pick up her purse and a small white paper bag on the passenger seat. Catori waved and walked over to give Edie a hug.

For a moment the two friends embraced. Catori stood back and grabbed Edie's hands in her slender fingers. Catori's eyes blinked several times. She released Edie's hands and placed her left hand on Edie's forehead while gently pressing her right hand on Edie's abdomen. After a few seconds, she cupped both hands under Edie's chin, and then embraced her once again.

They whispered a few words to each other, and Catori turned and headed back across the street. She got in her car and drove away, waving to Edie, with a big smile spread across her alluring Native American face.

With the carry-on bag and purse slung over her shoulder, and holding the small white paper bag, Edie walked up the porch steps and entered the house. Amber followed but kept back several paces. Steve stepped forward around the bar and gave Edie a long kiss. The two embraced, remaining silent.

"Did Catori leave?"

Edie nodded.

Steve smiled. "You sent her away because you couldn't wait to have wild, incredible sex with me?" He motioned with his head. "Out on the deck?"

Edie shrugged, a small smile on her face.

Amber sat staring at them both, her ears forward, head tilting in rhythm to Steve's words.

Steve placed one of the glasses back in the cabinet.

Before Edie responded, Steve filled the two remaining glasses.

"Ah… sorry, Steve, for now I'll skip the drink."

She walked over to Steve's desk and put the white bag next to the keyboard, glancing at the words typed on the screen. She turned back to Steve, leaning against the desk.

"I've kinda gotten used to how you've portrayed me in your books. Shy… easy-going personality. Tall and willowy… long, flowing blond locks… cascading over full, supple breasts… slim waist, transitioning to enticing, curvy legs."

Edie paused and Steve took a large gulp of his martini. "But she does have your amber eyes."

Edie's eyes narrowed. "Did I mention the slim waist?"

Steve placed the glass back on the bar counter. He took a few steps toward Edie.

Glancing at the small white bag on the desk, he said, "Is that for me?"

Edie pursed her lips and shrugged.

He took a closer look at the white bag. "Walgreens?"

They both looked down at Amber who was on her back and whimpering.

"Don't think we'll be needing it anymore. I just bought it to be sure…but I got a more reliable diagnosis from Catori. Never had much faith in these home test kits anyway."

Steve closed the rest of the gap and wrapped his arms around Edie. They held the embrace long enough for Amber to give up and pad outside.

Steve whispered in Edie's ear. "I was thinking about a similar conclusion for book number two… looks like you stole my ending."

"We can still get naked on the deck."

"I already covered that in chapter two. But it might need a little tweaking. I don't want to disappoint my readers."

Steve picked up Edie in his arms and nudged the patio door open a little wider. As he stepped onto the deck, he hesitated and then said, "With this news, I should give the president a call. Tell him we need to reconsider his offer." He gently lowered Edie back on her feet.

Edie reached out and touched his face. "No way, Steve. We need to make damn sure this baby has the chance to live in a world not on the brink of disaster. Too much blood has been shed already. This has got to stop, and I don't think we can look the other way."

Steve's finger gently tapped the lone tear flowing down Edie's cheek.

For a while Edie stared at nothing in particular. After a deep sigh, a small smile spread across her face.

"Those papers. That wound up in Clarissa Mendelschein's mailbox?"

"You mean Constantine's ranting about a stupid lunatic and those granite statues in Georgia?"

Edie nodded. "Apparently the president is interested in all this. I think he's even given the project a name. And

I've started my own investigation. Do you know why the Guidestones were placed in Georgia?"

Steve spread his hands out and returned her smile. "No. But maybe that's what the president has in mind for me and Amber. Don't tell me you've already found out the answer?"

"They're in a safe zone."

"Safe from what?"

"Let's just say your dad might've been on to something when he moved to the Idaho panhandle."

Steve wiped his hands over his face and stared back at Edie.

He waited.

"It's another safe zone."

"Again… safe from what?"

"One day all this could be gone," Edie said, waving her hands. "Our little hideaway in Sonoma will just disappear and the new Pacific coastline will be a short drive west of Coeur d'Alene, Idaho. The Spokane Valley could become very valuable beachfront property."

Steve didn't voice any response. Edie said nothing further, and they both relished the quiet.

They sat facing the distant mountains long after the setting sun gave up its display of colors to the emerging darkness. They held hands and contemplated the dawning of a new day and a better future for their unborn child.

THE END

Author's Notes

Targeted Validation is the fourth book in
The Amber Restrained Series.

   The series chronicles the escapades of two disparate individuals, Steve Casella and Edie Pauling, who surmount their differences and form an interminable bond that takes them on a journey to fight the injustices assailing the American dream. Together they challenge the seemingly unending barrage of incompetence and corruption that is ignored, facilitated, or orchestrated by the almost invincible power structure of an encroaching government. Along for the ride is Amber, a dog Steve has rescued from a fatal house fire. The sometimes disobedient canine companion is a constant source of frustration and amusement, but as part of their team, no one is more capable to assist when times get rough. As the nation and the world gather at the brink of extinction, Steve and Edie desperately try to gain traction against the slippery slope toward ultimate destruction.

<<ronvergona.net>>

Books by Ron Vergona

Opposition Reflex
Terrible Swift Sword
The Guarding State
Targeted Validation